About the Author

Jane Peart, award-winning novelist and short story writer, grew up in North Carolina and was educated in New England. Although she now lives in northern California, her heart has remained in her native South—its people, its history, and its traditions. With more than 20 novels and 250 short stories to her credit, Jane likes to emphasize in her writing the timeless and recurring themes of family, traditional values, and a sense of place.

Ten years in the writing, the *Brides of Montclair* series is a historical, family saga of enduring beauty. In each new book, another generation comes into its own at the beautiful Montclair estate, near Williamsburg, Virginia. These compelling, dramatic stories reaffirm the importance of committed love, loyalty, courage, strength of character, and abiding faith in times of triumph and tragedy, sorrow and joy.

Shadow Bride

Book Seven
The Brides of Montclair Series

JANE PEART

It was not like your gracious ways!
You went, with sudden unintelligible phrase,—
Upon your journey of so many days,
　Without a single kiss or a good-bye?
　　—Patmore

ZondervanPublishingHouse
Grand Rapids, Michigan

A Division of HarperCollinsPublishers

SHADOW BRIDE
Copyright © 1991 by Jane Peart

Requests for information should be addressed to:
Zondervan Publishing House
Grand Rapids, Michigan 49530

Library of Congress Cataloging-in-Publication Data

Peart, Jane.
   Shadow bride / Jane Peart.
     p. cm. –(Brides of Montclair series : #7)
   ISBN 0-310-67011-X (paper)
   I. Title. II. Series: Peart, Jane. Brides of Montclair series :
bk. 7.
   PS3566.E238S5 1991
   813′.54—dc20   91–19158
                                                       CIP

Edited by Anne Severance
Interior Design by Kim Koning
Cover Design by Art Jacobs
Cover Illustration by Wes Lowe, Sal Baracc and Assoc., Inc.

Printed in the United States of America

   92 93 94 95 / LP / 10 9 8 7 6 5 4 3

Part I

1875 to 1876

What? Gone without a word?

—Shakespeare

*To die and part is less an evil than to part and live; there—
there, is the torment.*

—Landsdowne

chapter

1

Cameron Hall

Fall 1875
Mayfield, Virginia

KATE CAMERON stood at the drawing room window of Cameron Hall, watching her son, Rod, take his chestnut gelding over the hedge at the end of the meadow, the horse's flowing mane and the rider's windblown hair almost the same russet gold.

On this early October afternoon, Indian summer lingered in the Virginia countryside although tinges of scarlet edged the leaves of the elms on the avenue of trees lining the drive up to the house.

As horse and rider cantered toward the stables and disappeared from sight, Kate turned away and walked back into the room with the slight stiffness of arthritis that sometimes plagued her at the onset of cool weather.

Even at sixty, Kate retained much of her youthful beauty, still slim and elegant, with only a few faint lines marking the passage of time, trials and tragedy endured showing in her face.

Seating herself in one of the wing chairs beside the fireplace, she looked appreciatively around the gracious high-ceilinged room. Kate had always loved this room from the first time she saw it when she came here as a bride from Savannah forty years before. Cameron Hall, built by her husband's Scottish ancestors who settled on a

King's Grant a century before, was one of the most magnificent of the James River plantations.

Only recently, at Rod's insistence, it had been refurbished. New draperies hung at the arched Palladian windows, its worn upholstery replaced, the carpets restored, everything brought back to its pre-war grandeur.

Under Rod's skillful management, the fortune they, along with most Southerners of their class, had lost with the Confederate defeat was slowly being rebuilt; and the Cameron Hall stables were becoming known as one of the finest Thoroughbred farms among horse-breeding circles.

Kate's heart filled with pride when she thought of how Rod had overcome so much to bring about the present success of the stables and farm. The place had been in disastrous condition when he returned after having been a Yankee prisoner of war. He had also had to face personal heartbreak, the death of his twin brother, Stewart, and the disappearance of the woman he loved—Blythe Montrose.

Kate sighed as her eyes rested upon the family portrait hanging over the mantle, painted when her red-haired twin boys were about eight and her daughter, Garnet, a pixyish three. How young even she and Doug looked then! How happy they had been in that sheltered, idyllic world before the war.

Her thoughts of the past were suddenly interrupted by the sound of the front door's slam and booted footsteps approaching along the polished hall floor. Kate turned her head in anticipation toward the drawing room door that a minute later opened, and a tall man in a tweed riding jacket stepped into the room.

At thirty-eight, Rod was splendid looking, *very much like his father, Douglas Cameron,* Kate mused, broad-shouldered, long-limbed, athletically built. As he had matured, he had grown even more handsome. His strong, well-molded features gave definition and character to his face. Kate liked the mustache he'd worn since the Army too; it gave him a certain dashing air to his almost too serious expression.

However, it was not her son's physical appearance that concerned Kate but his bachelor status.

"Good afternoon, Mother."

"Did you have a good ride?"

"Never better. My new hunter is coming along well. He'll be more than ready at the opening of the fox hunting season," he replied, running his hand carelessly through his hair.

"Isn't it a bit cold in here for you, Mother? There's quite a chill in the air these days."

Walking over to the fireplace, Rod took a log from the basket beside the hearth and tossed it into the fire.

"Is that better?" Rod asked after he had the fire going. "Are you feeling all right? You looked a bit pensive when I came in." Rod gave her a searching look. "Don't tell me you're still missing the *young ladies,* are you?"

Knowing he was referring to their former boarding pupils in the school she and Garnet and Dove had started to help their depleted financial situation after the war, Kate laughed.

"Who would have thought I'd miss all those harum-scarm girls with their giggles and shrieks? But I have to admit I do miss them once in a while." Kate shook her head. "After Garnet remarried, Dove and I couldn't possibly have continued doing it. No, that's a closed chapter, and I find plenty to keep me busy and happy, doing things I didn't have time for when we were runing the Academy. Such as visiting and seeing old friends. In fact,"—here she hesitated before continuing casually, "I've invited Elyse and Fenelle Maynard for tea. Perhaps after you've bathed and changed, you'd like to join us?"

An amused smile tugged at the corner of Rod's mouth, and he lifted an eyebrow. "Must I? Won't it be all tea, tiny cakes, and ladies' talk?" he teased, his eyes twinkling with the old boyish mischief.

Kate touched the cameo at her lace collar, replying nonchalantly, "Oh no, I don't think so, dear. Fenelle is quite charming and clever, and I'm sure they would both be disappointed not to see you while they're here. They've just come back from Richmond, you know, on a visit to Francis, who is in law practice there now. You could just pop in and say hello, couldn't you?"

"Oh, Mother, you *are* transparent!" Rod shook his head, chuckling.

"Perhaps only because I've hit a nerve?" She hesitated before adding earnestly, "Dearest boy, I am just thinking of your happiness. You rarely go out socially any more, turn down more invitations than most people receive! How do you expect to meet anyone . . . especially any eligible young ladies . . . if you don't socialize?"

Rod shrugged. Propping his arm against the mantel shelf, he stared down into the fire.

"Perhaps I'm not interested in socializing or meeting anyone . . . especially not any *eligible*—and by that, I take it you mean *marriageable*—young ladies!" There was an edge of sarcasm in his reply.

"Oh, darling, I don't mean to push. It's only that—well, Rod, isn't it time you thought seriously about marrying? With *you* the Camerons come to an end, you know." She made a sweeping gesture. "And all this, all that has been built here, has been standing for generations—this beautiful house, the land, the stables, the Thoroughbreds—who will it go to when we're gone? Will it be lost? Just as Montclair was lost and the Montrose dynasty ended—"

The mention of that name brought a stillness into the room. When at last Rod broke the silence, his voice sounded choked.

"I had hoped—well, Mother, you *know* what I hoped—" he broke off.

"Yes, darling, I *do* know, and I am sorrier than I can say that things didn't work out the way you wanted them to. But Blythe has been gone for years now. No one has the remotest idea where she went, where she is, what became of her. . . . Even Sara and Clayborn don't know—" Kate halted, recalling the letter she had recently received from Sara Montrose in Savannah. Sara had written that they had received a large sum of money through a New York law firm; they suspected the money had come from Blythe. Sworn to uphold the confidentiality of their client, however, the lawyers had refused to divulge the source when Clay tried to investigate.

"We surmise it must be part of the inheritance from the gold mine or ranch Blythe's father owned in California," Sara had written. "But that is only supposition. It seems the child has vanished into thin air. She was, I'm afraid, never happy in Virginia, so perhaps she returned to California. I wish her Godspeed. The money is some sort of trust fund from which we receive a generous monthly check. I am more than grateful, of course, for it gives us a needed sense of independence, even though sister Lucie could not have been more hospitable here in Savannah. I am confiding this only to you, dear friend. The lawyers were very explicit that we should not tell anyone else whom we suspect to be the source of our windfall. So I trust you not to share this information with anyone else, no one at all, not even your nearest and dearest!"

Had there been any information in Sara's letter that would have helped Rod locate Blythe, Kate knew she would have told him. But since this further mystery would only add to his burden, she had remained silent. By now, everyone in Mayfield—except Rod, perhaps—simply accepted Blythe Montrose's strange disappearance as a closed book. Kate feared that her son would never do so, that he would go on missing Blythe for the rest of his life, failing to even think of building a life with someone new.

Of her two sons, Rod had always been the more difficult for Kate to understand. It was a myth that twins, even if physically "as alike as two peas in a pod," were identical in other ways. Stewart had been so open, so quick to respond, but Rod was much more reserved, keeping his own counsel.

And after the war, he had withdrawn even further into quiet detachment. Of course, he had suffered the irreplaceable loss of his twin, and his prison experience had been brutal. Nevertheless, years had passed, Kate reminded herself. Shouldn't some healing have taken place by now? Characteristically, Rod never spoke of Stewart or Blythe, and Kate had no idea what he was now thinking or feeling.

Rod lifted his head and regarded her wearily. "I understand what you are saying, Mother, and I know how you feel."

Kate reached out her hand in a comforting gesture. "I didn't bring it up to hurt you, son. I wouldn't have said a word. It's just that—" She bit her lip.

"I know, Mother, I know. Believe me, your concern is valid. I think about all this, too." He hesitated before concluding, "I've been planning to go to Ireland on a horse-buying trip, and I thought this time I'd go to England—"

"That would be wonderful, dear! Garnet would be so pleased. She and Jeremy know so many lovely people there, and surely they would introduce you—"

Rod held up a warning hand. "Wait, please, let me finish. What I started to say was I intend to go to London. I've heard there's a firm there that specializes in searching for and locating missing people. I plan to consult them."

"About Blythe? In *England?*"

"It's as good a place as any to try, isn't it?" Rod said with a tight smile. "I've advertised in dozens of western newspapers, contacted every possible lead in California." He flung out his hands in a gesture of helplessness. "And nothing! So I can only assume that she has left the country."

Kate did not know what to say, so she didn't say anything.

In a moment Rod straightened his shoulders and forced an enthusiasm he didn't feel. "Well, I'm off to get washed, brushed, and curried to make myself presentable for your tea party." As he strode toward the door, he called back over his shoulder. "Don't worry about me, Mother. I'll be fine. Things will work out."

I pray so, dear son, Kate said silently. *Lord,* she prayed, *I believe you will bring about what is best, but I ask please make it soon.* She ached with sympathy for this man who had so courageously carried his heartbreak for the past six long years.

Just outside the drawing room door, Rod halted, clenching his jaw. Why couldn't he forget her? Why had every other woman since Blythe seemed so ordinary? He closed his eyes, wincing as if in pain, and her face came to his mind as clearly and vividly as when they had ridden through the autumn woods together and she had turned in her saddle to look back at him with her dancing brown eyes, her glorious hair streaming in sunbright strands in the wind.

Blythe, my love, where are you? Why did you leave without a word? Will I ever see you again?

With an effort, Rod dragged himself back to the present. Shoulders set firmly, he crossed the hall and mounted the stairway to his room, determined to make as pleasant a task as possible of the afternoon with the Maynard ladies.

A small, shabby buggy, drawn by an ancient mare, rounded the bend of the drive, bringing Cameron Hall into full view of its occupants, a plump dowager and a younger woman, sitting stiffly erect in the hard seat.

Elyse Maynard turned to her daughter and gave her a studied appraisal, flicking an imaginary bit of lint from the immaculate, if worn, afternoon gown. "Now, for pity's sake, Fenelle, if Rod comes in, don't sit like a bump on a pickle all afternoon. Be animated! Men like girls who can carry on an interesting conversation, can be witty as well as look nice."

Fenelle folded her lace-gloved hands in her lap and suppressed a sigh, bracing herself for her mother's usual instructional before any social visit. This one, of course, was especially important, at least in her mother's estimation. Rod Cameron would be joining them this afternoon for tea, the invitation had stated. And Rod Cameron, in Elyse Maynard's eyes, was a fine "catch."

"It's not as though you were still eighteen, Fenelle," her mother reminded her. "So many of our eligible young men lost their lives fighting for our glorious Cause, you know. It isn't as if you had the choices you once had, dear girl."

Fenelle needed no reminder that she would be thirty on her next birthday, although with a bland blondness—pale, smooth skin and cornflower blue eyes—she looked at least five years younger. Yet, as each birthday approached and she was no nearer settling down, her mother's anxiety increased. Fenelle could not remember when they had actually stopped celebrating birthdays. Now, her mother pretended to forget them.

"Not that anyone remembers birthdates—" her mother said philosophically and repeatedly. "Anyone who would ask a lady her age—well!" was a sentence that Elyse Maynard never finished, leaving the fate of such a gauche person to her listener's imagination.

Besides her delicate prettiness, Fenelle was shy and sensitive and suffered acutely from her mother's obsession with her continued spinsterhood. What was harder to endure was the fact that she was not even allowed to grieve the loss of Holt Chalmers, the young lieutenant who surely would have married her had he not been killed at Antietam early in the war. Her mother fluttered nervously if Fenelle even mentioned his name, and she did not approve the fact that her daughter kept his picture on her bureau with a small vase of fresh flowers before it.

"The war is long over, Fenelle. Not one southern family has escaped losing someone. I loved Holt and mourned for him as deeply as anyone who knew him, but it's been years now, sweetheart. You simply *must* get hold of yourself."

Why *must* I? Fenelle asked herself rebelliously.

Of course, she knew why her mother was so insistent that she put her ill-fated love aside. Since Fenelle's papa, Everett Maynard, had died, the two women were practically penniless. Having given generously to the Confederate cause, he had been left with nothing but stacks of worthless paper money. While walking home from his law office one summer afternoon in 1872—an office that had seen no paying clients in years—he had suffered a fatal heart attack. Fenelle, who had loved him deeply, was convinced that her father's heart had simply broken.

To keep a roof over their heads and food on their table, she and her mother had been forced to sell off valuable family treasures, piece by piece. Then, too, Fenelle's brother, Francis, who had been an undercover agent for the Confederacy, worked as a law clerk in a big firm in Richmond and sent home as much money as he could spare from his small salary.

But what Mrs. Maynard said they needed and was determined to arrange was a wealthy husband for Fenelle, one who could support all of them in fine style.

There were very few men left in the south who could fill her requirements—men of good breeding, excellent character, and unlimited resources. Rod Cameron was one of these.

"And don't talk about books!" was Mrs. Maynard's final directive as she firmly reined in in front of the curved welcoming arm steps of Cameron Hall. "I don't imagine Rod has the inclination or time to read nor is much interested in people who do! I wish you'd study up on horses," she added as an afterthought, again glancing critically at her daughter. "Now, straighten your bonnet and smile!" She gathered her skirts and placed a determined smile on her own face just as Kate Cameron walked out on the veranda to greet them.

chapter

2

Cameron Hall
Mayfield, Virginia

Rod looked across the room at Mrs. Maynard, perched on the edge of one of the wing chairs like an uneasy bird, balancing her teacup with one plump hand while propelling a dainty cucumber sandwich to her mouth with the other. A mouth that Rod noted with some annoyance, had not stopped moving since the Maynards' arrival.

"I do declare, Kate, I never cease to be amazed at the ways some of our dearest friends have managed to survive since the war. Why, just the other day when Fenelle and I were making calls, whom do you suppose we ran into just as we were getting out of our landau in front of Mamie Dunaway's?" She paused breathlessly to let Mrs. Cameron guess, taking advantage of the moment to pop another tiny triangle of bread into her mouth. Before Kate could answer, Mrs. Maynard had chewed, taken a swallow of tea, and was ready to continue.

"None other than Harmony Chance, who was, you remember, a cousin of the Montrose family . . . on the Barnwell side, I believe. Well, she was with her daughter, Alair . . . such a beautiful girl! . . . and so vivacious—" Here she cast a significant glance at her own daughter, who was demurely sipping her tea. "Of course, I was surprised to see them over here, all the way from Winchester, and

16

when I asked what in the world they were doing so far from home, you will never imagine what we were told!"

Mrs. Maynard surveyed her audience, her eyes moving from one to the other with the look of a secretive tabby cat just waiting to pounce.

Rod stirred restlessly in his chair. Mrs. Maynard was everything he disliked in a woman—a gossip, a whiner, a pessimist. Only his innate good manners kept him from displaying his utter boredom and distaste for the half-hour's monologue to which he'd been subjected. He had no interest in conversation that dwelt on the flaws and foibles of every person whose name had been mentioned during the afternoon. But nothing seemed to check Elyse Maynard's deluge of words as long as she possessed privileged information.

Satisfied that no one knew why the Chances happened to be in Mayfield, she resumed. "They were shopping for fabrics for Alair's trousseau!" announced Mrs. Maynard with a smug look, then folded her hands in her lap, looking around to gauge the impact of this piece of news.

"Alair? Getting married? But she's hardly more than a child!" exclaimed Kate.

"Eighteen her next birthday!" declared Mrs. Maynard. "But, my dear, you will never in all your born days imagine to whom she's engaged!" Another round of glances, then triumphantly, "Randall Bondurant! The blackguard who stole Montclair from Malcolm Montrose!"

In spite of herself, Kate Cameron drew in her breath in an audible gasp and set down her teacup. "You don't mean it!"

Mrs. Maynard nodded her head emphatically.

"I do indeed. I was every bit as shocked as you, my dear Kate. I tried not to reveal it, but I felt quite faint, didn't I, Fen?" She turned to her daughter for confirmation. "Harmony was so obviously pleased with the match that I wouldn't have spoiled it. But of course, she never did have a grain of sense, even as a girl, and I've known her all my life. And then Alair was so thrilled, showing off her ring—which is the biggest, most vulgar diamond I've ever seen!

I mean, my dear, what could I have said or done but admire it and wish the girl happiness?" She threw out both fat little hands.

During this recital Rod regarded Fenelle through narrowed eyes. Color had risen into her pale cheeks, and long lashes fluttered over downcast eyes. *Why, the poor girl is as embarrassed as can be over her mother,* he thought with sudden sympathy as Elyse Maynard rattled on.

"Well, I tried to be as polite as possible, but it was all I could do not to give Harmony a good piece of my mind right then and there. Remind her how Montclair came to belong to Bondurant, and how no one, absolutely *no one* in Mayfield has received him since he came here to live! Well, at least, none of the old families. I understand he *is* received in some homes and *particularly* in the homes of some of the Yankee newcomers, the *'nouveau riche'* who came here after the war—but *really!* " she huffed in exasperation. "What *can* Harmony and Clint be thinking of to let their only daughter marry such a— such—" Her words spun out like a spool empty of thread at last.

Even Kate, always the diplomat, seemed at a loss for an explanation.

"Of course, Harmony and Clint have had a very hard time," she suggested. "You know their home was occupied and left in shambles by the Yankees, and Clint was so badly wounded he has never been well since he came back from the war—I know Harmony grieved that they were not able to do for Alair what they would have if they had not lost everything. Perhaps, marrying someone like Bondurant, being mistress of a beautiful home like Montclair seems a good future for their daughter."

Elyse drew herself up indignantly. "Well, I'm not saying it's all their fault, Kate. Surely some of the blame has to be laid at the feet of Malcolm Montrose. It was he who squandered what was left of the Montrose estate—lost it in the end—"

Immediately Rod sprang to his old friend's defense.

"Malcolm was a casualty of the war as much as any soldier who died on the battlefield, Mrs. Maynard. He suffered irrevocable loss, may I remind you, in the tragic death of his wife, Rose—"

Mrs. Maynard seemed miffed at the implied reprimand and dismissed Rod's reminder with a wave of one hand.

"Of course, I know all that, dear boy. But there were others who suffered every bit as much—" The deep sigh and pursed lips made plain that the Maynards had had their *own* severe losses from the war, although she was too much a lady to bring it up!

Kate, hoping to avoid a verbal conflict between her guest and her outspoken son, hurriedly changed the subject.

"Has a date for the wedding been set?"

Mollified at the chance to relay more information on the startling piece of news she had furnished, Elyse chattered on.

"Oh, it is to be quite a lavish affair, Harmony says. The wedding will take place in the gardens at Montclair, which she told me have been fully restored and will be in glorious bloom in early spring. Alair says there will be at least a dozen bridesmaids and a European honeymoon to follow! Why, Montclair hasn't seen such an event in many a year. Malcolm was married up north, and then I suppose his second marriage took place in California—" Mrs. Maynard pronounced the name with distaste, as if it were as strange a place to be married as Tibet! She paused then and interjected, "Whatever became of that girl Malcolm brought home? The one from the West . . . what was her name?"

Kate, casting a quick, anxious look at Rod, replied for him. "Blythe. And she left after the house and property were taken. No one has ever heard where she went." She rushed on to fill the awkward silence. "So, tell us about your trip, Elyse. When do you and Fenelle leave for England?"

At the mention of Blythe's name, Rod felt the familiar pang, that wrenching blend of anger and frustration. Again her image flashed before him—those haunting eyes, sometimes alight with laughter, other times like dark woodland pools, unfathomable and mysterious; the sweet curve of her mouth, the apricot flush of her cheeks—

"More tea, darling?" His mother's voice reclaimed him, sparing him further painful memories.

Rod held out his cup and, as he did so, he caught Fenelle's gaze upon him and met it with a smile. He watched as she colored, and an answering smile played at the corners of her lips. *How shy she is,* he thought, *how completely different from her mother.*

"My brother-in-law, Webb, has booked us on one of the finest, newest British passenger ships." Mrs. Maynard beamed. "We sail on the tenth of April." Then leaning forward confidentially, she said, "You know, Everett's brother was smart enough to see the storm coming, and long before any of the rest of us recognized that war with the North was inevitable, he took his family—and, I might add, his fortune—and went to England, a country that was, as you know, most sympathetic to our cause."

Her loud sigh attested to her regret that her own husband had not followed his brother's wise counsel in the matter of business.

"How lovely for both of you. And such an educational opportunity for you, Fenelle," Kate murmured, including the young woman in the conversation which, up to this point, had been monopolized by her mother.

"Oh, yes, indeed. Webb has wanted us to come ever since the war ended, but dear Everett, as you know, was unwell and we did not feel he could withstand the journey. Since his passing—" Here Elyse reached into her small handbag and drew out a lace-edged handkerchief with which she dabbed briefly at dry eyes. "Webb has been urging us to come for some time. At length, *he* made all the arrangements for our passage himself. And Deidra, his wife, has all sorts of plans for Fenelle. A London season!" Mrs. Maynard simpered, adding significantly, with a sidelong glance at Rod, "It seems American girls are much admired and sought after in society over *there*. She has even suggested Fenelle may be presented at Court!"

"How exciting!" Kate smiled at Fenelle whose face was now quite rosy, reflecting the unwelcome attention focused upon her.

"Oh my, yes! We may even come home with a title, who knows?" Mrs. Maynard giggled girlishly and wagged a playful finger at Rod. "I must say American men may have to look to their laurels with such competition from English gentlemen. Our young ladies may become our most important export!"

Sensing Fenelle's embarrassment, Rod's compassion was aroused. "You ride, don't you, Miss Fenelle?"

She perked up visibly. "Oh, yes."

"Perhaps you would like to see my new hunter before you leave."

"I'd like that very much," she said, relief evident in her voice.

Rod got to his feet. "He's pastured in the near meadow. We could walk down and see him, if you like."

Fenelle turned to her mother questioningly. "Mama?"

"Yes, yes. You two young people run along." Mrs. Maynard looked pleased. "But don't be long, dear. We have other calls to make, you know."

As they strolled out onto the porch and down the steps to the terrace, then over the lawn toward the pasture, Rod gave the young woman beside him a measured look.

Fenelle Maynard was tall, slender as a wand, with the fine, delicate features of an aristocrat. Her blue eyes, when she turned to look at him, were almost at a level with his. Under his steady gaze she nervously raised a hand to tuck a straying strand of pale, blond hair under her bonnet.

At once, Rod felt a protective affection for her. Putting up with that dreadful mother of hers must be an ordeal. He had known and admired her brother, Francis, who had risked his life for the Confederacy during the war, and Rod considered that Francis's sister possibly possessed the same qualities of quiet bravery and endurance.

When they reached the fence, they leaned against the top rail and watched with silent pleasure as the chestnut gelding, golden mane flying, galloped in splendid freedom.

After a while Fenelle said softly, "He's very beautiful."

Rod followed the graceful movement of his horse with pride.

"Yes," he agreed. Presently he said, "I'm going to Ireland in a few months to visit a horse farm owned by a friend and purchase some horses for my stable." Eyeing Fenelle curiously, he continued, "You know my sister Garnet lives in England. When I finish my business in Ireland, I plan to visit her there. Since you'll be in London at the same time, perhaps I could call on you at your uncle's home."

He watched as a slow blush suffused Fenelle's translucent skin. She turned serious eyes upon him in which he saw, for the first time, a flicker of life and interest.

"I would like that very much, Rod."

The birth of her smile was a beautiful thing to behold.

"I'll give you Uncle Webb's London address, and I shall look forward to seeing you—"

Nothing comes to pass but what God appoints. Our fate is decreed and things do not happen by chance; everyone's portion of joy or sorrow is predetermined—Seneca

chapter
3

Victoria Station
London, England

GARNET DEVLIN entered her first-class compartment, accompanied by her maid, Myrna, carrying her mistress's valise and jewel case, followed by a porter with the rest of the baggage. While Myrna directed the stowing of the suitcases, Garnet seated herself for the two-hour train ride to her country home.

As the porter departed with a mumbled "Thankee mum" for the tip, Garnet realized that in her last-minute rush to the station, she had forgotten the new novel she had intended to bring along.

Annoyed at her own absentmindedness, she said fretfully, "Oh, Myrna, do run back into the station and buy me the latest edition of *Queen*. I forgot my book, and I need something to read on the way."

"Yes, madam."

Myrna opened the compartment door, ready to step out, when Garnet added, "Oh, and a box of caramel toffee, too, please. Do hurry, though. For once, the train might leave on time!"

The maid hurried off about her errand, and Garnet settled in, loosening her sable scarf and removing the hatpins from her velvet toque.

She wasn't particularly looking forward to this weekend. They would be entertaining some of Jeremy's business acquaintances, one of whom was an author newly acquired by the publishing firm. Garnet sighed. Writers were always so tedious—either completely self-absorbed or else tiresomely inarticulate. One had to make such an effort to draw them out on any subject other than their own writing project! To make matters worse, *this* one had a French wife, which meant she would be bringing her French maid and *that* would certainly upset the Devlins' household servants.

Garnet would have much preferred to entertain some of their own friends, or better still, to spend a weekend alone with her husband. Even after nearly six years of marriage, they still enjoyed each other's company more than any other.

Smiling, she preened a little. Jeremy was a devoted husband, making her feel as cherished and desirable as when he had first fallen in love with her. Now they had their precious little daughter, Faith, who was literally the "apple of his eye." Yes, it would have been nice if this could have been a family weekend.

The train whistle shrilled, and Garnet checked her diamond lapel watch, frowning. Where was Myrna? It shouldn't have taken this long to fetch the fashion magazine and a box of candy. Leaning forward, Garnet peered anxiously out the compartment window to see if her maid was coming.

Just at that moment, across the platform another train pulled in on the track parallel to hers. As compartment doors opened and passengers began to emerge, Garnet suddenly drew in her breath, her eyes widened in shock.

In disbelief, she watched as a young woman stepped out onto the platform, pausing there as if expecting to be met. She was stylishly dressed in a dove-gray suit trimmed with black Russian braid and wore a small black hat tilted forward with a sheer black veil drawn across her face and tied in back with a bow. This did not, however, hide her flame colored hair. A name formed soundlessly on Garnet's lips as the young woman began walking toward the station gates. Even so, she had stood there long enough for Garnet to get a good look.

Shaking, she sank back against the plush seat, her heart pounding. She couldn't be mistaken. Though she had changed, everyone changes in six years, she would have recognized *Blythe* anywhere!

Blythe! It *was* Blythe! Malcolm Montrose's widow, Rod's long-lost love!

Blythe, in England! This was the last place on earth Garnet would ever have expected to see Blythe Montrose. What was she doing here? Did she live in the city? Or had she, like Garnet, come on a shopping expedition, or perhaps to visit friends? And had she been here all this time since leaving Montclair under such mysterious circumstances? No one had ever known what had become of her.

Rod! Suddenly Garnet thought of her brother who had loved Blythe so hopelessly, even while she was married to Malcolm. Just this very week Garnet had received a letter from her mother saying Rod was coming to England. Garnet still had the letter. Now she drew it out of her purse and reread it.

Kate had written that Rod was sailing on the same ship as their old family friends, Mrs. Maynard and her daughter, Fenelle—the mother and sister of an old beau of Garnet's, Francis Maynard. According to Kate: "Fenelle has grown up to be a very attractive young woman, and Rod seems quite taken with her. How I wish something would develop between them. I long for him to find happiness again and yearn for Cameron grandchildren to make this house ring with the merry sound of children once more. And, of course, to carry on this proud name."

Just then Myrna, breathless from hurrying, entered the compartment. "Sorry, madam, but they didn't have a new *Queen,* so I brought *Ladies' Day* instead. I hope that is suitable? And they only had chocolate buds—no caramels."

Ordinarily, Garnet might have been cross at the substitutions, but today she was too preoccupied with her thoughts. She took the magazine and box of sweets her maid handed her, hardly aware that the engine whistle was shrieking again, and the train began to move slowly forward.

As the train gathered speed, Garnet wrestled with her dilemma. When Rod came, should she tell him she had seen Blythe? She had no idea on which train Blythe had arrived or where she was going or at which station along the route she may have boarded. She may have been visiting someone in the country or—oh, the possibilities were endless! It was enough of a mystery how she had come to be in England at all. And what a bizarre coincidence for Garnet to have seen her!

Garnet thought of her last trip home to Virginia and the haunted look in her brother's eyes. If anyone could recognize and understand unrequited love, it was she. Hadn't she loved Malcolm Montrose in vain for years? It was only after he brought Blythe from California and after Jeremy had come into her life that Garnet had finally been able to come to terms with her hopeless fantasy.

She remembered Rod's torment when Blythe still lived at Montclair in those last months with Malcolm, who had gone off on a binge, drinking and gambling, until at last, the ultimate tragedy—he lost his ancestral home in a card game. Within weeks, he was dead. A horseback accident. And Blythe? She had simply disappeared. The letter she had left explained the situation but gave no hint of where she was going or what she planned to do.

It had been a terrible time, and Rod was still suffering. Involuntarily, Garnet shuddered.

"Are you chilled, madam?" Myrna asked solicitously. "Here, let me put this lap robe over your knees. Should I order tea?"

Distracted, Garnet merely nodded, her thoughts spinning as fast as the train wheels, the question in her mind echoing with every revolution: *What shall I do? What shall I do?*

As the train wound its way through the city railyards and then picked up speed, rattling forward, Garnet leaned back against the cushioned seat.

Blythe! Here in England or perhaps in London! It seemed impossible, but Garnet felt sure she had not been mistaken. She had had a good look. That face with its small high-bridged nose, the proud set of her head, her graceful carriage—all were stamped indelibly on Garnet's mind from the first day she had seen her nearly eight years ago.

"Madam, your tea. Shall I pour for you?" Myrna spoke. Garnet looked up into her maid's concerned eyes as she offered her the small tray with a squat brown pottery teapot and a thick white cup and saucer she had obtained from the porter.

"Yes, thank you." Sipping the hot liquid, she stared out the window at the changing landscape. Grimy warehouses and rows of soot-blackened buildings gradually gave way to lush, rolling countryside. The train clattered over arched stone bridges, thundered through villages, stopped at flower-bordered stations, then started up again, passing through long stretches of meadow where sheep grazed and cottages nestled against the green hillsides.

Blythe . . . Blythe . . . Over and over the train wheels seemed to repeat the name.

Then, as it had long ago, Malcolm's voice intruded into Garnet's thoughts, "Garnet, may I present my wife—Blythe Dorman *Montrose.*"

Stunned at the word *wife*, Garnet had stared at the girl framed in the doorway of the pantry at Montclair. Even now she could feel the numbing shock. She had felt exactly as when she had fallen out of a tree as a little girl, landing flat on the ground. Although she had not been able to breathe or speak, Garnet saw that she was young and very beautiful. It was her eyes Garnet noticed first—large, dark, frightened as those of a startled doe, then the glorious auburn hair curling around her heart-shaped face from under the edge of an atrocious purple bonnet that looked very much the worse for wear. But even her peculiar outfit could not disguise a lovely figure.

Bewildered, Garnet had turned to Malcolm for some kind of explanation. But Malcolm had stepped away from her, distancing himself physically as well as emotionally, and she had looked into the eyes of a stranger.

Where was the Malcolm of old, the one she had loved so desperately all her life, the one who had broken her heart by marrying Rose Meredith, his Yankee bride? Would he now break it a second time?

Somehow she had managed to mumble that Sara, an invalid, must be prepared for her son's unexpected return, and for the surprising news that he had brought back a bride from California. Even now, so many years later, Garnet could still remember the blinding tears that crowded into her eyes as she had stumbled up the stairway toward Sara's room.

Betrayed! Every other thought was suppressed by this one fact. Betrayed by her own heart as well as by Malcolm—Malcolm whom she had worshiped as a child, longed for as a young girl, coveted as a woman. Malcolm, for whom she had hopefully waited during the years of her own widowhood, keeping his home, caring for his invalid mother and his little son, Jonathan, expecting that at long last all her yearning, dreaming, waiting would be rewarded. Then he had returned, and with him, Blythe.

"We're coming into the station now, ma'am," Myrna said as the train pulled to a stop. Garnet snapped back to the present and stepped out of the compartment onto the platform.

The Devlin coachman was waiting for them. He saw to the luggage and assisted Garnet into the small carriage. Springing to his perch in front, he lifted the reins, gave the two bays a flick of his buggy whip, and set off at a brisk trot down the road to "Birchfields."

The house Jeremy had bought for them in the country had a long and interesting history, dating back further than Garnet cared to hear. In the 1840s it had passed out of the hands of the original owners, been purchased by one of the newly wealthy industrialists, and refurbished and modernized. The place—surrounded by storied English gardens—provided a haven of peace after the busy social life Jeremy's work demanded of them in London.

Jogging along the winding country road, Garnet was still preoccupied. She was almost glad now that Jeremy wouldn't be down until tomorrow when he would arrive with their guests—the writer, his wife, and their entourage. Having this evening alone would give her time to think things through, to decide whether to write her mother about her strange sighting of Blythe at Victoria Station, to prepare Rod for the possibility that she was now living in England. Or would that be too cruel? Besides, what did she really have to tell them? Finding Blythe in London or wherever she was would still be like searching for the proverbial needle in a haystack.

Perhaps it would be best not to mention it at all.

By the time they drove up the curved driveway and halted at the front entrance of the timbered and stone Tudor mansion, Garnet was still undecided. Hadley, the butler, came down the steps to see to the luggage. Lined up in the front hall to greet her were Mrs. Cavanaugh, the housekeeper, and the three maids.

Even after years in England, Garnet still found it strange having white servants. She had learned one did not treat English staff with the same careless informality with which she had always interacted with her own family's black servants back home in Virginia; and certainly not with the intimacy she had enjoyed with Tilda, Carrie, and Bessie during the war years at Montclair.

"Good afternoon, Mrs. Devlin. I hope you had a pleasant trip down," Mrs. Cavanaugh greeted her.

"It was . . . all right," Garnet said evasively, then admitted, "Actually, I'm exhausted, Mrs. Cavanaugh. And with company coming tomorrow, I think I'll just have something light for dinner in my suite and get to bed early."

"As you wish, madam," the housekeeper replied. Then as Garnet started toward the stairway, Mrs. Cavanaugh asked, "Will Miss Faith be coming down this weekend as well?"

Garnet paused. "Yes, Nanny will be bringing her with her father on the morning train."

Continuing up the steps, Garnet thought fondly of how Jeremy adored their little daughter. Even when he was entertaining, he liked having Faith around, unlike most English fathers, who did well to give their children a pat on the head when they were brought down by their nurses before bedtime. She had yet to see an English gentleman lavish much love or attention on a child. She was blessed indeed, Garnet thought as she entered the master suite on the second floor.

Myrna, who had followed Garnet upstairs, helped her off with her coat and into a velvet-and-lace dressing gown, saying quietly, "I'll get you some hot tea, madam. That should relax you and help you rest."

"Thank you, Myrna," Garnet replied absently and went to look out the window overlooking the formal garden with its maze of boxwood hedges. "It will be a busy weekend—"

Her mind still on Jeremy, Garnet took out her hairpins, thinking of the unexpected way her husband had come into her life. Considering the circumstances, surely their meeting had been providential—

Toward the end of the war Garnet had been living at Montclair, her husband's home, while Bryce rode with Mosby's raiders. She, her widowed sister-in-law Dove, their cousin Harmony Chance, their children, her father-in-law, Clayton Montrose, and Sara, Garnet's invalid mother-in-law were alone there while the men fought for the Confederacy. After the death of Rose, Malcolm's first wife, Garnet assumed the care of their son while Malcolm served with Lee's army.

The four women had just been terrorized by a raid made by a small band of undisciplined Union soldiers who had threatened to return when Jeremy, then a major in the Union army, had offered them his protection.

Thereafter, though officially their enemy, he had come each night to guard the house against any unordered attack by renegade soldiers. Later, he had also returned Jonathan's little pony, Bugle Boy, confiscated by the troopers along with the rest of the livestock.

After the war, Jeremy had returned to Virginia and surprised Garnet one day by calling on her. Now a widow, she was overwhelmed by the darkness of her life, and she was touchingly grateful for the attention of this handsome and sophisticated man, now an executive with a prestigious New York publishing firm. To her further surprise, he had declared his love for her and his desire to marry her.

Jeremy finally convinced Garnet, who had never expected to know love again, that they could find happiness together. With the respect and admiration he had earned from her during the war came a dawning realization of love, and they were married at Cameron Hall.

After all the years of deprivation, Jeremy had given her a life she could never have imagined. With publishing offices both in New York and London, they divided their time between the two cities, combining Jeremy's business trips with interludes of pleasure. They stayed in some of Europe's grandest hotels, visited Austria and Switzerland, where Garnet was stunned by the sight of the spectacular Alps. They toured capital cities, saw the great works of art in museums, heard music played by some of the finest orchestras conducted by the most famous maestros of the concert world, took boat trips down the Rhine, viewing the fairy-tale castles from the decks of luxury yachts.

Life had opened into astonishing vistas for Garnet since her marriage. Still, although she appreciated and enjoyed her exciting new life, she was often homesick for Virginia, and it was a special joy for her to be able to travel often to visit her mother in Mayfield and to see her brother, Rod.

Her thoughts turned to Rod. It just wasn't fair! He had cared for Malcolm Montrose's neglected second wife with a devoted passion, and she had apparently abandoned him after losing Malcolm and Montclair. Now Garnet had seen her—Blythe, the object of his long search, the source of so much of Garnet's past pain and envy.

Garnet reached for the double silver frame on her dressing table and studied the photographs. On one side was a picture of her two brothers, Rod and Stewart, looking so handsome in their brand-new Confederate uniforms. The other picture was of Rod alone, ten years later.

He was still quite handsome. But there was something about his expression that had not been present in the first picture, she thought as she compared them—the indefinable look of someone who has been touched by tragedy. The eyes held a secret sorrow, a secret not hidden from his sister.

Again Garnet fretted. Would it diminish his heartache to know she thought she had seen the woman he had loved and lost? The one great love of his life? Or would it only prolong his pain?

chapter
4

Belvedere Square
London, England

"Good afternoon, Mrs. Montrose. The carriage is over here."

"Thank you, Barnes." Blythe replied, then followed the Ainsleys' coachman to the dark green carriage at the curbing outside the train station.

Barnes tossed a coin to the boy holding the reins of a sleek pair of horses, then opened the door for Blythe to get inside.

Seated in the luxurious interior as it rolled smoothly through the city, Blythe gazed with interest at the panorama unfolding outside the window. The crowded streets, bustling pedestrians all in an intense hurry to get somewhere, and noisy activity contrasted sharply with the quiet village where she lived.

It was a rare occasion, usually at her friend Lydia Ainsley's insistence, when Blythe could be persuaded to come up for a few days' visit. Although she enjoyed shopping and dining out at one of the fine restaurants before going to the theater, more and more she was reluctant to leave her serene life in the country and the delightful company of her small son.

This time, however, she had come to town for the specific purpose of seeking help on a decision that had been troubling her a good deal. She had delayed coming for weeks. Now she could no longer put it off. The decision must be made soon, or so Corin Prescott had told her.

Blythe frowned, remembering the conversation that a few weeks before had started her thinking about the whole matter. Corin, her friend and neighbor in Kentburne, had brought it to her attention. The discussion had disturbed her so that finally she knew she must put all her concerns before Edward Ainsley. As her son's godfather, he would be the logical one to consult.

Edward and Lydia Ainsley were dear and trusted friends. She had first met them through her father's New York attorneys. Recently widowed, absolutely alone in the world and pregnant, Blythe had faced an uncertain future. Evicted from Montclair three days before Christmas, just weeks after Malcolm's death, she had fled the shambles of her life in Virginia—but not before going through Malcolm's trunk, in which Blythe had found a letter addressed to her from her late father. In it were five hundred dollars in gold and instructions to contact the law firm of Cargill, Hoskins and Sedgewick in New York City. There she discovered her father had set up a trust fund for her after his first gold strike in California. Having invested in railroad, shipping, and other valuable stocks, he had made her a wealthy woman!

On the romantic whim that Malcolm's child should be born in England, the land of his favorite authors and poets, Blythe first planned to go there. Her lawyer, however, advised her that in her condition the warm climate of Bermuda might be a better choice and offered to write a letter of introduction for her to some friends who were wintering there.

In Bermuda, Blythe and Lydia had become immediate friends. Later, she sailed with them for England and stayed with them in their London town house until they helped her find Larkspur Cottage in Kentburne, a charming village about twenty-five miles from London, where she had lived ever since. When her baby was born that summer, the Ainsleys were the natural choice for his godparents.

But Jeff was no longer a baby, Blythe reminded herself, six years old and next year, starting school!

As the carriage turned toward Belvedere Square, the exclusive residential area where the Ainsleys lived, Blythe recalled that conversation with Corin Prescott.

Corin had stopped by with some cuttings from his own large garden for Blythe to plant in her smaller one, and they had stood together watching Jeff roll his hoop wobbily down the lane in front of her cottage.

"He's growing fast, isn't he?" Corin commented. "What a fine big fellow he's getting to be, Blythe. He'll make a cricket player his first year at his boarding school, I've no doubt."

"Boarding school?" echoed Blythe, puzzled.

"Of course, hasn't Ainsley looked into the matter for you yet?" Corin seemed surprised. "When there's no father, that's usually the godparent's job."

"No, he hasn't mentioned it. But I have no intention of letting Jeff go away to school!"

"But, my dear Blythe, all young boys must be sent off to school at his age," Corin explained patiently.

"Why must they? There's a perfectly good school right here in the village."

"Not for a *gentleman's* son," Corin corrected her.

Blythe thought that over for a full minute before saying, "But I don't want him to go away. I would miss him too much."

Corin's voice was gentle. "There's the boy to think of, Blythe. He needs other lads for playmates, fellows his own age as well as older boys for models. That's especially important for a lad growing up without a father or brothers."

Blythe gave him a rueful glance. "And in a household of women? *Doting* women, at that, I suppose?"

Corin laughed. "I didn't say that! But I do believe what I'm saying is true, Blythe. It wouldn't be for Jeff like it was for me. My parents were in India where my father was posted, and I had to come back to England to go to school. It was years before I saw them again. But you can choose a school fairly close, where you can see Jeff often. And then, of course, there will be holidays and vacations, when he'll come home."

Blythe hated the whole idea of sending her little boy away, having other people looking after him. But if, according to Corin, it was the best thing for him, she would have to consider it.

Seeing that it had made Blythe so uncomfortable, Corin tactfully refrained from bringing up the subject again. But Blythe knew she must consult Edward about a school for Jeff. She trusted his judgment, knowing that he himself was a product of the English "public school system," which, paradoxically, meant "private boys' boarding school."

After listening carefully to what Edward had to say, she would reserve her right, as Jeff's mother, to make the final decision.

Blythe sighed. Bringing up a child alone was so . . . lonely. Suddenly she thought of California, of the one-room schoolhouse in Lucas Valley where she had gone to school. How different her son's life would have been if, after Pa's death, she and Malcolm had stayed there to run the ranch.

Jeff would have lived a healthy outdoor life in the Sierra foothills—roaming the woods, wading, swimming, fishing, riding horseback—instead of fulfilling the expectations of an "English gentleman."

Had she made a mistake in coming here? Making a life for herself and her son so far from California? Or even so far from Jeff's Virginia heritage?

But there was no heritage now, no Montclair for Jeff. His father had lost it all on the turn of a card.

Thoughts of Virginia and Montclair were always bittersweet. She *had* loved Malcolm. Had he lived, they *might* have been able to work out their life together. Blythe was too honest not to admit the disturbing truth that it was her love for another man that had compelled her to leave without disclosing her whereabouts to a anyone. Carrying Malcolm's child, how could she have sought help from Rod or reveal the love she had for him?

Unbidden came the memory of riding horseback with Rod through sunlit autumn woods one particular day, when they had stood together on the rustic bridge over a rushing stream. She was certain that he had been on the verge of declaring his love. Panic-stricken at the thought of betraying Malcolm, she had run away, back to the dubious safety of her husband's home. Later, she had been forced to run again, putting as much distance as possible between them.

The carriage came to a stop. Blythe saw that they had reached the Ainsleys' impressive town house. Quickly, she thrust away her painful memories. *Better not to remember,* Blythe thought. *What was past was forever lost. It is the present and, most of all, Jeff's future that counts now.*

Lydia Ainsley came rushing down the carpeted stairway to greet her friend with a warm hug.

"Oh, it's so good to see you, Blythe!"

To the butler who was standing silently by, she said, "We'll take tea upstairs, Thompson, in my sitting room."

With an arm about Blythe's waist, Lydia led her to the stairs and started up. "Come along, Blythe. We have so much to catch up on. I'm eager to hear all your news!"

Lydia Ainsley's sitting room reflected her charm and good taste. Rose velvet draperies were drawn against the fog of the London afternoon, and a cheerful fire glowed in the small white marble fireplace. With a graceful hand Lydia waved Blythe to one of the matching curved loveseats.

"Do sit down and take off your hat, Blythe. Be comfortable."

As Blythe followed her hostess's suggestion, a discreet knock came at the door. A maid in a black uniform and white ruffled cap and apron entered, bearing a large tray.

Recognizing the maid as the same young woman who was always assigned to attend her whenever Blythe was a guest in the Ainsley home, she spoke. "Hello, Violet."

The girl darted a quick look at Lydia before answering. Blythe's easy American manners broke with the rigid protocol in this traditional upper-class English household, where the presence of servants was rarely acknowledged. Lydia gave an imperceptible nod.

"Good afternoon, Mrs. Montrose." Violet dropped a little curtsy. "It's nice to see you again, ma'am. And 'ow's little Master Jeff?"

"Growing like a weed, Violet!"

Violet set down the tray and stepped back, awaiting orders from her mistress.

"That will be all, Violet. Thank you."

"Yes ma'am." With another curtsy Violet exited, and the two ladies settled down to tea and conversation.

As she poured the steaming Oolong tea into shell-thin cups, Lydia said, "I was so happy to get your note that you were coming up for a visit, Blythe. We don't see half enough of you. And with Edward so busy here in the city, we don't get down often to see you in the country. And how is my darling godchild?" Lydia asked as she handed Blythe her cup.

"Thriving, and a real joy as well as a handful, of course!" Blythe laughed, beginning to relax in this atmosphere of affection and warmth. She always felt welcome here. "Actually, it is precisely because of Jeff that I've made this visit. I need to talk to Edward about him."

Lydia registered alarm. "Nothing wrong, I hope?"

Blythe shook her head. "No, not at all. I just need to ask Edward's advice about Jeff's education. He's very bright, you know. Already knows the letters of the alphabet, and he's always asking questions of me and Nanny, too, about how things work and why things are the way they are—" Blythe smiled a bit ruefully. "He's no longer satisfied by Nanny's standard reply: 'Now, now, Master Geoffrey, that's not for little boys to know.'" She shook her head. "Jeff gets very cross with Nanny when she gives that response, I'm afraid."

"And well he should!" Lydia remarked. "Jeff's far too intelligent to be put off with that kind of nursery prattle." She passed a plate of flaky scones to Blythe who took one.

"I've been told it's time . . ." Blythe hesitated, unwilling to name Corin as the source of this information. Lydia would be likely to pounce on the fact and read far too much into it. That Blythe had been discussing such a personal decision as Jeff's education with the handsome retired Army officer might lead her friend to a wrong conclusion about their relationship. Carefully amending her words, she continued. "I mean, I understand that most little boys in England are sent to boarding school when they are seven or eight."

"That's true," Lydia agreed, stirring sugar into her tea. "I know my brothers were and Edward, too, of course. I'm sure he will be more than happy to advise you, although, be prepared, he will most certainly be prejudiced in favor of Barcliff, his old school."

"Well, of course, Jeff's only six," Blythe said quickly. "There is still plenty of time—"

Wide-eyed, Lydia gazed at her . "Oh dear, no, Blythe! Actually it may be too late! Don't you realize to get into some of the best schools, parents sometimes register their sons at birth?"

Aghast, Blythe stared back. "Really?"

"Oh, yes, indeed. However, if you do decide on Barcliff for Jeffy, I feel sure Edward could be of tremendous help. You see, one of his old classmates is now headmaster there, and there are always a few strings one can pull," Lydia reassured her.

The conversation then shifted to the plans Lydia had made for Blythe's visit—shopping and lunch tomorrow and, this evening, a small dinner party.

"Just a few friends and their wives. And tomorrow evening, we have tickets for the theater and supper afterward. I so wish you were going to be here longer, Blythe. There are some lovely people I'd like for you to meet, some Americans we've recently become acquainted with—"

Blythe was only half-listening. Already, she found her thoughts drifting to the cozy little house nestled in its old-fashioned garden in Kentburne. By this time Jeff would be in from his daily outing with Nanny, would have had his bath and was probably sitting down to his own tea.

"Nursery teas," Blythe had learned, were actually light suppers before the children's bedtime. These were more substantial meals than the dainty sandwiches and tiny cakes it was customary for adults to have before their formal dinner hour at eight-thirty or nine. She missed being there to read to him, cuddle him, hear his prayers. She could almost feel his little arms around her neck, smell the clean, warm scent of him as she tucked him into bed—

Lydia's voice brought her back from her longing thoughts. "I suppose you'd like to have a little rest before changing for dinner, wouldn't you?" she asked, reaching for the tapestry bellpull to summon the maid.

Violet appeared as if by magic. "Yes, ma'am?"

"Will you take Mrs. Montrose to her room and see that hot water is taken up for her bath?"

Lydia rose and walked with Blythe to the door, giving her an impulsive hug. "I'm so glad you're here. I've missed you! It's been weeks since we've had a good visit. You mustn't be such a stranger." She wagged her finger playfully in Blythe's face.

Blythe couldn't tell her friend that she found her trips to the city an ordeal, something she put off time after time. The Ainsleys had no children of their own, so she knew Lydia would not understand that even a night or two away from Jeff was difficult for Blythe. Perhaps Lydia would even caution her about making her son the center of her world.

The guest room had been redecorated since Blythe's last visit. Lydia's artistic talents were well-employed in her home, but Blythe knew her friend filled up the emptiness of her childlessness, of which she never spoke, by endless shopping for furniture and fabrics.

The end result is the creation of a restful, eye-pleasing environment such as this, thought Blythe, looking about her with pleasure. Apricot velvet draperies swung back from starched lace curtains. The ornate mahogany bed was covered in a flowered chintz in muted green, golds, peach colors. There were matching plump chairs on either side of the fireplace, over which hung a delicate floral watercolor.

On the bedside table was a hand-painted porcelain lamp, a popular new novel, a book of poetry, and a moiré-silk writing case filled with stationery embossed with the Ainsley crest.

In the small adjoining dressing room was a full-length mirror. An armoire had been placed alongside a satin upholstered reclining couch. The dressing table held crystal containers for powder, perfume atomizers, eau de cologne, silver-backed mirror, brush and comb.

Violet brought in the large brass vats of hot water for Blythe's bath along with scented French soaps and thick, thirsty towels. Before she left, the maid spread a mist-soft knotted throw on the chaise for her, and although Blythe did not feel particularly tired, she stretched out, indulging herself in a rare moment with nothing to do but rest and prepare herself for the evening's festivities.

"I'll be back in time to help you dress and do your hair, ma'am," Violet said softly as she left, closing the bedroom door quietly behind her.

How shocked the maid would be to know that Blythe managed very well every other day, dressing herself and doing up her own hair, Blythe mused. Again her thoughts drifted to her son.

It was probably good for both of them for her to get away from the cottage once in a while. He had the constant watchful care of his Scotch nanny, the affection of Cook and Emma, the thrice-weekly housemaid.

Blythe admitted she was, as the English say, "besotted" with her son. But then right from the beginning Jeff had been an ideal "picture-book" baby, the kind that grandmotherly ladies in the park made cooing sounds over when he was wheeled out in his pram.

He looks so much like his father must have looked at the same age, Blythe thought. Malcolm's other son, Jonathan, came to mind. Though she had never seen him in person, she had seen the portrait of him as a very young child, painted with his mother, the beautiful

Rose Meredith, who had died so tragically in a fire. She wondered if Jonathan was happy living up North with Rose's relatives.

The reddish fluff that had crowned Jeff's head as an infant had darkened as he grew older, and now he had the same silky dark curls as his father. Instead of the dark eyes Jonathan had inherited from his mother, Rose, Jeff's were large and intensely blue.

Yes, Jeff was a darling—loving and lovable. But he was also independent, strong-willed, stubbornly intent on having his own way more and more.

"Needs a man's hand, that one does," Nanny declared often, giving Blythe a knowing glance. "A houseful of women won't do for that lad," she would say, as even at a year or fifteen months, Jeff had strained out of her arms, wanting to be put down to take his own tottering footsteps on his way to explore some new delight.

Jeff would stand for only so much hugging, being held. He would give Blythe a tight, choking clasp around her neck, then move out of her arms at the first opportunity. Her eyes often followed him on these early explorations, thinking how different everything would have been if—but Blythe never allowed herself to dwell too long on the past.

She had done what she had to do. If it had been a mistake, there was no point in fretting about it now.

Early on, Nanny began insinuating that Blythe would do well to marry again, find a good but firm stepfather for the little boy. Diplomatic at first, she became more outspoken as the years passed and Jeff grew from a toddler into a sturdy little boy. After all, as Nanny pointed out, Blythe was only twenty-four and looked even younger.

Her hints became even broader when Corin Prescott started calling. Fond of quoting Scripture, she would sometimes say, "Well, ye know, Mrs. Montrose, 'weepin' endures for a day, but joy comes in the mornin',' don't ye know?"

It was time to put away mourning, she would murmur when Blythe dressed in black to go out or to church on Sundays. Gradually, giving in to the old nurse's urging, she removed the crepe veil from her bonnet, then added crocheted white collars and cuffs from Nanny's own needle to relieve the severity of her traditional mourning costumes. The first time she went up to London to shop with Lydia, Blythe bought a gray caped coat and bonnet; and the next time, pale lilac and bright blue. Nanny was extravagant in her approval of these changes.

"Are you ready to dress, ma'am?" Lydia's little maid broke into Blythe's long reverie.

Later, sitting at the dressing table in front of the mirror, Blythe felt wickedly indulgent and allowed Violet to brush, braid, and coil her hair.

"Oh, ma'am, 'tis a real pleasure to do *your* hair. So thick, and such a glorious color!"

Blythe smiled at the compliment and at once was thrust back in time to an incident in which someone else had said almost exactly the same thing.

Amelia Thompson! Her cabin-mate on the boat trip from San Francisco to New Orleans when she and Malcolm, newly married, were on their way back to Virginia and Montclair. Because of overbooking on the ship, Blythe had had to share a cabin with Amelia and her infant daughter rather than with her new husband. What was to have been their "honeymoon" trip was anything but, she recalled, though she remembered Amelia and little Daisy with real affection.

Amelia had been lively, talkative, and friendly. Blythe, fresh from the frontier town in northern California where she had lived with her rancher father most of her life, was introduced by Amelia to fashion, the latest hairstyles, and some fascinating tidbits about married life that brought a blush to Blythe's cheeks, even in retrospect.

Bonded by the intimacy of their mutual quarters, their natural affinity for one another, and the youthful need for companionship, the two young women had become fast friends on the tediously long journey. But this came to an abrupt and ugly ending when they docked in New Orleans and Amelia's husband, an army officer, met his wife and baby. When Malcolm saw Major Thompson's blue uniform, he refused to shake hands and walked away, leaving a bewildered Blythe to attempt an explanation. Later, when she asked Malcolm why he had behaved so rudely toward her friend's husband, he had turned on her savagely.

As a former confederate officer who had lost not only his own brothers but also many of the men under his command, Malcolm declared his hatred for that uniform. Anyone wearing it was his enemy.

"What jewelry did you wish to wear, ma'am?"

Violet's question startled Blythe back to the present. She shook her head unconsciously, looking down at her left hand where she still wore the plain gold band Malcolm had placed on her third finger in the wooden church in Lucas Valley nearly eight years ago.

Violet looked disappointed, and Blythe thought how the girl's eyes would sparkle to see the ruby and diamond Montrose bridal set that was safely locked away with some of the few things Blythe had taken with her when she had fled from Montclair that dreary December day. She had never worn the set. She had only looked at it once or twice, wondering if Rose, Malcolm's first wife, had ever worn it. She knew that Sara, Malcolm's mother, had. She was wearing them in the portrait hanging over the drawing room mantel at Montclair, a portrait painted when Sara was a bride, fresh from Savannah.

A knock at the bedroom door announced Lydia, splendid in a cranberry faille dinner gown, who exclaimed, "How lovely you look, Blythe! The emerald green is so becoming! Now, aren't you glad I persuaded you to buy that material and pattern to have made up from the model we saw at Madame Berthe's salon on your last visit?" she asked with a satisfied expression. Then tucking her hand through Blythe's arm, she said, "Come along. Edward is already downstairs and eagerly waiting to talk to you about Barcliff before our other guests arrive."

What Lydia had described as a "simple little dinner party" proved to be an elaborate affair, with Thompson presiding over the serving of an eight-course meal by two white-gloved footmen. Beginning with a cream of celery soup and ending with a delicate carmelized custard followed by a selection of fruit and cheese, the dinner amused Blythe as she compared it to her simple evening meals at her Kentburne cottage. How could Lydia's elegantly gowned lady guests keep their wasp-waisted figures if they dined out four out of five nights a week, as she had been told most of them did?

At a signal from Lydia, the ladies adjourned to the drawing room, leaving the gentlemen to their brandy and cigars.

Only half-listening to the conversation swirling about her, Blythe gazed around at her surroundings. Quite suddenly, Blythe was transported from the ornately furnished Victorian parlor to the main room of the Lucas Valley ranch, her childhood home.

For some reason, this had been a day for reminiscing. Blythe saw it all vividly—the big black stove she had taken such pride in polishing, the fire glowing through its scrolled open-work door lettered with the brand "Kitchen Queen," the sizzle of the kettle boiling on one of the back burners, the smell of simmering coffee in the glazed blue pot. In the center of the room was the scrubbed oak table and, over by the window, Pa's old rocker, pulled close to the bookcase where he shelved his prized copies of Charles Dickens and Sir Walter Scott.

How far I've come since those days, Blythe thought incredulously. Replacing that scene was another—the high-ceilinged drawing room at Montclair as she had first seen it, shrouded with dustcovers over all the furniture, making them appear to loom before her like gray ghosts. *And that's what they are*, Blythe thought, *ghosts of another lifetime*, from a world she did not know whose happy voices and dancing feet echoed in the haunted air—

Unconsciously Blythe shivered, and immediately Lydia's concerned voice asked, "Are you cold, Blythe? I do hope you're not taking a chill. Move over here a little closer to the fire . . . or should I send Violet upstairs to fetch your shawl?"

Denying her hostess's solicitous inquiries, Blythe quickly made an effort to enter into the conversation around her. Soon the gentlemen came strolling in to join the ladies.

While trying to concentrate on a rather rambling story told by Aurelia Holmes of all the problems she had encountered in a French hotel, Blythe caught part of a conversation between Edward and Captain Rolfe Pender. She heard the name of "Cameron Hall," and she was instantly alert.

"Yes, we plan to go to Virginia in the spring," Captain Pender was saying. "I want to look over some of his stock. I've been hearing quite marvelous things about the yearlings from his stables."

"Then I would be most interested in hearing your opinion when you return," Edward responded. "My brother is keen on adding to his stables also, and I'd like to look into getting a gentle mare for Lydia to ride when we go down there weekends."

Cameron Hall! They were talking about Rod's home, his stables. At the time she had fled Montclair, he had just begun to build up the stables again after their devastation during the War Between the States. Apparently they had now regained their legendary reputation as a fine horse-breeding farm. She was so glad for Rod!

At the same time all the pain and longing she had thought was behind her surfaced once more, all the old emotions! She had tried to put him out of her thoughts as completely as she had put herself out of his life. Now she realized she had failed.

She saw him as she remembered—his tall, erect figure, walking so straight one scarcely noticed the slight limp from his war wounds, the thick, tousled hair, the set of the shoulders, the line of his firm jaw, those clear truthful eyes that seemed to penetrate straight through one. Blythe drew in her breath at the memory.

"Don't you agree, Blythe?"

Lydia's question startled her, and before she could stammer an apology for not having heard it, she was rescued by Edward's request for his wife to play for them. He stood at the piano, already placing the sheets of music on the rack, so Lydia rose with her question unanswered.

As the notes of the piece began to fill the room with melody,

Blythe resolutely banished Rod's image and arranged herself in an attitude of attentive interest. She would give herself only to this moment, to her friend's recital. The love she had never fully acknowledged was a thing of the past. She had left it behind—at least three thousand miles and another lifetime ago.

The next day was filled with shopping, a delightful lunch and tea, then home to the house on Belvedere Square to rest until time to dress for the theater. The hours passed in a kind of blur for Blythe. Although she did her best to be congenial, underneath she felt the strong tug of home.

Lydia insisted on coming to the station to see Blythe off. And, with an exchange of hugs and promises to see each other again soon, she departed.

chapter

5

Larkspur Cottage
Kentburne, England

THE LONDON TRAIN shrieked to a stop, and Corin Prescott, waiting on the platform, stopped pacing to watch the passengers file out of the first-class compartments. When he spotted the tall, graceful figure he was looking for, his usually steady pulse quickened. Though he had known her now for almost six years, he felt as he had the day he met Blythe Montrose for the first time.

Soon after he returned to Kentburne from Her Majesty's service in India, he had noticed the solitary figure walking the lanes early on misty mornings. When he inquired who she was, he was told she was an American, a widow who had taken the Larkspur Cottage. Corin lived only a stone's throw from there, in Dower House on the estate of Monksmoor Priory, the crumbling mansion on the hill above the chalk cliffs. When he had finally met her through the local doctor, Reid Wilson, he had been enchanted by her glowing beauty, her dark brown eyes.

Now, as he caught sight of her moving briskly along the platform, willow-slim in a traveling suit of soft blue tweed and a rust-feathered bonnet, he waved his hand, calling, "Blythe!"

She turned and smiled, and he hurried toward her, all his proper English reserve forgotten in the joy of seeing her again. Grinning like a schoolboy, he stammered out breathlessly, "I—'ve missed you."

She seemed both surprised and amused.

"Why, Corin, I didn't expect anyone to meet me. You shouldn't have—I could certainly have managed on my own," she said as the porter trundled up with a small cartload of packages.

"With all these?" Corin lifted an eyebrow skeptically. "It looks as if you bought out all the stores in London! My buggy is over there." He directed the porter, who tipped his cap, picked up the cart handles again, and started down the platform ahead of them.

Blythe tucked her hand into Corin's proffered arm, and they followed.

"How was your visit with the Ainsleys?" he asked.

"Oh, very nice, as usual. But I was ready to come home."

"You can't be away from that boy of yours long, can you?" Corin frowned. "You've no cause to worry about the lad, Blythe. I've stopped by every day to see him—"

Blythe tried to look apologetic. "Oh, it's not that I don't appreciate what you've done, Corin. You're always so good to see about him when I'm away. And, of course, he's in capable hands with Mrs. Daugherty, now that Nanny's gone to another family—"

"You're going to have to get used to being without him, you know, once you've decided on his school. Was Edward of any help there?"

"Very helpful. Naturally, he's keen on his old school, Barcliffe, but I haven't really decided—" Blythe broke off, not yet willing to share with Corin just how much her thinking had changed in the two-hour trip from London.

He helped her into his barouche, paid the porter, then climbed in beside her.

"It's good to have you back," Corin said, lifting the reins and urging the horses forward. "The village . . . I . . . nothing is the same when you're not here."

Blythe returned the smile but felt again the inner warning, that little signal that Corin Prescott was growing much too fond of her.

His feelings for her had obviously progressed beyond an affectionate friendship, and Blythe knew she would have to do something about it.

She did not want to hurt him, nor did she want to give him false hope. But how could she explain that there was no room in her heart for anyone else . . . because Rod Cameron was still firmly lodged there?

The short distance from the train station to Blythe's home was spanned in a matter of minutes. As Larkspur Cottage came into view, Blythe thought how fortunate she was to have found the rambling two-story house, much larger than it looked, with spacious rooms comfortably arranged. She particularly liked the quaint diamond-paned windows and the stone wall that surrounded a garden through which a path meandered to the blue arched door.

But it was not the house that she craned forward in her seat to see. As they pulled to a stop in front, the door burst open and a little boy came running out.

"Mummy! You're back!" Jeff shouted and flung himself upon Blythe almost before she had had a chance to step out of the carriage.

She lifted him up into her arms, and his own chubby arms went around her neck in a tight hug.

"Oh my, it's good to see you, Jeffy!" she cried as he scrambled out of her embrace and, tugging on her hand, tried to pull her into the house.

"Wait, Jeff dear, where are your manners? You haven't even spoken to Captain Prescott."

"But I've seen him today already, Mummy." The child halted and looked up at Corin for confirmation. "He brought—" he began, but stopped mid-sentence as Corin put his forefinger to his lips. Jeff's eyes twinkled conspiratorily, dimples deepening in his rosy cheeks. "Oh, I forgot! It's 'sposed to be a surprise!"

Blythe gave Corin a wary glance. "What's this? What have the two of you been up to?"

Corin shook his head slightly. "It's nothing really, just a welcome-home."

"Well, come in and have tea with us," Blythe invited.

Again Corin shook his head. "No, I think this reunion should be just you and your son. I'll stop by again tomorrow."

"If you're sure . . . Thank you, Corin, for meeting my train and escorting me home . . . and for the mysterious surprise, whatever it is!"

Corin looked at the charming, girlish woman, unself-conscious and serene, content with simple joys. Never had he loved her more. Was she—he wondered, beyond his reach?

Blythe had not missed the expression in Corin's eyes as he had gazed at her with Jeff. It was so apparent that she knew she must do something about Corin before it went any further.

With a wave of his hand he drove away. Blythe and Jeff stood at their gate, watching the handsome buggy make the turn of the road, then hand-in-hand, they went into the house together.

Just inside the front door a portly, gray-haired woman stood waiting.

"Welcome home, Mrs. Montrose," she greeted Blythe, taking the packages and helping her off with her jacket.

Mrs. Daugherty had come just after Nanny Bartlett left to take charge of another newborn. When Blythe protested her leaving, Nanny told Blythe she never stayed longer than four years in any one place.

"I love babbies," she had said in her thick Scotch burr. "But when they get to walkin' and talkin', I like to move on. That way you don't get too attached to a young one so that it makes it verra hard to leave when they go off to school."

Blythe recalled that practical bit of philosophy. It didn't make her decision about Jeff's education any easier.

Mrs. Daugherty was a godsend, highly recommended by the agency to whom Blythe applied for a housekeeper. The day she arrived and took off her astonishing hat, bobbing with cherries, Anne Daugherty had taken charge of Jeff, the house, and Blythe.

Jeff, just learning to talk, could not manage the name and promptly dubbed her "Dotty." The nickname, approved by Mrs. Daugherty herself, stuck.

"It's so good to be home, Dotty!" Blythe said happily, lifting her veil and removing hatpins and hat.

"And it's good to have you back, it is, ma'am. Now I've put the kettle on for a nice cup of tea, which you'll be needin' after your trip," said Dotty as she bustled off down the hallway toward the kitchen.

Blythe stood for a minute, relishing in the familiar surroundings, and at once saw that the room was filled with flowers from Corin's garden—freesias, day lilies and some other kind of white bloom whose name Blythe could never remember. Not that it mattered. The flowers spoke eloquently of Corin's thoughtfulness. An envelope addressed to "Blythe" in his distinctive handwriting was propped against one of the vases. She reached for it but was interrupted by Jeff who was digging into one of the parcels.

"Is this one for me, Mummy?"

She had promised him a new car for his toy railway train, and although he could not read yet, he did know his letters and recognized the box from the toy store and held it up with an eager look on his face.

"Yes, darling, that's for you."

As she answered Jeff's question, Blythe slid Corin's note into her pocket to read later, grateful for the delay.

After they had enjoyed Jeff's favorite tea—thin wedges of cinnamon toast and Dotty's marmalade cake, baked in honor of Blythe's homecoming, she read to him from his new book about King Arthur, then let him play with his train set until bedtime. She tucked him in with prayers, hugs, and kisses.

Pulling Jeff's door shut behind her, Blythe went to her own room and almost reluctantly drew Corin's note from the pocket of her skirt and read,

My dear Blythe,

Strangely enough, it was only this week while you were away that I fully realized how much you have come to mean in my life. Everything seemed gray when I returned from putting you on the train to London last Thursday. People commented on the fine weather we were having, but everything seemed overcast to me.

I wish I were more skillful in putting my thoughts on paper. Unfortunately, I'm no poet. Perhaps I will do better in person the next time I see you, very soon, I hope. I must travel to the city tomorrow to see my lawyers about some legal matters concerning the estate, but I will call when I return. Until then, hold me in your thoughts as I always hold you.

> With kindest regards,
> Ever, Corin Prescott.

Reading so much between those few lines, Blythe was unable to sleep long after she had returned the note to its envelope. She sat in the windowed alcove of her bedroom, looking out at the night. In the distance through the trees, she could see a single light burning in Dower House where Corin lived.

Tradition had it that the widow of the lord of the manor came here to live when her son married and inherited the title. Corin was a distant relative of the Marsh family, who had owned the estate called Monksmoor Priory and the property for generations. The family had long ago scattered or died out. Even Corin could not trace his connection to them through the maze of English family lineage. When he had tried to explain it to her, Blythe had laughed and told him it sounded much like the long and complex genealogy of Virginia families.

The light in Dower House made Blythe wonder if Corin were sleepless, too. She could almost see him in his booklined, oak-paneled library, sitting in one of the worn leather chairs before the fireplace. Was he perhaps thinking what her reaction to his note might be? For all his world travels, his education and upbringing, Corin was basically shy. A deeply private and reserved man, Blythe knew it must have been difficult for him to suggest such deep feelings.

Her mind sifted through all the conflicting ideas, plans, suggestions, advice she had received over the past few days. From the moment she had been sure she was to have Malcolm's child, her every thought had been focused on his future. She had come to England with the idea that somehow Malcolm would have shared and understood her reason for wanting his child to be born in the mythical Camelot of his boyhood hero, King Arthur, where the highest ideals of chivalry, honor, and service to God were upheld. When money ceased to be a problem with the discovery of her father's generous provision for her in his will, she resolved to put her plan in motion.

Admittedly, it had been a strange, secluded time of her life. She had purposely set out to erase the trauma of learning that hers had been an arranged marriage, a bargain struck between Malcolm and her father. No amount of money could heal that kind of heartbreak, but it had eased the way for her to give her son—and Malcolm's— the best life had to offer.

If one only knew *what* was best for him. To rear him as an English gentleman might negate his true heritage. After all, Jeff was an American, a Virginian. And Blythe's own background, though very different from Malcolm's, was equally American. Her mother, a courageous gypsy girl and her father, a brave Kentuckian, had both possessed adventurous spirits that led then to the frontier west. Surely Jeff had inherited some of those same qualities, as well as the aristocratic legacy of his well-born Virginia father.

The more she thought about it, the more Blythe's conviction grew that before she made any commitment, she should take Jeff back to the United States to meet his grandparents, Sara and Clayborn Montrose, now living in Savannah. Then perhaps to Virginia, to Mayfield, where Jeff could see his home, Montclair, if only from a distance.

With growing confidence, she rose from the window seat and went to her desk. Taking out stationery, she dipped her pen into the inkwell and began to write:

"Dear Mr. and Mrs. Montrose—"

Part II

Parting and forgetting? What faithful heart can do these? Our great affections never leave us. Surely they will follow whithersoever we shall go.

—*Thackeray*

Whether happiness may come or not, one should try to prepare one's self to do without it—George Eliot

chapter
6

Near Dublin, Ireland
Spring 1876

ROD TOOK THE TRAIN from London to Liverpool, then boarded the evening steamer for Dublin. As the ship eased into the Mersey for the crossing, he leaned on the deck's railing, watching the lights of the port city recede. His mind juggled a dozen thoughts simultaneously, but returned again and again to the interview he'd conducted in London the afternoon before.

In retrospect, maybe he should have been alerted right away when the cabby brought him to the old brick building in a questionable part of the city. Entering a dark foyer, he had mounted a steep, narrow stairway, then made his way down a series of labyrinthine hallways to stand in front of a door. The sign, lettered in garish gold overleaf, read: "Bristow and Burnham, Private Investigators."

His hand on the doorknob, Rod debated the wisdom of what he

was about to do and hesitated. Then, deciding that having come this far he could not turn back now, he twisted the knob and went inside.

In the dingy office a man, seated behind a desk, looked up over small, square spectacles punctuating his sallow, moon-shaped face. Sparse strands of hair were combed precisely over his balding head.

He squinted curiously at Rod. "Yes, sir, may I help you?"

Rod felt an instinctive revulsion. As if his errand were not questionable enough, it seemed he must solicit the help of a man whose very appearance was reminiscent of a pulp novel.

"Mr. Burnham? Mr. Philip Burnham?"

"The same, sir."

"I'm Rod Cameron. We've had some correspondence and—"

The man nodded and replied in an oily voice, "Quite so, quite so. I have your letter here someplace. Do have a seat, sir, until I locate it—" Burnham rummaged through a sheaf of papers cluttering his desk while Rod sat down stiffly in a chair opposite.

"Ah, yes, here it is." Mr. Burnham retrieved a dog-eared folder from the pile that threatened at any moment to topple over. "I see you're looking for someone you have reason to believe is in England. Am I right?"

Almost before Rod had finished giving a brief description of Blythe and his reasons for extending his search for her to England, the man was shaking his head.

"Mr. Cameron, the trail for this young lady is nearly five years old. You do understand that it has cooled off considerably by now. People trying to lose themselves usually move very fast, covering their tracks the first few months when it might be easiest to catch up with them."

"I didn't say she was *trying* to—" protested Rod, but the man ignored the interruption and resumed his lecture.

"Besides, you've given me very little to go on. A physical description is usually of little use, especially in finding a woman determined *not* to be found. Women can do all sorts of things to change their appearance—dye their hair, pad themselves to look heavier, wear a different style dress, affect an entirely new manner—It's surprising what good actresses the ladies can become."

Mr. Burnham's eyes took on a gleam of admiration. "I recall a Miss Tillie Murgesson, a real 'stunner,' she was, too. A shopgirl who had cleverly absconded with the store's entire monthly payroll and—"

Rod stirred impatiently, and Mr. Burnham adjusted his eyeglasses and returned to the papers in his folder. Drawing out a letter Rod recognized as the one he had written just a few weeks ago, the man cleared his throat. "Now was this . . . Mrs. Blythe Montrose . . . an employee? Someone you suspect of taking the family silver, or perhaps her mistress's jewelry or—" Here Mr. Burnham looked up, eyeing Rod across the desk with a certain sly look. "Or does she have some letters in her possession, perhaps written in the indiscretion of infatuation, that you now wish returned?"

Rod felt a rising fury he could barely restrain. "I don't think I've made myself clear, Mr. Burnham. I am *not* trying to trap anyone. I simply want to know if this . . . this young lady is well." Rod's voice took on a firm authority that Mr. Burnham was quick to acknowledge.

He hastily put down the letter he was reading and brought out a legal pad, making scribbled notes as Rod dictated.

"Let's go over the description once more then, sir. Approximately five feet seven . . . hmm, tall for a lady, isn't she? Red hair—oh yes, dark auburn, you say. Color of eyes?" He wrote rapidly, his pen noisily scratching across the sheet of paper. "What sort of occupation might this lady now be employed in, do you suppose? Domestic service, clerk, waitress?"

This question gave Rod pause. He could not think of a possible answer. What would Blythe do, alone, without money, friends or family, in a strange country? Maybe his mother was right. After all, why would Blythe have left America? Still, all the leads Rod had followed so far had led nowhere. The one most promising had suggested that Blythe took the train from Mayfield to Richmond and on to Washington. From there, the only reasonable direction would be to go north to a big city like New York or Boston. Why? But, then, that was still the most puzzling, unanswerable question of all. *Why,* indeed?

When the Camerons had found out about Montclair and learned that Blythe was gone, they had discussed every possibility. It seemed to Rod, after his fruitless efforts to locate her in California, that she must have stayed in the east. Left penniless by Malcolm's profligate gambling, where would she go, what would she do with limited formal education and no work experience? Seek work as a housemaid or children's nurse? Rod had never known a woman who had to support herself. His mind had drawn a blank then, nor had he been able to offer Mr. Burnham a satisfactory suggestion.

At length, he left the office feeling as frustrated as before. He also felt a little degraded for having discussed Blythe with that man who was probably more accustomed to dealing with the lowest types of criminals and evaders of the law. As distasteful as it had been, Rod's determination to leave no stone unturned in his search for Blythe was stronger than ever. If this character could come up with any helpful information, it would have been worth it.

Rod now pounded his fist on the ship's railing. Where was she? And if he couldn't find her, why couldn't he forget her?

He shivered in the swirl of mist and fog now encircling the open deck. Turning up his coat collar, he went below to the small, cramped cabin where he spent a restless night in a narrow berth too short for his long legs and awoke, sore and exhausted, to the sound of ship horns announcing their arrival in Dublin harbor. He was in Ireland at last.

Dan McShane was there on the dock to greet Rod with a wide smile and a hearty handshake. When he took Rod over to his fine polished carriage drawn by two prancing black horses, a freckle-faced, rosy-cheeked boy of about twelve was sitting in the driver's seat, proudly holding the reins.

"This is Sean, my oldest," Dan introduced him. "I let him take off the day from school to help me greet our American guest."

The road from the docks wound through the city and out into the countryside. Rod was struck by the variegated shades of green so brilliant that the landscape seemed to shimmer in an iridescent mist. They passed through a village of thatch-roofed, white-washed cottages, scattering barefooted children and squawking chickens in their wake. Friendly villagers waved as the carriage rolled by, and Dan shouted his own lusty greeting.

Off the main road, a narrow lane threaded its way between undulating pastureland. Here Rod first glimpsed the herds of fine horses from Dan's stables. Good horseflesh!

His excitement mounted as at last they drew up in front of a gray stone house, its entrance bright with flowers.

Dan tossed the reins to Sean. "Take the horses down to the stables for a good rubdown, there's a good lad." To Rod, he said, "Come along and meet my better half." He grinned broadly.

As they got down from the carriage, the top half of a polished oak door swung open, and a handsome woman with dark wavy hair and blue, laughing eyes beckoned them inside.

"Welcome, Mr. Cameron! I'm Maura." She unlatched the full door and held it open. "And would you be ready now for a good Irish breakfast? The girls and I are just getting it on the table."

A few minutes later Rod was sitting at the broad table in the sunny dining room. There were slices of succulent pink ham, mounds of fluffy eggs, yellow butter, potatoes cut thick and browned lightly, fresh-baked oat bread, and steaming hot sweet tea. He ate with an appetite fueled not only by the abundant food, but by the warmth of the good people in the home.

That was the first day of his week-long visit to the McShane farm, each day thereafter a pure pleasure. Their hospitality rivaled the legendary Southern hospitality with which Rod had grown up.

The McShanes' four children, three boys and a pretty little girl, were as friendly as their parents and rode their own ponies like veterans. Maura McShane, a real "stunner," as Mr. Burnham might have described her, was obviously in love with her big, rugged husband, who adored her unashamedly.

It was an environment that both charmed and saddened Rod. He could not deny a twinge of envy as he observed their happiness, the contentment of their life together. It made his own solitary status, his unfulfilled dreams, his loneliness, even more acutely unbearable.

Rod spent the first part of his stay looking over Dan's stock, selecting the brood mares he planned to buy to enhance his own stables at Cameron Hall. In frequent consultation with Dan about his distinctive techniques of horse-training, Rod took note of the subtle differences in training technique that Dan used for riding from those he used for raising hunters.

By the end of the week, Rod had acquired a tremendous respect for Dan—his knowledge, his way with the animals, his expertise— and accompanied him to the lawyer to sign the bill of sale for the horses Rod was arranging to ship back to Virginia.

Just before he was to leave for England and his visit with Garnet, Rod told the McShanes good-bye to do a little exploring on his own. Taking a room at an inn near Dublin, he set off one fine, misty morning for a long hike.

A few miles from the village, he had been told, was the site of an ancient abbey situated on the cliffs high above the ocean. It was here Rod sat on a flat, sun-warmed rock to eat the lunch the innkeeper had packed in his haversack.

While he munched on ham and cheese between thick slices of homemade bread, Rod contemplated the magnificent view—emerald green Irish hills against a cerulean sky, the golden sands below, the turquoise water dancing with white crests of foam.

So far from home and all that was familiar, Rod experienced a strange melancholy. His eyes roved the glorious landscape, its wild grandeur and haunting beauty. That there was no one to share this splendid moment, no human heart to understand his mood and echo his sentiments was overwhelmingly oppressive.

He finished his lunch, stood up and walked a few yards farther toward the abandoned abbey. He had been told it had been built in 1062, supposedly one of the finest examples of ecclesiastical architecture in which early Irish Christians worshiped. Later, it was destroyed by Cromwell's men and finally gutted by fire, its treasures stolen. Now all that remained was a rubble of stone, part of a wall and arch.

Rod stepped among the ruins, wondering what this structure, built to the glory of God, must once have been like. Beyond the nave, now open to the sky, were the remnants of a graveyard with a few granite Celtic crosses and broken headstones. Rod strolled through the scattered stones of the church out onto the coarse tufted grass and wandered through the burial plots.

Most of the epitaphs were nearly undecipherable, probably carved in old Gaelic. But as he continued to wander among them, the inscription on one caught Rod's attention, and he stopped to read it.

"Eileen of my heart, Eileen of my love, ere the world should end my love for you remains ever"—Aidian Wyre, 1640"

What stonecutter, having lost his beloved, had composed this heartrending promise? Whoever he was, Rod felt instant empathy with him.

From that ancient graveyard he walked slowly back over hillocks studded with wind-sculpted yew trees, then down along a sparkling clear stream. As he turned toward the village back to his room at the inn, Rod came to a decision.

He could not spend the rest of his life mourning something irretrievably lost, something that, for all his searching, he had not been able to find. Life was not meant to be empty and meaningless. Life was meant to be shared; love, to be given; the future, to be anticipated.

The words of a proverb came to mind: "Hope deferred maketh the heart sick." Well he was heartsick, all right, tired of hoping for what appeared to be hopeless, tired of the emptiness of his life. He longed for fulfillment, for love, and the promise of happiness.

He would be leaving for England in the morning. There he planned to visit Garnet and Jeremy at their country house before sailing for America and back to Virginia.

But first, he decided, he would stop in London and call on Fenelle Maynard, who was staying at her Uncle Webb's home.

This decision made, Rod began to pack. He knew he had reached an important crossroads, one that should make him feel more settled, less uncertain. Why, then, did he feel such doubt, the void in his heart still unsatisfied?

The withholding of truth is sometimes a worse deception than a direct mistatement—Lord Napier

chapter
7

The Birchfields
Near London, England

GARNET BUTTONED the close-fitting jacket of her elegant black gabardine riding habit and scowled at her reflection. Why, of all times, the only weekend Rod could manage to come down before departing again for America, did she have a house full of guests?

If only Rod had let her know the *minute* he returned from his horse-buying trip to Ireland instead of lingering in London, then casually stopping by Jeremy's office to send a message that he would be down the following weekend!

"It appears he was involved in some social events he had promised to attend with your old Virginia friends, the Maynards, and was not able to extricate himself politely," Jeremy explained at Garnet's indignant protest.

"It's not fair!" she fumed. "Allotting me just four days of his month-long stay in the British Isles! How did he get himself so hopelessly entangled with the Maynards anyway?"

Jeremy smiled. "I got the impression that he was rather pleased and looking forward to escorting the daughter, Miss Fenelle Maynard, to a series of soirées and balls."

Garnet glared. "Mrs. Maynard has always had her eye on one of my brothers! While Fenelle was still a little girl, her mother was setting her cap for either Stewart or Rod, and it didn't seem to matter to her which one. Now poor Rod is the target."

"A not unwilling target, if I'm not mistaken," Jeremy put in mildly.

Garnet was too upset to continue the discussion. The fact that she was sure she had seen Blythe at Victoria Station just a few weeks ago and had not yet told Rod was still on her conscience.

But how could she have told him? There hadn't been a chance. When she and Jeremy had gone to meet his ship, Rod was already in the company of the Maynards. And if the truth were told, she had to concede that he did look quite as if he were enjoying it.

"Well, there was nothing to be done about *that*," Garnet told herself.

At least she had made plans for them to go for a morning ride alone, and she would make sure to tell him then about seeing Blythe and about her feeling that the young woman must be somewhere in England. Possibly somewhere near London. She must tell him before—

She stared into the mirror, confronting her fear. Before what? The answer was starkly chilling: Before Mrs. Maynard succeeded in her long effort to manipulate Rod into marriage with her daughter!

Fenelle *had* grown up to be a fragile beauty, Garnet had to admit, if you admired the ethereal type. But her mother! Elyse Maynard had often been the subject of Garnet's most wicked imitations, performances which used to send her father and twin brothers into paroxysms of hilarity. Even Kate had to suppress her amusement, while chastizing Garnet for her lack of charity.

If only it were not too late! She thought of the long voyage, notorious for promoting romance, and more time spent together at the theater, at dinner parties and balls in London—before Rod's side trip to Ireland. And instead of coming directly to the Devlins' country place, he had "dallied" again in London, squiring Fenelle to various and sundry events. Garnet was more than a little piqued at him!

Setting her mouth determinedly, she picked up the black velour hat with its saucy plume and set it carefully on her head, tying the velvet ribbons of the snood under her hair. Then, hooking the loop on her skirt over her wrist, she swept out of her dressing room and down the stairs.

The sound of voices from the dining room alerted her that most of her guests were already at breakfast. Sunlight streamed through the tall windows all along one side of the high-ceilinged room where a half dozen people were gathered around the long polished table. On the mahogany sideboard was an array of silver chafing dishes and platters containing pheasant, lamb chops, bacon curls, sausages, racks of toast, compotes of fruit and linen-covered baskets of crumpets. Footmen stood at either end, ready to refill cups with a choice of hot beverages.

With a motion of one graceful hand, Garnet acknowledged the gentlemen who had stood at her entrance and smilingly bid everyone good morning. Going directly to the silver pot, she poured herself a cup of steaming black coffee. Cup in hand, she turned and spoke directly to Rod.

"Are you ready for me to show you our riding trails?"

Rod lifted an eyebrow. "No breakfast, little Sis?"

His use of the family's pet name for her from the old days brought a quick lump to Garnet's throat. How much she loved her brother, how much she coveted happiness for him, the same kind of happiness she had come to know with Jeremy.

"We can always eat later. Come on, the beautiful morning's wasting. I've already sent to the stables for our horses, and the grooms will be bringing them around any minute."

"I didn't know you had horses available to ride!" spoke up

Delaine Medby, a notorious flirt. "I wish you'd said something earlier." She pursed her soft red lips in a pout, giving Rod a sidelong glance.

"Yes indeed, you have a wonderful stable, Mrs. Devlin," remarked Blanton Ethridge, an editor at Jeremy's publishing firm. "Your husband gave me a tour yesterday."

"Then why didn't someone show *me*?" fumed his pretty wife.

Garnet bit her lip in frustration, alarmed that her plan for a private time with Rod might turn into a group riding party. She was determined not to spoil her one chance to be alone with Rod, no matter what. She glanced over at her husband, and a silent signal passed between them.

Jeremy gallantly rose to the occasion. "I'll do the honors later this morning, if you like, Mrs. Ethridge," he offered smoothly. "And I'll select a special horse for you to ride, Miss Medby."

Garnet quickly set down her cup. "Come, Rod, we must be off!" she said brightly. "If I don't ride now, I'll not have another chance all day." Sending a charmingly apologetic smile in the direction of her guests, Garnet beckoned for Rod to follow and started out of the room.

Hurrying through the long hallway to the front terrace, Garnet heard Rod's booted footsteps behind her and called over her shoulder with a mischievous grin. "That was a close call! For a second, I was afraid we were going to have the whole troop with us!"

Outside, the grooms held the heads of two magnificent horses— one, a dappled gray; the other, a sleek roan. They mounted and cantered down the drive. Garnet had always been a skilled horsewoman, and Rod was "born to the saddle." The Dartmoor country was interestingly different from the lush Virginia countryside with its rolling hills and woodland stretches.

Soon they were far beyond the manicured grounds of the manor house, climbing a broad path rough with stones. At the top of a hill they reined in and surveyed the panoramic view spreading out before them—acres and acres of barren ground and jutting boulders, the famed moors. But as they rode on farther, what had seemed a sweep of thick brown turf was in reality a varicolored carpet. Golden gorse bloomed alongside purple heather. Clumps of pink and blue wildflowers crowned the hillock and dotted the vast landscape.

Garnet drew her mount to a halt. "Let's get down and walk a bit," she suggested.

Leading their horses loosely by their reins, brother and sister strolled companionably for a few minutes. The wind was ever-present—a low sighing through the rough grass. Above them, silhouetted against a vivid blue sky, a hawk soared and spiraled.

Garnet considered a way to bring up the subject of Blythe, but before she could speak, Rod was asking her a question.

"Are you happy, little Sis?"

Surprised, Garnet exclaimed, "Oh, yes, Rod! *Very* happy!"

"I'm glad," he said, stopping to let his horse nibble at some brush. "I've done a lot of thinking about happiness lately—how unexpectedly it comes and how swiftly it can go. Jeremy is a fine man, Garnet—" he gave her a quizzical smile—"even if he did fight on the wrong side in the war. But then that's all in the past. So much is in the past, and we have to move on." He patted the horse's nose and continued.

"Like many other Southerners, I've spent entirely too much time dwelling on the past. Now I'm determined to look to the future, build for it." He squared his shoulders. "You know I stayed at Dan McShane's farm while I was in Ireland. And seeing him with his family about him, his life there brought it all clear to me how much of life I've missed. Dan's teaching his sons to love the land and plant themselves deep in its soil. They're building a good foundation for the future, Sis. It forced me to think about my own future—"

As he paused, his face still averted, Garnet felt her hands under the leather gloves tighten on her horse's lead.

Rod turned to face her. "Garnet, I'm the last of the Camerons, you know. As Mama has pointed out on several occasions—the family line ends with me. That is, unless, I marry and have children of my own."

Now! Something inside Garnet's head exploded. Now is the time to tell Rod about seeing Blythe! It might be the one clue he's been searching for. But her throat constricted, and she waited, dreading Rod's next words, which were, "I'm going to ask Fenelle Maynard to marry me."

While her maid strategically placed a marcasite comb in her elaborately coiffed hair, Garnet glared at her reflection. She had not slept well the night before, as the circles under her eyes attested, and with houseguests and more guests arriving for dinner, she needed to look her best.

But she had gone to bed burdened by Rod's announcement and the secret that weighed on her so heavily, and had awakened, unrested and anxious. She had been short with her maid when Myrna brought in the morning tea, an English custom Garnet had never fully embraced, and she had sent her back down to the kitchen for coffee.

Now she had been tense all day. Her guests' conversation had seemed especially boring, the requisite bridge game in the afternoon, tiresome, and she could not wait to escape to her bedroom for the hour or two before dinner to be alone. Even this respite had not proved helpful. Over and over she had berated herself for not telling Rod about seeing the woman she was certain was Blythe in Victoria Station.

"How is that, madam?" asked Myrna, handing Garnet a mirror, then stepping back to admire her own handiwork.

Still distracted by her uneasy thoughts, Garnet tipped her head from one side to the other, checking her hairdo.

Just then a knock sounded on the boudoir door.

"Come in," Garnet called.

A middle-aged woman in a dark blue dress collared in white and wearing a fluted lawn cap set squarely on top of her gray head, hesitated in the doorway.

"Beg pardon, madam, but Miss Faith is begging to come in and see you. I wasn't sure whether you were dressed or wanted her to—"

"Of course, I want her, Nanny." Garnet twisted around to face her daughter's nurse. "My hair has taken so long that I didn't realize it was so near Faith's bedtime. Have her come in, by all means."

"Yes, madam. I'll send her right in then." The woman backed out the door, closing it quietly behind her.

Garnet turned back to study her reflection again. "Yes, Myrna, I think you've outdone yourself. It looks *trés chic*."

"Thank you, madam. It's ever so becomin', if I do say so. I saw a picture of the Princess of Wales with hers done much the same, and from what I read, Princess Alexandra has the exact same coloring as you, mum."

Amused at her maid's extravagant praise, Garnet declared, "Then I must look stunning because the Prince of Wales's wife is quite a dazzling creature from the mere glance I once had of her riding out in her carriage."

"Oh, she *is* that. At least, from all the reports of her in the papers," Myrna replied seriously, unaware that Garnet was teasing.

Another quick rap came at the door, then it burst open to admit a little whirlwind with dark, flying curls, wearing a ruffled nightie and pink wrapper. She came running toward Garnet, arms outstretched, losing a small furry bedroom slipper in the race.

"Mummy! Mummy! You look beautiful!" she said, flinging herself into her mother's embrace.

"Look sharp, now, Miss Faith!" Myrna said in quick alarm. "Mind you don't muss your mother's dress."

"It's all right, Myrna." Garnet laughed as she gave Faith a hug, then set her firmly back down on her feet, and gazed fondly at her only child.

Faith Devlin promised to be a beauty, having inherited Garnet's pert expression, the impudent turned-up nose, and her father's shiny coal-black hair, his gray, long-lashed eyes.

Faith stared, awe-struck at her mother as Garnet turned slowly, holding out the skirt of lemon-yellow glacé-silk drawn back in the new style with ruffles cascading into a small train. She adjusted the decolletage slightly, then smiled at her small daughter, who was regarding her with adoring admiration.

"Oh, Mummy, you look like a fairy princess!" Faith sighed.

Garnet reached out and cupped the rosy cheek with a cool hand. "Thank you, my darling!"

Garnet sat down again to examine the contents of the velvet jewel case Myrna had opened for her.

"Mummy, can't I stay and watch the company coming?" Faith begged as she climbed into Garnet's chaise lounge and watched as her mother slipped pearl pendant earrings into her lobes, then took a pearl choker from her jewel box for Myrna to clasp about her slender neck.

"Oh, I suppose so, this once." Garnet's thoughts drifted back to the days at Cameron Hall when she had perched at the top step of the graceful double staircase, her face pinched between the banister rails, looking down to see her parents' festively attired guests as they arrived for the many parties given at their palatial Virginia home.

"Then be sure and tell Nanny I can, or she'll make me go to bed just like a baby!" Faith said firmly.

Garnet laughed at her daughter's imperious tone. For the dozenth time she thought how much like herself at the same age Faith was! Garnet prayed, however, that she would not grow up as stubborn and willful as *she* had been. Most importantly, that Faith would not repeat her mother's grave mistakes in love, that she would find someone from the beginning who was the right one!—

Abruptly, Garnet dismissed these thoughts. She certainly had more immediate problems than Faith's future romances, she reminded herself, thinking of Rod—Rod and Blythe, Rod and Fenelle Maynard.

Her brother's declaration still troubled Garnet like a stone in the heel of her riding boot. It wouldn't go away unless she did something about it. And right now, Garnet did not know what to do.

Just then, Faith's piping little voice interjected itself into her confusion.

"Mummy, don't you think Uncle Rod is the handsomest of all the gentlemen here this weekend? I *do*! Except Papa, of course. Nobody is as handsome as Papa." Faith paused for a second before she went on. "What do you 'spose happened in Ireland, Mummy? Uncle Rod seems so happy since he came back."

Garnet stared at her little daughter in surprise. How right she was. Rod did seem much happier, happier than Garnet had seen him in ages. Assured, confident of the future. His planned engagement to Fenelle Maynard had apparently made the difference. Perhaps Fenelle had given Rod back his lost purpose in life, his self-esteem, his optimism.

It was then Garnet made her decision. It would be useless even to mention Blythe at this point. Rod was set upon a new, hopeful path. And Garnet, for one, was not going to do anything to cast a shadow on the sunshine now glowing so radiantly in his life.

And what about Blythe? Surely, by this time, Blythe had found her own new happiness. Perhaps she had put all that had happened to her in Virginia behind her. Surely, her memories of Mayfield could not be ones she wanted to hold and cherish, even if she had once thought she loved Rod.

No, Garnet decided, *the best thing to do is to say nothing*.

Never one to dwell for long on vague probabilities, she rose from her dressing table, gave Faith a kiss, and said, "I must go down to our guests now, precious. I'll tell Nanny to let you peek over the balcony until everyone comes and we go into dinner. But then you must go right to bed, understand?"

Faith nodded solemnly. "Yes, Mummy, I promise."

Having assured herself that she had made the right decision about Rod, Garnet swept out of the room and down the stairs, ready to step into the role she played with such verve and style, that of the charming hostess of Birchfields.

Part III

Life unfolds in a continuous succession of expectations and experience; all that happens is through the mercy of God.
—anonymous

chapter
8

The Guest House
Savannah, Georgia

LYING ON HER reclining chair in the sunshine, Sara Montrose watched the hummingbirds hovering above the hanging baskets of trailing red and pink fuchsias suspended from the fretwork of the porch. It had become a morning ritual for Clay to settle her here on the sunny terrace while he went to pick up the morning mail. Here she could enjoy not only the birds, but also the lush beauty of the surrounding blossoming azaleas and camellia bushes. It was especially pleasant now in April since the weather had become so balmy.

The guest house where she and Clay now lived, set in a grove of gnarled oaks hung with Spanish moss, occupied a portion of the spacious grounds of Sara's younger sister Lucie's home a few miles from Savannah.

Six years ago Sara and Clay had come to spend the winter. They were still here. Unforeseen circumstances had prevented their returning to their Virginia home, a fact that had not surprised Sara. Although she had not confided her foreboding to Clay, she had had a feeling when they left Montclair that they would never return. No one could have anticipated the tragic turn of events that had brought her premonition to pass.

Courageously, Sara had set about to make a new life, for Clay's sake more than for her own. She had left Savannah as a bride in a rebound marriage, glad to escape her unhappy memories. Now she made the effort to renew old ties, invite old friends to call, create a congenial social circle for them. Even though the long-ago riding accident had left her a semi-invalid since the age of thirty, Sara was still elegant and fascinating. In spite of her obvious fragile health, people always came away from a visit declaring how witty, bright, and marvelously entertaining Sara was.

Sara never spoke of the other tragedies that had wounded her spirit. Only Clay knew the secret sorrow of her heart, the hurts that had never fully healed—the loss of her three sons, of the magnificent home over which she had presided for many years, of a sense of being in control of her destiny. As ever, he was her devoted companion, admirer and lover, always eager to do whatever would make her more content, happier, or more comfortable.

As she saw his tall figure coming now through the lushly flowered garden toward the cottage, Sara felt her heart soften with affection. How dear Clay was, how steadfast through all the vicissitudes they had suffered together in their long marriage.

As a girl, Sara was considered extraordinarily beautiful. It was said that every young man who met her fell in love with her. She had had dozens of proposals, but she knew why she had chosen Clay. It was not just that she had been cruelly disappointed by her first love, but that she realized, even then, Clay loved her in spite of her flaws. And with each passing year, she appreciated him more.

Sara sat up a little, noticing that Clay's step was quicker than usual this spring morning and that he was smiling and waving an envelope in one hand.

In fact, she could see that her husband was trembling with excitement.

"You may find this as hard to believe as I, my dear—" he said in a voice that shook slightly. "But this is from Blythe!" And he handed her an envelope bearing an English postmark.

Startled, Sara took it and read the return address. "Kentburne? Where is that? England?"

Clay nodded. "Open it, my dear. Let's see what it says," he urged her.

Sara's heart was beating rapidly as she picked up the ivory-handled letter opener and slid it along the flap of the envelope. She unfolded the three pages of thin writing paper, her eyes skimming the first line. Then she wet her dry lips and began to read aloud.

Dear Mr. and Mrs. Montrose:

I know you have wondered about me all these years, and I ask your forgiveness for my long silence. My only excuse is that I was too young, too devastated by the events that led to Malcolm's death and my eviction from Montclair to think rationally. I only recall thinking what a blow it would be to you both, and simply didn't have the courage to face you, nor the wisdom to help you bear these dreadful tragedies.

It was months before I could sort things out for myself, I suppose. As you will note, I came to England—for sentimental reasons. Through Malcolm's love of this country, I too had come to think of it as a kind of haven where I could somehow recover from my sorrow and build a new life. That new life included Malcolm's son—

Sara drew in her breath and raised her eyes to meet those of her husband's.

"A son!" she repeated. Clearing her throat, Sara read on.

His name is Arthur Geoffrey Paul, after Malcolm's favorite boyhood hero, King Arthur and St. Paul, the great lion of God. But I call him Jeff.

Jeff is a handsome boy. He looks much the way I imagine Malcolm might have looked at this age. He is very bright, with a happy disposition. On his next birthday he will be six, old enough to travel. Therefore, I am planning to bring him to America next month.

If it is agreeable with you, we will be coming from New Orleans and look forward very much to visiting you in Savannah next month.

I regret any pain my actions over the past years may have caused. I am most anxious to make amends and to see both of you again. As Malcolm's parents, and Jeff's grandparents, you hold a special place in my heart.

Affectionately,
Blythe Dorman Montrose

"Well!" was all Sara could say as she folded the letter and replaced it in its envelope.

"Well, indeed!" Clay agreed. "Isn't it wonderful, Sara, dear? To see a grandson we didn't even know about? And in only a few weeks!"

Sara's mouth twisted slightly. "You would think she would have let us know about this sooner! I mean, for all intents and purposes, we lost Jonathan to the Merediths. It seems quite unfair that Blythe would have kept Malcolm's other son from us, too!"

Clay reached over and patted Sara's hand. "Now, my dear, best to let bygones by bygones. Blythe is older now, wiser. She even admits she acted impulsively. Says she's sorry for any grief she has caused. Let's welcome her with open arms, not bring up any unpleasantness from the past."

Sara regarded her husband affectionately. "You're right, of course. Turn the other cheek. What a fine Christian man you are, Clay. I sometimes envy you your ability not to harbor bitterness about anything. I'm afraid I sometimes allow myself to be overwhelmed with regrets, old sorrows." She lifted her chin and smiled at him, her eyes brighter. "I wonder if Jeff really *does* resemble Malcolm? Malcolm was such a handsome child."

"We'll soon see, my dear," Clay reminded her, smiling happily. "We'll soon see."

Riding from the Savannah dock in the open carriage Sara's sister had sent for them that early spring morning, Blythe gradually noticed a subtle difference in the air. The sharp, tangy dampness of the wharves gave way to the soft, flower-scented air.

The quiet streets were ablaze with blooms—long beds of azaleas, from frosty whites to palest pinks and fiery reds and waxy-leafed bushes laden with velvety camellias. Begonias spilled riotously over the iron-lace balconies. And from behind scrolled wrought-iron fences and the gates of hidden gardens peeked pink day lilies.

Savannah homes were stately, Blythe decided, mostly of Regency architecture built of stone or stucco and etched with exquisite ornamental work like black lace against the pastel of the walls. It was a city of churches, too, Blythe noted as they passed first a white-spired building, then a twin-towered cathedral facing the square.

Blythe took a long, deep breath, hoping the mingled fragrances would soothe her nervousness. The thought of seeing Malcolm's parents after all these years was daunting. Yet both of them had responded to her letter, expressing their delight at hearing from her and their happy anticipation of her visit.

"I cannot tell you how your message cheered Sara," Clayborn had written in his fine Spencerian hand. "She is counting the days until your ship docks and you and our grandson will be here."

In spite of these reassurances, Blythe still felt some apprehension. Before she had left Montclair and Mayfield, she had sent them a letter, explaining as best she could the disastrous circumstances under which their home and land had fallen. Written in the shock and grief of Malcolm's death and the loss of the Montrose estate, the letter had contained only the bare facts. Blythe herself had acted in panic and run away.

For many complicated reasons, Blythe had never felt really welcome nor accepted at Montclair. Even though she was carrying Malcolm's child at the time, she had felt the best thing she could do for them was to disappear from their lives. Maybe, if there were no reminders of Malcolm's unfortunate second marriage, they would recover all the sooner.

But now, nearly seven years later, she was coming back into their lives. What happened next was in God's hands.

Before they left England, Blythe had bought a book about the southern part of the United States, full of pictures. She and Jeff had pored over it for hours, turning the pages as she read to him about the places they would see. Now, it was all coming alive for them.

She looked over at her handsome son, sitting up so straight, looking from right to left as they rode along. Now they were at the outskirts of town, turning into the country road leading out to Sara and Clayborn's cottage on Lucie's plantation. The road was lined with tall pines on one side and on the other with vast marshes where herons and spindly-legged cranes waded.

"Look, Mummy!" Jeff exclaimed, pointing to the strange-looking birds, his eyes shining.

How handsome he is, Blythe thought, feeling that sweet little jolt of love and tenderness as her eyes rested on her son. The morning sun had dusted his dark curls with a golden light, giving his hair a mahogany sheen. He looked like Malcolm, and yet she could see something of herself in him, too. Blythe wondered for the hundredth time what the Montroses would think of Jeff.

The carriage slowed, then made a right turn through gates onto a crushed-oyster-shell drive shaded by arching live oak trees hung with mysterious gray moss. The drive led to a majestic, white-pillared house at the far end. As they came closer, Blythe realized she was actually holding her breath. Almost before the carriage came to a complete stop, she could see the graceful figure of a woman gliding out from the house to stand at the top of the steps.

This must be their hostess, Lucie Leighton Bowen, Blythe thought as the driver opened the carriage door and handed her down, then lifted Jeff out to stand beside her.

"Welcome to Windhaven," the lady called to them in a softly accented voice.

"Thank you," Blythe replied, and she and Jeff mounted the steps to the porch.

"I'm Sara's sister, and, of course, you're Blythe." When Lucie spoke, the cadence was low and musical, the distinctly southern one Blythe had all but forgotten.

Lucie held out both hands to Blythe, then leaned down to hug Jeff.

"And I'm *your* Aunt Lucie, young fellow. Come along, I'll take you right to Sara. She's been on pins and needles for days, waiting for you two to come!"

Following her into the cool interior of the house, Blythe was struck by both its simplicity and its quality. The hall, hung with mirrors on either side, extended the length of the house, seemingly endless. Through this hallway they walked out onto another veranda, the twin of the one in front, down steps and along a flagstone path to a small house nestled under the thick shade of towering oaks.

"We built this as a guest house for overflows in the days when we did much more entertaining," Lucie explained. "And when Clay suggested Sara would be better off in our milder winter climate, this seemed made to order for them. Everything's on one floor, so much easier for Sara, and it's convenient to our house and for the servants—" Lucie's radiant smile utterly transformed what might have been described as a rather ordinary face.

Recalling Sara's remarkable beauty, Blythe had been a little surprised that her sister was so very different in appearance, but there was a sweetness of expression and a tranquility that she had always found lacking, even in the perfection of Sara's features.

"Sara! Sara, they're here!" Lucie called as they neared the flower-edged brick terrace. There curlicued white iron furniture was arranged, and overhead purple wisteria garlanded the trellis, giving both color and shade.

Lucie caught Jeff's hand in hers. "Come, darling, don't be shy. Come meet your grandmother," she urged gently.

Jeff looked to Blythe for reassurance, then marched up onto the terrace just as Clay's tall figure filled the cottage doorway. Blythe drew in her breath sharply. Mr. Montrose looked much as she remembered him, yet decidedly older. His wavy white hair was smoothly combed, the flowing cravat and ruffled shirt of his white linen coat, immaculate.

"My dear Blythe," he said, his voice husky with emotion. Then his gaze fell on the little boy who had halted on the threshold. There was a moment of absolute stillness when the only sound to be heard was the slow rustling of the wind stirring high up in the trees, the muted flutter of bird wings.

After a long minute he said, "So this is Jeff. What a fine boy you are, and very like your father. Wait until your grandmother sees you." Over Jeff's head Clay's eyes met Blythe's. "Thank you for coming, my dear, thank you for bringing our grandson." Then he called over his shoulder, "Yes, yes, Sara, darlin', we're coming!"

He took Jeff by the hand and led him inside, and Blythe followed.

In the small parlor just off the entrance hall, Sara waited on a lounge chair placed between the French windows opening out onto the terrace.

Though Blythe had expected to find her mother-in-law aged, she was surprised to see that Sara was still lovely. Gowned in a lavender taffeta dress, its neck and sleeves ruffled in lace, she held out her arms, tears darkening her blue eyes to sapphire gems.

"Darling boy!" she said as Jeff stepped shyly forward. "How I have longed for this day!" Her eyes feasted on him, then she looked past him to Blythe. There was only a second's hesitation before her smile included the boy's mother in its welcome.

"Blythe, if you don't look every inch an English lady!"

Blythe's cheeks flushed hotly. Sara's compliment was ample reward for the time and care she had taken in dressing for this, their first meeting after all these years. She had chosen a walking suit of taupe bouclé-knit expertly tailored to sculpture her slimly curved figure, its cream-colored revers and cuffs decorated with trapunto embroidery, the skirt fashionably gathered into a short train in back. Completing her stylish ensemble was a biscuit straw hat, trimmed with beige grosgrain ribbons and set artfully atop her coppery curls.

That first afternoon the four adults, their attention centered on one small boy, sat on the shaded terrace enjoying a refreshing tea of delicious iced lemonade, a feather-light pound cake, and the first fresh peaches of the season with a lemon sorbet. The conversation was pleasant, with no sad memories brought up nor any sort of recriminations for Blythe's long silence. There would be time later to speak of the years between. It was enough now to enjoy this unexpected reunion and speak only of happy subjects.

When Clay took Jeff to explore the large garden with its goldfish pond and waterfall, Sara reached for Blythe's hand and squeezed it gratefully.

"How good of you to come all this long way, my dear, and bring this darling child so that we could get to know him a little." She paused, "You have done a magnificent job with him. He has obviously been brought up with a good balance of love and discipline . . . something, I'm afraid, I never accomplished with *my* sons. I loved them extravagantly and spoiled them totally." Sara sighed, then gave a small, involuntary shudder. "I'm only sorry that we've already missed so much of his childhood . . . But—" she shook off the negative thought—"we shall just make the best of the time we have!"

The next time the two women had to be alone was on an afternoon when Clay took Jeff to the harbor to see the many ships being loaded and unloaded with their exotic cargoes of cotton, hides, wood, wine, fruit—merchandise from all corners of the world. It was then Sara and Blythe first spoke of Malcolm and the self-destructive end of his life, weeping unashamedly in their mutual loss of this man they had loved.

"It wasn't all Malcolm's fault," Blythe told Sara. "I was the wrong wife for him. If he had married someone strong like Garnet, he might not have slipped into despair. I was too young, too ignorant to help him—" Her voice broke.

"You mustn't blame yourself, Blythe, nor burden yourself with guilt. What's done is done. We'll never know if what we did was right or wrong until eternity. Each of us lives out his or her own destiny. We make decisions that, once set in motion, affect us and everyone around us." Sara sighed deeply. "My deepest regret is that Malcolm did not live to see this wonderful boy, his son. It would have given him something to forge a new life for, a reason to bring Montclair back into the Montrose family."

Seeing Blythe's teacup nearly empty, Sara poured another steaming cupful. "You know, of course, that Montclair has been taken over by the very man who won it in the card game with Malcolm?"

Blythe bit her lip and nodded. How well she remembered that awful day, just before Christmas, when the county sheriff's messenger had delivered the eviction notice. Later, on the very same train she was taking out of Mayfield, Randall Bondurant had passed her on his way to his private car through the day coach where she sat grieving.

"In spite of everything, Blythe, I think you should take Jeff to Virginia, back to Mayfield, let him see Montclair—if only from a distance. He has a right to know his heritage. Who knows? Maybe he will be master there yet!" Sara shook her head. "One thing I have learned is that one never knows what lies ahead. Life presents such twists and turns that one should never give up hope."

Blythe could never recall a time in which her mother-in-law had looked on the hopeful side of things. But as the leisurely days passed, Blythe glimpsed more and more of this new Sara.

Of course Sara had aged. The dark wings of hair were now predominantly silver, framing the perfect oval of her finely lined face, the toll of years of illness and many sorrows. But there was a new serenity in Sara that Blythe had never seen, and she wondered if she would learn its secret.

This came about on one of the last afternoons of her visit, when Blythe decided at the last minute to decline Lucie's offer to go calling on some of her friends and see some of Savannah's historic homes and sites. Instead, she said she thought she would spend the time with Sara.

Sara seemed pleasantly surprised when Blythe appeared at the little cottage. Almost simultaneously, a small black boy came shyly onto the terrace where Sara was reclining on her chaise.

After greeting Blythe, Sara turned to the child. "Tell the other children we'll not have a reading lesson today, Toby. Miss Blythe's visiting me this afternoon, so you tell Bessie and Joel to come over tomorrow and we'll read the story about Daniel and the lions' den, all right?"

The little fellow nodded. His big dark eyes rolled toward Blythe curiously, then he ran through the garden and back toward the kitchen area of the big house.

"Am I upsetting your plans?" Blythe asked.

"No, my dear, not at all. One day is the same as the next to children." She smiled. "That was Tobias, the cook's boy. I'm teaching him and his sister and cousin to read. And at the same time they're learning about the Bible." As if slightly embarrassed by this admission, Sara shook her head. "Who would ever have believed it of me? Rose would be so pleased, if she knew."

Blythe sat down opposite the older woman, gazing at her thoughtfully.

As if reading her mind, Sara said softly, "Oh, yes, my dear, I've changed. You bend or you break, you know."

The two women began talking quietly, Blythe sharing with Sara some of her uncertainties about Jeff's future.

"There are some fine schools in Virginia," Sara reminded her. "I never approved of sending Southern children up north to be educated, and I suppose I feel the same way about American boys going to English boarding schools."

"Maybe I'll look into some while I'm there," Blythe said. "I've decided to follow your suggestion and take Jeff to see Montclair."

"What a good idea, my dear!" Sara commented as if she had not suggested the idea. "And if you were not so far away, you could come for visits and we would really get to know our grandson."

As the sun shifted, shadows fell onto the terrace where they were sitting, and Sara gave a little shiver.

"It's getting cool out here. I suppose we should go inside before we get a chill."

Blythe rose, then hesitated. Light as Sara was, could she manage to carry her into the house alone?

At this moment, Sara pointed to the latticed screen behind her chaise lounge. "Please hand me my crutches, Blythe."

Startled, Blythe stared at her mother-in-law. She had never

known Sara to use crutches. Always she had been carried or wheeled about in an invalid's chair.

Sara met her glance with a wry smile.

"Yes, I use crutches. I have for years, though no one knew about it. Now you will discover another dark truth about me, Blythe. When I was first injured, it was thought I would be bedridden for the rest of my life. However, gradually, due to my basically strong constitution, I suppose, my back mended even though my legs were useless. The doctors I consulted said I could manage to get around on crutches."

Sara shook her head. "Although I learned how to use them, my movements were so awkward and ungainly that I was bitterly resentful. I had always been light on my feet, a graceful dancer, and an accomplished rider and could not bear to have anyone see me struggle to cross a room so wretchedly. Of course, Clay knew and my maid, Lizzie, but no one else. Oh, Blythe, I was so proud, so vain! I deprived myself and my family of a much more mobile, more involved wife and mother! I am ashamed to confess it, but it is true."

Spontaneously Blythe leaned down to embrace Sara, then found the crutches and helped her stand. Bonded now in a new understanding, the two women went into the house.

"Will you call on the Camerons while you are in Mayfield?" Sara asked the day before Blythe and Jeff were to leave for Virginia.

The question caused Blythe's heart to beat erratically. She was sure that Sara had never suspected the strong attraction she and Rod Cameron had had for each other. Why should she? As far as Sara was concerned, the Camerons were just family friends whose sons had grown up with her own.

Now she hedged her answer. "I don't know, I'm not sure. They may have forgotten all about me."

"Oh, no! I'm sure they would be delighted to hear from you and especially to see Malcolm's son."

"I'll think about it," Blythe murmured, then added, "But please don't write that I'm coming. I'll decide when I get there."

Sara looked puzzled, but acquiesced gracefully. "Of course, that's up to you."

The time of their departure for Virginia was bittersweet. New memories had been made, replacing in part the strained and tenuous ties of the past. Clay and Sara were now more than Malcolm's parents. They were Jeff's grandparents and, perhaps even more significantly, her friends. Leaving them now brought a kind of sadness for what might have been.

chapter
9

Mayfield, Virginia

BLYTHE HAD NEVER planned to return to Mayfield. In fact, until her long talk with Sara, Mayfield was the very last place she ever imagined going. But Sara's argument had been convincing.

On the sunny days aboard the boat traveling up the coast from Savannah, Blythe thought often about that afternoon she and Sara had spent together and how Sara had confided in her so intimately, as if she felt compelled to share with Blythe all that she herself had learned so tragically.

"It's the things I didn't appreciate that I miss most," Sara had said. "Now, I *know* that joy in most lives is as fleeting as a summer rainbow. And we *must cherish those times*. The day of my accident that changed my life forever was such a happy one. Clay had just given me a beautiful new Arabian as a gift after Lee's birth. I recall mounting, then turning back to see Clay and Malcolm standing on the porch steps, and thinking how wonderful my life was!" A sad smile touched Sara's lips. "So, you see, as it says on the sundial in Noramary's garden at Montclair: COUNT ONLY THE SUNNY HOURS."

Upon their arrival in Mayfield, the train's conductor informed Blythe that the Mayfield Inn always sent a carriage to pick up prospective guests. An official of the inn would then take care of the passengers' luggage, and they would be driven to the front entrance. At his suggestion, Blythe signaled the driver, and soon she and Jeff were seated in the open carriage en route to the Inn.

On the way, Blythe was amazed to see how well Mayfield had recovered from the ravages of war. The first time she had seen the town, it had borne the scars of frequent skirmishes between Union and Confederate forces. As a county junction, Mayfield and its railroad were strategically located and had been fought over, won, and lost a half-dozen times by each side, and in the last year of the conflict, had been occupied by the Yankees. Now it had the look of a flourishing community.

When they drew up in front of the imposing new façade of the inn, Blythe would not have recognized it as the shabby, weathered building she had known. Everything about it had been refurbished, from the nattily uniformed porters and bellboys to the plush carpeting and baroque furnishings of its interior.

As she approached the desk, a smiling clerk greeted her.

"Welcome to Mayfield, ma'am." To Jeff, he said, "Howdy, young fellow." Then he dipped a pen into the inkwell and handed it to her as he pushed the registration book forward. "And how long will you be staying with us?"

"I'm . . . not sure. I have some business to attend to. Actually . . . I am looking for some property—"

"That's mighty fine." The clerk beamed. "I know of just the person for you to contact, ma'am—Richard Pembruck, as fine a gentleman as you will ever meet. Deals in properties of all kinds. I know he'd be happy to show you around. Now, if I might have your name—"

Blythe hesitated. One of the risks of coming to Mayfield was the name "Montrose," so readily associated with the prominent family. The hyphenated "Dorman-Montrose" she had used in England had gone unnoted, since that usage was fairly common. Here in

Virginia, however, it might seem pretentious and draw unwanted attention, or worse still be immediately recognized and beg questions.

"Mrs. Blythe Dorman—" she said finally, rationalizing dropping the last name. It was protection, a precaution, not really a lie, she told herself.

"With your permission, ma'am, I'll let Mr. Pembruck know of your interest in seeing some of the available places hereabouts, and then you may make an appointment at your convenience."

Blythe signed her name with a flourish. "Perhaps in a day or so, but I think I'd like to look around on my own a bit first. Could you arrange for me to have a carriage and driver for a few hours tomorrow?"

"Anything you say, ma'am," the clerk agreed heartily.

Their room was a spacious one, with a large canopy bed for Blythe, and a small trundle bed for Jeff. The windows overlooked Mayfield Square. Here, surrounded by flower beds, the statue of a confederate soldier at parade rest presided over an octagonal park. Placed at random intervals were benches where people sat chatting or simply meditating on all that the stone soldier represented.

Later, when Blythe and Jeff went down to the elegant dining room for the early dinner service, they were shown to a table by a dignified, white-coated black waiter, who introduced himself as Clarence.

Jeff, as friendly as a puppy, soon struck up a conversation with him as their glasses were filled with ice water. From Clarence, they learned that the inn maintained a large play yard with slides, swings, and a merry-go-round for the children of guests.

"Oh, could I go there, Mummy?" Jeff asked eagerly.

"Yes, dear, perhaps—" Blythe murmured as she studied the menu.

"Now?"

"Too late this evenin', suh," Clarence told him. "Play yard closes down at five. Mebbe tomorrow, if yo' mama says—"

"Tomorrow then, Mummy?"

Blythe glanced over the top of her menu at his excited little face.

"Well, not tomorrow, Jeff. I thought we'd take a carriage ride. There's something I want to show you."

His look of keen disappointment changed to curiosity.

"What is it, Mummy?"

"A house—"

Jeff's face fell. "A *house?*" he repeated. "Why would I want to see a *house?*"

"It's a very special house, Jeff. It's where your father grew up, where he lived when he was a little boy. It's called Montclair."

Clarence, who was waiting to take their order, shook his head. "Beg pardon, ma'am, but it ain't called Montclair no mo'. That place b'longs to Mr. Randall Bondurant who married Miss Alair Chance. So they call it 'Bon Chance' now."

Silently Blythe repeated the new name. The words felt strange on her lips—*Bon chance*—with her limited knowledge of French, Blythe knew it meant "Good luck." How ironic, for a house lost to a gambler in a card game. It might have been *his* good fortune, but not Malcolm's, and certainly not Jeff's.

The next afternoon Blythe and Jeff waited on the veranda of the inn for the hired carriage.

"Drive out along the river road," she instructed the driver as she climbed in.

The tree-lined country road had not changed quite as much as the town, but Blythe noticed freshly painted white fences surrounding lush pastureland on which well-fed cows and sleek horses grazed. The passing panorama kept Jeff busy and interested. But the farther into the country they drove, the more Blythe felt a nervous anticipation—an indefinable mixture of longing and dread.

The closer they came to the familiar bend in the road where she knew the Cameron property began, the faster her heart beat. She leaned forward, her gloved hands twisting in her lap, as they passed the stone gates of Cameron Hall.

The old pain clutched her throat, old questions surfaced—the ones she usually did not allow herself to dwell upon. What had the Camerons thought when they learned that she had left without telling them why she was going? How ungrateful Mrs. Cameron must have thought her, after all her many kindnesses to Blythe. And Rod—what must he have been thinking all these years?

But what else could I have done? Blythe agonized.

Just then the driver's voice broke into her anguished thoughts, as he called down to her. "We're coming to 'Bon-Chance' now, ma'am. Want me to ring the gatehouse bell?"

"No, we're not going up to the house. Just stop outside the gate, please."

"Why can't we go in, Mummy?" Jeff asked.

"Because we don't know the people who live there now."

He looked puzzled but accepted her answer.

When the carriage came to a stop, she said, "Come along, Jeff." When Blythe got out, he scrambled out behind her, then ran ahead to the closed gates. Leaning over her son's head, Blythe gripped the railings, squinting her eyes through the masses of blooming pink and white dogwood for a glimpse of the house she had last seen on that drizzling, long-ago December day.

All she could see was a long stretch of velvety manicured lawn and, in the distance, a section of the gleaming white columns on the deep porch, the slanted slate roof, the sparkle of sunlight on the windowpanes framed by dark blue shutters.

"I can't see anything, Mummy!" complained Jeff. "Can't we go in?"

"No, Jeff."

"But if it was my father's house, won't they know us?"

"It was a long time ago, Jeff. Your father's dead. Someone else owns it now." Her voice was unusually sharp as she struggled with her own reaction to seeing Montclair again after all these years.

The little boy was quiet for a moment as if pondering his mother's meaning. Then he ran back and forth along the stone wall, stopping now and then to try to peer through the railings. Tiring of this activity, he ran back and tugged at Blythe's skirt. "Let's go now, Mummy. I've seen enough."

I have, too, she thought, her throat swelling with sadness as she looked down into the upturned face of her small son. *This* should all have been *his.* There should be no locked gates keeping him out.

With one hand she touched his curly head, then his plump cheek. "Yes, darling, it's time to go."

She took his hand and together they walked back to the carriage and climbed inside. As the carriage started back toward Mayfield, Blythe was sorry she'd come. It had probably been a dreadful mistake!

On the way back to town, Blythe stared unseeingly out the carriage window. She had not been prepared for the storm of bittersweet memories that stirred within her—that early spring afternoon when Malcolm and she had traveled this same road as newlyweds, Malcolm's old homeplace, the first sighting of the mansion, her heightened anticipation. The meadows bordering the grounds of the house had been golden with daffodils that day, and when they had gone inside, they had found Garnet arranging armfuls of them into vases. Garnet!

Blythe thought of the stricken look on Garnet's face when Malcolm had introduced Blythe as his wife. Unbeknownst to Blythe, Garnet had been in love with Malcolm even before his marriage to Rose Meredith and had loved him with a desperate passion for years—

Love can be so cruel, as *she* knew—

"Mummy! Mummy, look! Here comes a man on a horse!" exclaimed Jeff, pressing his face against the carriage window.

Jolted back to the present, Blythe turned her head in the direction Jeff was looking and saw a horse and rider approaching on the other side of the road.

It was like a dream out of the past. His wind-tossed hair and the horse's mane were nearly the same tawny color, and there was something heart-catchingly familiar about the way the man sat in the saddle. Suddenly Blythe knew it was no dream. Instinctively, she drew back, forcing herself against the leather seat, out of sight of the passing rider. Even before he cantered by the carriage, she recognized him. It was Rod Cameron!

Back in her room at the Mayfield Inn, Blythe battled her turbulent emotions. That passing glimpse of Rod had unnerved her. All the thoughts and feelings she had thought so safely locked away had sprung open—a Pandora's box of memories.

Seeing him on horseback recalled their rides together through the lush woodland trails adjoining their two plantations. One unforgettable day demanded remembering. They had ridden deep into the woods, and had dismounted and sat in the grape arbor of Eden Cottage, the honeymoon house for Montrose brides and grooms. That day they had come close to declaring the truth in their hearts of a love forbidden to them by all they both held sacred.

Blythe knew Rod to be a man of honor, strong loyalties, and firm faith. He lived by a code he would never betray.

But what of now? What would happen if she suddenly reappeared in Rod's life? Would he now declare that love? Or was it a hope she had preserved in her heart alone? The thought had a paralyzing effect.

Blythe knew it was dangerous to remain in Mayfield where, at some unplanned moment, they might encounter each other again. She wrung her hands, stifling the moan that sprang to her lips. There was so much guilt surrounding their relationship—guilt that she, a married woman, had been in love with her husband's best friend, guilt for the shabby manner in which she had treated his family—

It had been particularly difficult for Rod's mother, Kate Cameron, who was always the soul of grace and tact, even though Blythe's coming had meant a second heartbreak for her daughter Garnet. And Rod's cousin Dove had welcomed her as a sister-in-law. No, she must not take the chance of meeting Rod unexpectedly.

Blythe knew now that if she planned to stay in Virginia so Jeff could be educated in the land of his fathers, it could not be in Mayfield. It would have to be somewhere else.

She wished she had not made the appointment with the realtor for tomorrow. But the desk clerk had already made the arrangements, and Mr. Pembruck had followed up with a note, saying he was sure he had some properties in which she would be interested.

Yes, she would have to keep the appointment. But after that, she would take Jeff and leave.

Jeff, left in the care of a cheerful black maid named Mattie, was playing happily in the play yard of the inn when Blythe accompanied Mr. Pembruck the next day on a tour of houses and lots in the Mayfield vicinity.

She looked at all the property he had in mind for her and listened politely as he cataloged the selling points of each one, waiting until the appropriate time to tell him she would prefer something a great deal farther from the town.

"You see, I really don't intend to stay much longer in Virginia on this trip, Mr. Pembruck. My son and I will be leaving soon for our home in England. But I would appreciate it if you would keep in touch with me and let me know if you should find something suitable," Blythe told him when he escorted her back to the inn.

"Most assuredly, Mrs. Dorman. You have been explicit in outlining your needs—particularly proximity to a good school for your son. Be certain I will be in touch with you." He tipped his hat and bowed as he left her at the front entrance. "It has been a pleasure to meet you, and I hope the two of you will soon be Virginia residents."

Blythe thanked him, passed through the lobby of the hotel, and went up the stairs to her room. Doubts about the wisdom of planning to live again in Virginia troubled her. And yet it had seemed so right when she discussed the possibility with Sara. Maybe it was having seen Rod that had disturbed her so much.

Suddenly she felt an overwhelming urgency to pack and leave Mayfield as soon as possible. Even though she had booked passage on a ship sailing two weeks from today, she could take Jeff up to Richmond and Washington to see some of the historic sites there— Yes, she would notify the management that she would be leaving sooner than planned, ask them to prepare her bill and make train reservations at once.

Feeling weary after the long day of viewing property with Mr. Pembruck, Blythe decided to ring for room service and relax for a while before Jeff, with all his boundless energy, returned from the play yard.

When the maid appeared with tea and tiny sandwiches, Blythe noticed a folded newspaper on the tray beside the silver pot. It was the latest edition of the *Mayfield Herald*.

"I didn't order a newspaper," Blythe told the maid.

"It's a courtesy of the Inn, ma'am," she replied, bobbing a little curtsy as she left the room.

Blythe poured her tea, then unfolded the paper, thinking it might be interesting read the local news. Later, she was to think it strange that she had not the slightest premonition, not one, of what she would find when she turned to the society page. There, in bold black print, she read: TWO PROMINENT LOCAL FAMILIES TO BE UNITED.

"Mrs. Elyse Maynard announces the engagement of her daughter, Fenelle, to Mr. Roderick Cameron of Cameron Hall—"

The words blurred before Blythe's eyes. She read the rest of the article rapidly, registering only phrases here and there—"wedding plans undetermined at this time. Miss Maynard . . . visiting relatives in England . . . where she will enjoy a London season this summer."

Blythe's hands were shaking when she put the paper down. She rose from the chair and went over to the window. It was open to admit the soft, spring breeze, but she shivered and pulled the window shut. She felt cold. Weak. Devastated.

But why? Had she really expected Rod to wait for her, without a word, without hope? How could she have been so foolish? Still, she knew that in her heart she had secretly harbored a dream that somehow she and Rod would—*What? How?*

You fool! she chastised herself. *Why didn't you contact Rod when*

Jeff was born, when you were both free? Blythe shuddered and turned away from the pale afternoon sunshine streaming through the window. Even the sun had grown cold.

How much later, she was never sure, she began to remove articles of clothing from armoire and bureau drawers. There was no question in her mind now what she should do.

"But why do we have to leave?" protested Jeff when she told him that evening. "I like it here!"

Blythe looked up from her packing. "It's time we went back home, darling. Don't you want to see Dotty? I'm sure she misses us. And Captain Prescott's Labrador, Jet, must have had her puppies by now. He promised you one, remember?"

Seeing this seemed to satisfy Jeff temporarily, Blythe pressed her advantage. "You liked sailing on the ship, didn't you, Jeff? Well, we'll be going back on an even bigger one this time—" While her voice sounded cheerful enough as she embellished on the pleasures of their return ocean voyage, Blythe's mind was far removed from what she was saying.

"I guess so—well, yes, I did like that!" Jeff agreed. Then he jumped down off the bed. "What shall I call my puppy, do you think, Mummy? I like the name Rex or Prince, don't you?"

Thank goodness, Jeff was so amenable, so ready to accept whatever came along, Blythe thought with relief. This was such an easy age. If he had been older, it might not be so simple to explain her change of mind.

Two days later, all her arrangements were complete, and the morning they were to leave for Richmond, Jeff was so eager to be off, that, in desperation, Blythe sent him down to the lobby to wait for her there.

"Go tell Clarence good-bye, why don't you, darling?" she suggested.

"Oh, that's a good idea, Mummy, I'll do that!" he said, and went skipping off down the stairs.

Blythe put on her bonnet and adjusted the veil. Her small chin was set determinedly, her mouth firm, but she felt the turmoil within her, the terrible churning, the heaviness in her breast that made it difficult to breathe.

Feeling faint, she sat down on the edge of the bed to regain her equilibrium. *Just a case of nerves,* she thought. Good thing she was so very healthy, though she hadn't quite been herself since seeing Rod on the road back from Montclair.

Would she ever get over Rod Cameron? The sad truth was that she had lost him twice. If she had acted sooner, written him, anything . . . maybe . . . Blythe shook her head at her reflection in the bureau mirror. Too late, too late—

Resolutely, she rose from the bed, picked up her handbag and gloves, and left the room. The carriage from the Inn would take them to the Mayfield station for the train to Richmond. But first, she had to settle her bill and check out at the desk.

Descending the stairs into the main lobby, Blythe heard Jeff's voice. She halted, glanced around the lobby, and spotted him talking to two men. Their backs were to Blythe, but there was something familiar about the set of the taller man's shoulders, and her hand tightened on the banister. Instantly aware of her thundering heart, she moved behind one of the columns, where she could see and hear but was herself hidden. Every nerve quivering, she heard that deep drawl she recognized immediately.

"So, young fellow, what's your name?"

Blythe held her breath as the confident reply came, "Jeff!"

"Ah ha! Jeff, is it? Well that's a fine name for a Virginia lad."

"Were you named for our famous native son, Thomas Jefferson?" the other man teased. "Or, maybe, for our illustrious Confederate president, Jefferson Davis?"

Blythe bit her lower lip and made an unconscious gesture as if to stop him. What if Jeff had given his full name, Jeff *Montrose!* Then what would have happened?

From her vantage point, she saw Jeff tip his curly head to one side, evidently puzzled by the questions. Almost at the same time he caught sight of Blythe. "There's my mother! I'll ask her!"

To her dismay, the two men turned in the direction of Jeff's pointed finger. There was nothing Blythe could do but continue down the steps with as much dignity as she could muster. Her heart throbbed in her throat; her breath was shallow; her hands under her gloves, clammy. But what else could she do?

Rod stood motionless, watching the tall, slender woman move toward him. It was the reality of a thousand dreams, yet vastly different from his fantasies.

She was still lovely, her features visible through the froth of blue veiling, her auburn hair swept up under the saucy flowered and beribboned bonnet. But this was no coltish girl recently come from a western ranch. This was a fashionably attired lady of elegance and style.

Rod stiffened. His bearing became almost militarily erect. As Blythe came closer, she could see character lines in his handsome face, and the sun-bronzed russet hair was threaded with silver.

Waves of emotion threatened to overwhelm her. Then something in his eyes halted her—something undisguised, transparent, full of remembering, and she caught her breath.

As they stood looking at each other, she saw her agony mirrored in his expression. To her horror, the blue eyes glazed over, hardening into steel. For the first time she knew how awful these years must have been for him. Somehow the silence between them was worse than any words they might have spoken.

"Mummy, Mummy, who am I named for?" Jeff's high-pitched voice broke through her trance-like state. She felt his little hands grab hers, swinging slightly as he persisted. "Wasn't it some knight from King Arthur's court?"

Blythe felt her mouth tremble as she forced it into a smile.

"Rod," she murmured.

"Blythe!" Her name on his lips sent a thrill coursing through her.

As if Rod suddenly became aware of his companion, who was looking with curiosity from one to the other, he introduced them.

"Blythe, may I present Francis Maynard?" Rod hesitated a fraction of a second. "Francis, Mrs. . . . Montrose."

The other man acknowledged the introduction with a friendly smile.

"Delighted, ma'am. I presume you're related to old friends of mine, the Montrose family?"

Blythe nodded, somehow able to utter the confirming words: "Malcolm Montrose's widow."

Evidently Francis Maynard was sensitive enough to perceive there was something unusual in this meeting. "If you will excuse me, ma'am, Rod, I'll go on ahead and join our friends in the gentlemen's lounge. You'll join us later, Rod?" He bowed again, saying as he left, "You've a fine boy there, Mrs. Montrose."

Finally Rod spoke, breaking the long awkwardness between them. "I'm truly at a loss . . . I can't believe you're really here . . . I don't know what to say."

"I know." Blythe swallowed over the ache in her throat. "I never meant . . . this shouldn't be the way—" She gave up. "Jeff and I have been here just a few days. We've been in Savannah, with Mr. and Mrs. Montrose. It was she who suggested—" Blythe drew Jeff closer to her—"that I bring my son here to see Montclair—"

"You must know it's been taken over by Randall Bondurant—"

"Oh, yes, of course. I knew that . . . that's why I left—" she broke off helplessly. Again, the enormity of what she had to explain threatened to dissolve her. Rod's eyes were impenetrable, searching her face, seeking answers to the many questions that must be crowding his mind.

Rod saw the trembling mouth he had so often longed to kiss. She looked so vulnerable that Rod's heart felt sore, then it hardened. How dare she come back here *now!* Of all times! Hadn't she left without a word? Hadn't she proven her lack of trust in him by keeping her plans to herself? Hadn't she betrayed their love by all these years of silence? Now—when it was too late—here she was!

He found his voice at last and was surprised at its harshness. "And this is Malcolm's son?"

"Yes, this is Jeff. Jeff, short for Geoffrey. It was a name Malcolm liked very much," Blythe replied, thinking how stiff and formal she sounded. How odd to be speaking with the man she had loved all these years as though to a stranger.

Panic spread through her, and she groped for something more normal to say. "How is your mother, Rod? I thought of sending a note asking to call, but then . . . it didn't seem the right thing . . . especially now that I—" she stopped abruptly, feeling her cheeks burn. "I mean, we are here for such a short time. . . . Well, we must go now, we have a train to catch and—"

Here Jeff supplied the rest of the information. "Then we're taking a big ship, going back to England! And I am to have a puppy as soon as we get home!"

Rod smiled down at him. "That's fine, Jeff, every boy should have a dog." His eyes rested on the handsome little boy with interest and liking, all the while thinking, *This could have been my son. Mine and Blythe's*. He turned to Blythe. "What time does your train leave?"

"In an hour," she replied. "I have to settle my bill—"

"There's another train to Richmond later today. Take that one, instead." Rod's tone was authoritative. "We must talk, Blythe. We can go into one of the private parlors here. Don't you think you owe me that much?"

Blythe hesitated. What use was there in talking now? It would only make things worse. Her anguish was already unbearable. But how could she refuse?

Leaning down, she cupped Jeff's cheek. "Darling, how would you like to run out to the play yard, find your friends Tom and Jimmy, and play for a while so Mummy can have a visit with her old friend, Mr. Cameron?"

"Oh, yippee, yes!" Jeff said excitedly. "I didn't get a chance to tell them about the big ship we're going on!"

He was already heading for the side door as she called after him, "Try not to get too dirty!"

Rod smiled knowingly. "Aren't you asking the impossible of a small boy, Blythe?"

"I guess you're right," she agreed ruefully.

"Now, shall we go?" he asked, gesturing toward one of the alcoved parlors, curtained with looped velvet draperies, that circled the lobby. He motioned her forward and there was nothing to do but follow his suggestion. As she did so, Blythe now dreaded the very encounter she had dreamed of. What could possibly come of any discussion between them now?

The little room, heavily decorated in the ornate style set by England's Queen Victoria, was almost smothering to Blythe. She seated herself on one of the carved armchairs. A pink marble-topped table separated her from Rod, who lowered his long frame into the opposite chair.

Glancing over at him, Blythe could read the hopelessness in his eyes, the same despair she felt. They were as trapped now by their feelings for each other as they had ever been before. But she knew he was expecting an explanation of her actions six years ago. He deserved that much. In a breathless rush, she began to tell him how frightened she had been, how lost after Malcolm's death when she had been ordered out of Montclair, but Rod held up his hand and stopped her midway.

"Didn't it even occur to you that we . . . all my family . . . that *I*, in particular, wanted to help you in any way possible way, Blythe? Didn't you know I loved you?"

Tears stung her eyes and she nodded wordlessly.

"But I was carrying Malcolm's child, Rod. I thought it would be wrong to accept your help when I could promise you nothing in return—"

Rod shook his head as if he still did not comprehend.

Once the dam was broken, Blythe's words tumbled one over the other, pouring like flood waters as she told him about what she had discovered about her father's legacy, how she had acted on impulse, first going to Bermuda and meeting the Ainsleys who had taken her under their wing, and how she had ended up in England.

"I tried to find you," Rod said at last.

"I didn't know. I thought . . . I wanted you to forget me."

"*Forget* you? Did you really think I could do *that?*"

Her lips were stiff as she said, "Rod . . . I know you are engaged, that . . . you are getting married."

At her remark the pupils of his eyes widened slightly, and slow color rose into his cheeks. But he did not look away as he answered her. "Yes, quite recently to Fenelle Maynard, the daughter of old family friends."

"From Mayfield, then?"

"Yes."

"Are you to be married soon?"

"A date has not yet been set. Fenelle is abroad, visiting relatives in England. She won't be returning to Virginia until the fall. Her cousin has arranged a London season for her—" His words drifted off, spoken almost impatiently as though what he was saying was of little importance.

Blythe tried desperately to think of something appropriate to say, something, *anything,* but her mind drew a blank. She felt the rush of adrenaline that made her pulses throb. Rod's eyes held her prisoner, and she could neither move nor turn her head away.

His next words were so low she unconsciously leaned forward to catch them. "Why? *Why,* Blythe?"

She knew what he meant. Why had she left without telling him? Why had she not sent for him in her distress? Why had she disappeared from his life, leaving no clue as to where she was going or where he might find her?

She shook her head dumbly, looking down at her gloved hands pressed tightly together in her lap.

"I don't know, Rod. It was such a long time ago. I was a different person then . . . I can't remember what I must have been thinking—"

"Didn't you know I would have done anything, gone anywhere . . . if I had known?"

Without lifting her head or looking at him, she nodded miserably.

"If I had only known . . . maybe I should have guessed. But I tried . . . thought I should respect your . . . grief," Rod said. "I thought you *knew*. . . given time, I would have . . . we could have . . . Blythe, don't you understand? Didn't you know how much I loved you?"

"Don't!" she gasped. "Don't say it!"

"I *have* to say it!" Rod retorted almost harshly. "I've waited nearly six years to say it. How much can a man bear? Can you imagine the agony I've been through not knowing where you were, if you were all right, if you might be in want? Blythe, I never imagined you to be so cruel."

Blythe felt a quiver all through her.

"I'm sorry," she whispered.

"*Sorry?*" he echoed, a tinge of irony in his voice.

She felt the sting of tears at the back of her eyes, and she blinked them away before Rod could see them.

Just then Jeff came running in from the lobby.

"Mummy, our carriage is here. The doorman says it's time to leave for the train station!"

Startled, Blythe jumped, then spoke hastily. "Yes, darling. Go along. I'll be right there." Jeff lingered a moment, studying his mother with a quizzical expression, then he turned and ran off in the direction of the front entrance.

"Blythe, don't go yet—" Rod pleaded. "There's so much more to say—"

"No."

"There must be some way—"

She shook her head. "But there isn't. This is for the best—" Her fingers fumbled with the clasp of her handbag. "I must go," she said, but she did not move.

"I can't let you go like this . . . not again!" he declared. "I won't—" He put out his hand as if to restrain her physically.

Instinctively she drew back. "Don't! Please!" she cried in alarm, knowing that if he touched her she would weaken.

With all the force of her will, she got to her feet, avoiding his outstretched hand, and moved quickly across the room. At the archway, she paused briefly, then, afraid to look back, she walked through the door.

In the lobby she went over to the desk. She stood there, her slim figure rigid, while her bill was figured and presented.

"I hope you enjoyed your stay with us, Mrs. Dorman, and that you will come back soon." The desk clerk smiled.

Steadying her voice, Blythe murmured what she hoped was a suitable response. When the clerk signaled to the bellhop waiting with her luggage, she thanked him. Then, head held high, she swept through the entrance, down the steps, and into the carriage where Jeff was waiting.

As soon as the carriage door closed behind her and she felt it move forward, Blythe drew a long painful breath. She smoothed each finger of her kid-gloved hands, responding to Jeff's childish chatter distractedly. Her mind seethed with all the unsaid things her heart had longed to say. She wished she could weep. She wished for any other emotion than what she was feeling.

Determinedly she lifted her chin. She could not, would not think of the past, only the future . . . a future forever without the man she loved so dearly.

In the small parlor off the lobby, Rod slumped back into the chair, put his head in his hands, and kept it there as he heard the sound of the carriage wheels rattling down the driveway.

Happiness is not the end of life, character is—Harriet Beecher Stowe

chapter
10

At Sea
En route to England

BLYTHE'S HAND tightened on Jeff's small one as she made her way across the bustling wharf to board their ship for the Atlantic crossing. Noise and confusion surrounded them as they pushed their way through the crush of people—passengers accompanied by family and friends seeing them off, sailors hurrying past, porters trundling carts of baggage, dock hands shouting instructions—all made up the mix of humanity at the Norfolk Harbor waterfront.

Blythe, her face flushed and mouth tense, almost managed to reach the gangplank with Jeff in tow. However, now he lagged behind, fascinated by all the dockside activity.

"Come along, Jeff!" she urged him.

Above them on the ship's deck a young officer leaned on the railing to observe the scene on the dock and saw the little tableau below. Watching the slender, attractive young woman in a stylish beige traveling suit coaxing the handsome little boy forward, he thought with anticipation that this routine trip from America that he made twice a year might be more interesting than usual.

But if Lieutenant Michael Walden had any hopes of striking up a pleasant companionship during the trip to England, they were soon dashed. In polite but coolly definite terms, Mrs. Dorman-Montrose made it perfectly clear that she desired to spend her time in her deck chair reading, or with her son.

The boy, however, was all over the ship, making friends with everyone from stewards to the captain himself. But a "Good morning," "Nice day," or "Good evening" were about as far as the hopeful lieutenant was able to get with the mother.

For Jeff's sake she tried to be cheerful when they were together, but his sociable nature led him to seek out others, and she was alone during much of the time on ship. Blythe had much to occupy her mind. The depression that had gripped her in the wake of leaving Mayfield returned to plague her; all the haunting "might-have-beens" remained.

She felt terribly young and vulnerable, "storm-tossed', as the composer of one of her favorite hymns described a troubled soul. Never had she felt more alone than on this voyage.

She struggled against the self-pity of a parent left alone to bring up a boy. Since she had lost Malcolm and now Rod, the only man she had truly loved, she must be both father and mother to Jeff. With that thought came the realization that she might have to face the rest of her life alone.

Filled with self-reproach, she remembered her failure to reach out for what Rod Cameron was offering. What a wonderful father *he* would have been to Jeff! She had no doubt that Rod would have accepted Malcolm's son as his own and brought Jeff up in the long tradition of honor and loyalty that was his own.

Whenever she had found herself lacking clear direction, Blythe turned to the one Source which had been her strength and mainstay through all the lonely years. At night in her cabin, with Jeff sound asleep in the next bunk, she opened her Bible and searched diligently for words of encouragement.

It comforted her to read the stirring assurance from the book of Joshua that had bolstered her sinking spirits at other times: "Be strong and of good courage; do not be afraid, nor be dismayed, for the Lord your God is with you wherever you go."

Blythe knew it was useless to look back, too late to imagine what she should have done all those years ago. What was important now, as Paul admonished in Philippians 3: 13, was to "forget those things which are behind and reach forward to those things which are ahead—"

As the ocean voyage drew to its close, Blythe realized that the days on shipboard had not been wasted. The time she had spent studying the Scriptures had given her new insight and renewed resolve to go on and, with God's help, to build a life for herself and Jeff that would enrich them both.

The night before the first faint green rim of the Irish coast was sighted, Blythe stayed up late, reading and praying for some word of guidance she could cling to in the days ahead. Just before she closed her Bible, she felt led to turn back to the well-worn pages of Isaiah. There she found what she had been looking for.

"Remember ye not the former things, neither consider the things of old. Behold I will do a new thing; now it shall spring forth; shall ye not know it? I will even make a way in the wilderness, and rivers in the desert."

Suddenly, Blythe felt new energy surging through her. God had never failed her when she had called upon Him. He would not forsake her now. No matter that there would be times of regret, times of self-recrimination, as there would surely be, she would memorize this verse, hold fast to it, believe that in her "wilderness," in her "desert," God *would* make a way for her.

Part IV

From England
to the Edge of Time

To every thing there is a season, and a time for everything under the sun.

—*Ecclesiastes 8:1*

chapter
11

Larkspur Cottage
Kentburne
Summer 1876

EVER SINCE her return to England, Blythe had felt unsettled and vaguely disquieted. The little house and garden that had so delighted her before no longer held the same fascination. She seemed unable to regain the contentment she had known before her trip to America.

Of course, she knew the source of her new restlessness. Blythe thought she had made her peace with the passions of the past. But seeing Rod again and learning the news of his forthcoming marriage had unnerved her. Not only that, but finding that her feelings for him were as strong as ever was even more disturbing.

What had she expected? That he had stopped living? Had ceased to be a man with desires, needs, longings? Had she supposed he had dwelt only in the past with his dreams of her? How selfish could she be? She herself had borne a child, made a home for both of them half a world away. She had a whole new life with people about her who cared for her. Could she wish anything less for Rod?

Yet she knew nothing of how Rod had spent those years, though it had taken only those few minutes with him to bring sharply into focus what she had thrown away.

Her foolish decision to leave Mayfield forever came back to taunt her now. Suddenly the loss was unbearable. She thought of all the years she had been alone, all the difficult, lonely years when she had longed to have someone strong to lean upon, to counsel and advise her, to love and be loved by in return. "I have only myself to blame!" she reminded herself over and over. But it only made her regret more devastating.

One early July day Blythe forced herself out into the garden to spend some time weeding, hoping this menial task would banish useless self-reproach. Donning a wide-brimmed straw hat and gardening gloves, she knelt by her pansy bed, willing herself to concentrate on the task at hand and not go wandering off into pointless paths of "what-ifs."

"Good morning, Blythe!" She looked up to see Corin leaning over the stone wall. "You look determinedly industrious," he commented with a smile.

Blythe sat back on her heels. "Well, after all, gardens do require regular attention, and since I got back, I'm afraid I've been neglecting mine."

"To say nothing of your friends and neighbors!" he chided her gently.

Blythe felt the subtle admonition in his tone.

"I know. I'm sorry. I just haven't been very good company lately."

"Can you put aside your spade for a few minutes and walk over to Dower House with me?" he asked. "I have something to show you that I believe you'll find very interesting."

"Like this?" Blythe glanced down at her denim pinafore as she got to her feet.

"You look fine to me. Besides, this is not an invitation to a royal tea party," Corin teased. "I've been doing some gardening of my own. Well, actually I've been overseeing Alec who's been clearing out some tangles of ivy that were about to take over the whole side of the house. I've wanted to get rid of it for quite a while since it provides a habitat for rats."

Blythe gave an involuntary shudder.

"It's all cleared away, now," Corin reassured her. "I wanted to show you what we uncovered. Come along." He opened the gate for her.

Together they strolled down the lane that led to Dower House. Even before she met Corin, Blythe had admired the mellow red brick house just beyond the gates of the Marsh estate. It had been built in the seventeenth century as the dwelling place for ladies of the manor superseded by daughters-in-law married to sons who had inherited the title, land and property. Maybe to those replaced matrons the house had seemed small and cramped after the high-ceilinged spaciousness of Monksmoor Priory. But Blythe thought it a perfect country house with a magnificent view of the river from the front and of the ocean cliffs from the rear. It did, however, seem more suitable for a family than one lone lady. Or, as was the case now, a single gentleman.

Corin led the way around to the side of the house where Alec, his gardener and handyman, was piling huge bundles of ivy into a wheelbarrow. There was a cleared space of about three feet in width from the stucco foundation.

Alec tipped his cap to Blythe, a crooked smile creasing his weathered face, and Blythe acknowledged him with a cheerful greeting. As the man rumbled away with his loaded cart, Corin beckoned Blythe over to the now exposed cornerstone.

"Come over here, Blythe, and look at this."

She did as he suggested. He was pointing to something carved into the plaster, and she had to crouch down to read it. Her lips moved, forming the words she now read aloud: "JEDEDIAH DORMAN, Master Pargeter 1678."

She felt Corin's firm hand under her elbow, helping her to her feet again. She gazed into his face where a smile played around his mouth, his eyes twinkling.

"What does it mean?" she asked, puzzled.

"Well, my dear Blythe, what I think it means is that your ancestors must have come from these parts. *This* Jedediah Dorman was the craftsman who did the pargeting on this house." He paused, waiting for the significance to dawn on her. "*Dorman,* my dear. It could be that *this* Dorman is an ancestor of yours. Is it possible that your father's family might have originated from this part of England?"

Blythe shook her head slowly. "I don't know. All Pa ever said was that he came from Kentucky, that they had settled there very early. But we never discussed—"

"Well, pargeting is pretty much a lost art. The few who have retained the knowledge are employed for restorations, that sort of thing. I'm not really sure how old Dower House is. I believe it was built some time after the Priory itself, or the mansion might even have been built on its ruins."

"What, exactly, *is* pargeting?" Blythe asked. The term was new to her.

"Pargeting was a skilled craft in the fifteenth, sixteenth and seventeenth centuries. You've noticed the ornamental plastering above the front door here, haven't you? The imprint of the Marsh family coat-of-arms? That is pargeting. But it does seem more than a coincidence, doesn't it? The name, Jedediah Dorman, being the same as your father's."

"Yes . . . but could it really be the same?"

Corin shrugged, pocketing his hands in his jacket. "Quite possibly. The techniques required an artisan who was highly skilled. A coat-of-arms was not an unusual request for a person building a house in those days. However, sometimes the manor lord wanted the pargeter to create something original, a family crest, or something else symbolic, like the one above the front door."

"I'm ashamed to say I never noticed it. Let's take a look," Blythe said eagerly, stepping around a pile of brush on her way.

At the front of the house Blythe examined with new interest the panel of ornamented plaster over the doorway to Dower House.

"Jedediah Dorman must have been a master at his craft, for there's not a single line or crack in this panel, and it has lasted all these many years," remarked Corin.

"How is it done, do you know?"

"I believe they first made a mold, usually of oak or some other hard wood. The ingredients of the plaster itself were usually an individual 'recipe' created by the artisan himself, most often kept secret and passed on from father to son, or loyal apprentice.

"Something like this is sketched first, then transferred to a mold." Corin stepped back for a better look. "Then, while the plaster is still moist, the mold is pressed into it for a matter of minutes to set the impression.

"I've read that the finest craftsmen made up their own plaster, pulverizing red bricks to mix into the plaster to get this pale pink shade. They would use the best oxhair for stiffening, which made the mixture that much stronger and more durable. *Your* Jedediah Dorman was a real artist. Maybe I can find out more about it in one of my books on the craft guilds. I'll see if I can look up some more information for you," he promised.

Blythe thanked him and walked back to Larkspur Cottage, thinking how strange it was to have come full circle across oceans and continents, and inadvertently finding a link to one's unknown past.

Two days later, Corin brought over a book from his extensive library. The book on pargeting was richly illustrated with examples of this unique, intricate skill. That evening after Jeff was in bed and asleep, Blythe sat up reading until very late. Even when she eventually closed the book and put it aside, she was thoughtful.

After she had fled Virginia for the second time, Blythe's depression had deepened. On the ship headed back to England, she could not shake the feeling that she was depriving Jeff of his rightful home and heritage for selfish reasons.

Again and again she questioned her motives. With what was she replacing all that she was robbing him of? What possible link did *she* have to England or with its history that she could pass on to her son? By the time they had docked, traveled by train down to Kentburne, and returned to their cottage, she felt disheartened and empty. Surely this was not enough to build upon!

But Corin, pointing out the possibility that the pargeting on Dower House had been wrought by an ancestor gave Blythe something new and different to consider. Somewhere back through the centuries, a skilled artisan—probably her ancestor—had lived and worked with honor and pride here in this same small village. Later, some other adventurous relative had decided to try his luck in the New World and had risked the rigors of a sea voyage. In America, still another had pushed back one frontier after another, braving the wilderness of Kentucky, until at last one had crossed the plains and prairies into California—her father, Jedediah Dorman. Who knew what brave creative blood coursed through her son's veins?

Indeed, Jeff had more than his father's Virginia legacy. He had a long and proud history through her as well. From her ancestors, Jeff was heir to something unique and special. And there was yet another missing piece of Jeff's inheritance that should also be explored. Blythe's mother—Carmella Montrero! Spain!

Blythe's heart gave a curious little leap as an extraordinary idea was born. Why not take Jeff and go to Seville, trace her mother's people, learn a little more about their Spanish background?

She said nothing to anyone, but her mind was filled with the plans she was making. She would go to Spain in September, she decided, when the heat of the Mediterranean summer was past. There was still a full year before Jeff would have to start school, and by that time she would have made the decision that was always hovering at the edge of her consciousness.

July slipped away into August, and the warm English summer began to wane. Though the garden was bright with color—the blue of delphiniums and larkspur, from which her cottage took its name, the pink and red of the rose bushes, heavy with blooms—Blythe noticed a shortening of the twilights now, and dusk came down quickly, cooling the air with just a hint of autumn's chill.

Although she had not even mentioned her plans to Dotty, not a day passed that Blythe did not turn over in her mind the idea of going to Spain. Some days she was sure that she would go; on other days, less certain. On still other days, she even doubted her ability to choose the wisest course for them.

Jeff, unaware of his mother's inner turmoil, grew stronger and brighter, more self-confident every day. Observing him with pride and pleasure, Blythe realized this would be a fine time to travel with him. He was old enough not to demand special care, yet still young enough to easily absorb new surroundings and situations and retain the memory.

Then one Sunday, as she walked over to the little village church to attend evensong, the words of Psalm 42 repeated themselves in her ear, voicing her own state of mind: "Why are you downcast, O my soul? Why so disturbed within me? Put your hope in God."

It troubled Blythe that thoughts of Rod Cameron still came unwanted into her mind, casting a shadow over the happiness that should be hers. He was probably married by now, she told herself, which made her longings even more disturbing, even sinful. She wished she could erase all thoughts of him, but it seemed impossible.

It was in this frame of mind that she stepped into the cool, dim vestibule of the church and entered the sanctuary.

Blythe had found the atmosphere here entirely different from that of the unadorned wooden church of her California girlhood. Its plain oak benches and rectangular windows contrasted sharply with St. Anselm's carved choir loft and stained-glass windows, each depicting one of the twelve apostles. The altar was draped in fine linen and lace, and there was a sculptured stone pulpit and pews with individual kneelers. But the God she sought was the same.

She slipped into a seat at the side and then to her knees in the customary private prayer before the service. Even though she felt her prayer inadequate and awkward, it was sincere.

"Lord, I'm ashamed of my confusion. You have promised in your Word to be a lamp to my feet, a light for my path, yet I seem to wallow in darkness. You have blessed me in so many ways, and I *am* grateful. But I still feel lost and alone. I need Your wisdom, Your guidance . . . I need to know if what I'm thinking of doing is the right thing—"

Slowly an almost tangible peace flowed over her, calming her spirit. She took a deep breath, feeling comforted in the absolute stillness of this quiet sanctuary.

How unlike Reverend Burke's church in Lucas Valley, where people greeted you heartily, clapped their hands to lively hymns, and "Amened" loudly throughout the service. And it was entirely different from the tent revival that had changed her life one summer in Mayfield. But *the mystic quality inherent in these Church of England chapels must be equally pleasing to God*, she thought. Like His children, each is part of the whole, the Body of Christ on earth.

The wheezing sound of the ancient organ striking the first chord of the preparatory hymn alerted Blythe that old Mrs. Templeton had taken her place, signaling the start of the evening prayer service. Rector John Ashford, preceded by two acolytes, both rosy-cheeked village boys in starched surplices and carrying lighted candles, came in and took their places on either side of the altar behind the chancel rail. The congregation rose to its feet, and there was a great scraping sound followed by the ruffling of pages turned as prayer books were opened.

"Almighty God . . ." intoned the Reverend Ashford in his deep, theatrical voice as he led the people in the responsive readings.

After this, he mounted a few steps into the pulpit where he could look down at his assembled parishioners.

"Our first Scripture is taken from the Old Testament, Second Samuel, the seventh chapter, twenty-fifth verse."

Blythe listened, almost mesmerized by the minister's mellow tones, only a phrase here and there catching her attention. In this chapter David was speaking to the Lord in the intimate way he had that Blythe always envied slightly. Imagine, being on such terms with God! Still, she could relate to David's pleas and praise, his thanking God for blessings and asking him for more.

The rector then said, "I am taking my homily from David's own question to the Lord in Psalm 8, verse 4: 'What is man that Thou art mindful of him?' We ourselves might well ask: 'How do we know God hears us when we pray and why should we expect Him to answer?'"

Blythe almost gasped. The subject was so nearly her own heart's cry.

The short sermon was simple: We should expect God to answer our prayers because He has promised in His Word to do so.

Next came a reading from the New Testament—the Gospel of John, fifth chapter. The passage recorded an incident in which Jesus healed a man crippled from birth. First, He had asked him: "Do you really want to get well?" then had instructed, "Get up and walk."

Those words went straight to Blythe's heart as if spoken directly to her. *Do you want to get over your melancholy, your useless longings for a man who is pledged to another woman? Do you want to be healed of your heartbreak?* she heard. Then, *Get up and walk!* Or, more to the point, *Get on with your life.*

She would do just that. She would go to Spain and allow God to heal the old wounds, the old regrets, reconcile the mistakes of the past.

The service ended with another quotation from a psalm, this time Psalm 119: "Do good to your servant according to your promise," followed by one last hymn and a benediction pronounced by the rector.

As Blythe came out of the church, it was still light, the sky a lovely lavender. Just outside the door, she saw Corin waiting for her. As they strolled together along the road leading to Larkspur Cottage and Dower House, Corin spoke of his own plans for his annual hiking vacation in Switzerland the next month.

Although she had not intended to tell him until all her arrangements were complete, somehow she could not help herself. Impulsively, Blythe blurted out her plans to travel to Spain and her reasons for wanting to go.

By the time they reached her garden gate, the sky had gradually deepened into purple. In the shadowy light, Corin's expression was thoughtful.

"How long do you intend to be away?"

"A few weeks, maybe longer . . . I'm not sure."

He was silent a moment before he spoke again.

"I was planning . . . to wait until my return from Switzerland to say this," he began haltingly. "I suppose I wanted to see if my being away would make a difference, if you might realize you missed me." He paused, "Now, I dare not take a chance." He turned back to look at her, but his face was in shadow and she could not read the expression in his eyes.

"You have not been the same since you came back from America, Blythe. So I must ask you—did something happen there? Something that altered your feelings about England, about living here? Perhaps, somehow, touching your native roots created a longing in your heart to go back. I've been afraid to ask. But, now, I feel I must . . . because—" Corin's voice grew husky with emotion.

He hesitated, as if expecting Blythe to interrupt his recital. But she, amazed at his sensitivity, could find nothing to say.

"Now I feel I can't wait, Blythe, because . . . I love you. I want to ask you to marry me."

After the words were spoken, they hung there, bringing a tension never before felt between them.

Corin reached for Blythe's hand and took it in both of his, raising it to his lips. "I've loved you for a long time, Blythe," he confessed. "May I hope? Is there a chance for me, for us? I love Jeff, too, you know. It would be very easy for me to love him—as my son."

"Oh, Corin, I wish you hadn't—" Blythe began.

"Don't give me your answer now, please," Corin interrupted her. "Wait until we both come back. That will be time enough. We have so much together, Blythe—friendship, common interests, like values, shared faith . . . It could be a wonderful marriage—"

"Corin, I'm honored that you should ask but—"

"Is there someone else, then, Blythe? Someone in America?"

She thought of Rod and felt the old heart hunger even as she knew it was hopeless to keep on thinking of him.

"Not exactly," she replied, wondering how truthful she should be with Corin. "I thought something was over, and I found it wasn't, but I know we can never go back—" She hesitated. "I hadn't thought of anyone else—"

"Then *do*, Blythe. I'll wait until you're ready. I'll not pressure you, and if you can't accept the possibility of . . . marriage . . . then we'll go on as before. I wouldn't want to lose you, not even as a friend."

"Corin, you are so very kind. I wish I could promise you more—"

"There's no need, Blythe. It will mean so much more if you give yourself time to get used to the idea. Now good night, my dear." He leaned forward and kissed her lightly on the cheek. Then he walked away through the gathering dusk.

Blythe stood at her gate and watched his departing figure until he disappeared into the darkness of the summer evening. Then with a sigh she walked slowly into the house.

Dotty was in her upstairs sitting room mending a rip in Jeff's trousers when Blythe reached the top of the steps and looked in on her.

"Was it a nice service?" Dotty asked.

"Very nice."

"Captain Prescott walked you home?" Dotty's comment was more statement than question.

"Yes." Blythe nodded. Then, because there was no way to ease into the subject, she said in a rush, "Dotty, tomorrow I want you to get down my traveling cases. I'm planning to take Jeff to Spain the first of September, and I had thought that while we're away you might want to visit your sister."

"Maybe so," Dotty said noncommittally, but her bright blue eyes probed Blythe sharply. She put down her sewing and, with the license of long familiarity asked, "What are you running away from, ma'am?"

Blythe's shoulders stiffened, and she wondered if somehow Dotty had witnessed the scene with Corin in the garden. Averting her gaze, she answered enigmatically, "How do you know I'm not running toward something?"

Since we cannot always get what we want, let us be content with what we get—Spanish Proverb

chapter
12

Spain
September 1876

FROM THE MINUTE she arrived in Granada, this city of her maternal ancestors, Blythe had the strange sensation of recognition.

The first morning after their arrival, as if responding to some inner call, she awakened early and stepped out onto the little balcony of their hotel room and was met by a breathtaking view. Beyond the hills rimming the city, snow-capped peaks glistened in the dazzling sunshine like jewels against a blue velvet drape.

For the next week, often leaving Jeff playing happily with the innkeeper's grandchildren to whom language seemed no barrier, Blythe went sightseeing. On sun-warmed afternoons she walked down the cobbled streets winding narrowly through the city. A soft, clear light Blythe had never seen anywhere else bathed the ochre-colored stucco houses and red-tiled roofs in a mellow gold tint and gave brilliance to the flowers overflowing ornate black iron balconies. Buildings and centuries-old walls bore the patina of time. Blythe felt moved back into another time period.

An undeniable romantic aura permeated the very air she breathed. The quiet streets held their own secrets; the historic stones told their own stories.

Before coming, Blythe had read to Jeff everything she could find on Spain, its history, its people, its legends. They learned that the Moors had come to this country as conquerors, later merging their culture with that of the peoples they conquered. Remnants of the hundreds of years of their occupation were evident in the variety and style of architecture—arches and domes of the Moorish structures standing side by side with the spires and towers of Christian churches. When at last they were forced to surrender to the armies of Ferdinand and Isabella, they left behind them an amazing blend of the two cultures that lingered hauntingly.

Blythe had particularly looked forward to seeing the Alhambra, the magnificent palace built by Moorish caliphs. But neither pictures nor words had prepared her for the reality of its architectural perfection. Through a maze of fantasy gardens with dozens of fountains, courtyards opened out into smaller courtyards. She had read that the Moors, coming from their desert country, had attempted to recreate their vision of a paradise on earth, since in their Koran, heaven is described as "a garden flowing with streams." *The sound of splashing water must have been soothing music to the thirsty souls of the first Moorish kings who had lived here*, Blythe thought, as she wandered in a dream-like state through the arched rooms exquisite with tiled mosaics and twisted marble pillars.

How the one-time conquerors must have hated leaving this beautiful place. She recalled the story of the last Moorish ruler of Granada who had paused in defeat to look back from a place called the Suspiro del Moro to mourn the loss of his kingdom. His mother, Queen Aicha, had mocked him cruelly in his grief, saying, "Cry like a woman for what you did not know how to keep like a man."

That bridge was now called "the sigh of the Moor," and once

Blythe had seen the Alhambra and Granada for herself, she understood the name.

When it was time to leave for Seville, Blythe had mixed feelings. Her father had told her what little he had known of her Spanish mother's background. Blythe knew only that she had been born into a gypsy family from the region of Granada. With a little research, she learned that the gypsies lived in caves in the Sierra Nevada foothills above the city, a self-contained world with its own laws, traditions, language, and customs. Children were educated according to their system, and their religion combined Christianity with superstitious beliefs and rituals handed down from one generation to the next. Thought to have been descended from nomadic tribes migrating from India, the people were a fiercely beautiful race, highly sensitive and emotional.

Carmella Montrero, Blythe's mother, the dark-eyed dancer with whom Jed Dorman had fallen madly in love on sight, had been "sold" as a child by her gypsy stepfather to the leader of a traveling dance troupe, and it was with this band of gypsy dancers that she had come to the American West where she had met the lanky young gold miner who became her husband.

Blythe realized her own looks were a blend of the two. Her velvety brown eyes and high coloring were surely inherited from Carmella; her height and hair from the lean, red-headed Kentucky mountain boy.

What she wondered most about were her personality traits. The strong, independent part of her nature must be Jed's legacy, while the sensitive, emotional side, her mother's contribution. Did they battle or blend? She sometimes felt torn between the two different pulls of her character. And what an odd combination to pass on to Jeff! What strange forces from the past shaped his life.

One afternoon upon her return to the inn after a day of sightseeing, Blythe encountered her landlord in the lobby, who told her, "Señora, you asked about the gypsy dancers? They will be performing at the cantina tonight! It will be a festive occasion. You can take the *niño*. It is an evening for families."

As darkness began to fall, Blythe and Jeff were seated at one of the tables in the patio of the cantina. Ornamental lanterns swung from the walls while bright flowers trailed from clay pots and circled the tiled space in the center, reserved for dancing.

Jeff had taken to Spanish food as though he were a native, Blythe observed, and was busily eating his plate of paella, a typical Andalusian meal of rice, chicken, and shellfish in a spicy sauce. This was served with vegetables—tomatoes, onions, and artichoke hearts, along with chunks of toasted bread sprinkled with cheese. Blythe sipped a cup of strong coffee and waited impatiently for the entertainment to begin.

Some deep chord of familiarity echoed within Blythe at the first strum of guitars. Then with a shout of "Olé!" the dancers swept onto the stage, feet clattering, the women swishing their bright-colored skirts like so many vivid "whirligigs," the men in tight, black pants and balloon-sleeved white shirts.

The rhythmic sound of the tapping shoes beating out the famous "flamenco" was hypnotic. Round and round they stepped in measured movements as ritualistic and yet seemingly spontaneous as the melody. Behind the thrumming guitars was the rat-a-tat of the castenets held in the dancer's hands, precisely snapping in tune with the exciting music. The dance increased in intensity as the music grew louder and more insistent. The dancers circled wildly, stamping their heels with the click of the castanets, until it ended suddenly in a final climactic synchronization of sound. "Olé!"

The applause that followed was deafening, and Blythe found herself clapping her hands until her palms tingled. She had been caught up in the fiery dance, imagining her mother as she was pictured on old playbills in her trunk—satin-black hair pulled back at the nape of her neck, the stylized curl at her cheek, the glint of gold hoops swinging from her ears, the flashing eyes.

One dancer had caught Blythe's eye from the first. Watching the slim figure in her ruffled gown, the twirl of fringe on her silk shawl, the flying high heels with their silver buckles, she felt a subtle kinship. And when the dancers took their final bows, this performer did a last little flip of her scarlet skirt, and for a single moment her eyes met Blythe's. An instant communication as fleeting as quicksilver seemed to pass between them—an invisible bond flowing from one to the other, uniting them with the child who had been bargained for and taken to a far country to become Blythe's mother.

Blythe knew that the connection was part fantasy, part memory of the poster advertising Carmella as the "Spanish Gypsy." But for an instant the beautiful flamenco dancer had recreated her mother in Blythe's mind. From this time on, Carmella would remain young, beautiful, and alive, as if the daughter had actually seen the mother dance in the place from which she had come.

Later, as Blythe took a sleepy Jeff back to their rooms at the inn, she could hear the music still playing in the cantina. She knew some of the people would stay on to dine and dance long after the gypsies left. But she had seen enough. This night would linger forever in her memory, linking her with another important part of her past, and Jeff's. She knew now what had drawn her so irresistibly to Spain.

It was in Spain that Blythe's thoughts about Jeff and his future became both more complex and clearer. It seemed increasingly urgent that this son of hers and Malcolm's should know the best of each separate inheritance. And wrong, somehow, to bring him up in England, with no real understanding, knowledge, or affection for the country of his parents' birth.

It was during this time that Blythe made her decision. Jeff must be educated in Virginia. She must take him back to America.

But, first, she must give Corin his answer. . . .

chapter

13

Switzerland

BLYTHE DECIDED to return to England by way of Switzerland while it was still early enough in the year to avoid the extreme cold and snow of the Alpine country. This stop would give her an opportunity to tell Corin her decision on neutral territory.

Before they had left for Spain, Corin had urged Blythe to bring Jeff to the village where he spent his annual mountain-climbing vacation. He told her he would like to introduce the boy to the exhilarating sport. Of course, Blythe knew that Corin also wanted her to share a special part of his life she had never seen.

The train from Lucerne wound steeply through mountain valleys from which sparkling sun-crested, snow-capped peaks were visible. The view was awe-inspiring and a bit frightening as they chugged up the inclines, the train whistle tooting shrilly, sounding for all the world like the whistle on Jeff's toy train set.

The train climbed steadily, hugging the mountainside, past deep valleys of soft purple shadows and clear mountain streams. Dollhouse chalets dotted the floor of the valley and nestled snugly against the foothills. Herds of cows, their bells clanging in a strange kind of symphony, munched on the last of the sweet grasses.

When they finally came to a stop and Blythe and Jeff stepped out on the platform at the picturesque station, the air was crystal clear, so pure it almost hurt their lungs to draw it in.

Corin had made reservations for them at the same hotel where he always stayed, and they were greeted by one of its representatives who was attired in a braided, beribboned uniform resembling that of a military general. He quickly transferred their luggage to an open carriage, and they started up a mountain road, climbing higher and higher with each turn, their route marked by pine forests standing guard like tall sentinels on either side of the road.

The hotel overlooked a lake so blue it dazzled the eye. Built of natural woods, it had a sloping roof and dozens of balconies with decorative designs of birds and flowers and flower boxes brimming with pink and red geraniums. Although the building was very large, its architecture reminded Blythe of one of those amusing little carved clocks whose doors pop open on the hour to emit a tiny wooden cuckoo bird.

Welcomed as expected guests by the hotel staff at the desk in the lobby, Blythe and Jeff were escorted to their suite. The room was typically Swiss. Starched lace curtains hung at the windows. Alcoved beds were piled high with eiderdown quilts and fluffy pillows.

The scene from the window looked like a Christmas card—all frosted evergreens and soft mounded snowdrifts and tiny houses set into the hillside like the toy villages some people place beneath their Christmas tree.

After depositing their luggage, the uniformed bellboy told Blythe, "Herr Prescott left a message for you this morning before he went for his day's mountain climb that he would meet you for dinner at seven."

That evening in the lobby a smiling, sunburned Corin seemed so happy to see them that Blythe decided she could not spoil their first evening together by disappointing him with her answer. *There would be a better, more appropriate time later,* she procrastinated.

They spent a pleasant dinner hour together, Corin full of plans for their stay in the village he had visited a half-dozen times in as many years. He was eager to show and share its delights with Blythe and Jeff.

Though Blythe had every intention of seizing the very next opportunity to tell Corin of her decision, no such opportunity presented itself in the full agenda of the next few days. There was so much to see and do, and the hours passed quickly.

On the third day Corin had planned to take Jeff on a day's hike. But first, the boy must be outfitted with sturdy boots and the traditional Alpine climber's lederhosen and a jaunty brimmed hat with its feathered brush. Then the right size knapsack for Jeff to carry on his back must be selected and purchased.

Jeff awakened early, without being called, and could hardly be persuaded to eat a good breakfast, so eager was he to be off. Corin was waiting in the lobby, boyishly eager to initiate Jeff in the basics of the sport he himself enjoyed so much.

Blythe waved them off. Then, left on her own for the day, she took the twelve-mile train trip into Lucerne to shop. Armed with a guidebook, she did all the touristy things one does in Lucerne, visited the historic churches and other noteworthy sites.

In the shopping district she browsed in the many stores on either side of the long street, astonished at the variety of intriguing merchandise on display—the exquisite embroidery, the jewelry designed in vari-colored tiny mosaic stones, hand-painted wooden triptychs of religious subjects, toys of all kinds. In one store she debated long over a wonderful Noah's ark, wondering if Jeff were too old for it, then on second thought decided against the purchase of all fifty pairs of animals! She went on to another gift store, lingering over a wide selection of music boxes, looking for just the right one to take back to Dotty.

As the afternoon wore on, Blythe's feet began to tire; and after seemingly endless debate, the only purchase she ended up making in the last store was a small paperweight, a domed scene of skaters that produced a miniature blizzard when shaken. Wearily, she found a seat at the table in an outdoor garden restaurant facing a flower-bordered square, promising herself she would come back another day during her stay to do some serious shopping. While she waited to catch her train for the return trip to the village, she ordered an ice and chose a layered cake from the pyramid pastry stand, which proved too rich for her to finish.

An hour later she settled at last into the windowed compartment on the train returning to the village, marveling at the magnificent scenery along the route.

As Blythe came in, a tired but still enthusiastic Jeff was just entering the hotel lobby with Corin, both talking at once in their desire to share the events of their day. Jeff declared he had had a "capital time," and Corin announced Jeff had the makings of a "real Alpine climber."

Pleasantly exhausted, they had an early dinner and retired early, even Jeff willing to call it a day. Blythe's last thought before drifting off to sleep was that she really must make the opportunity to talk with Corin privately. She had only arranged to stay in Switzerland for a week, and time was passing quickly. At the end of the week she and Jeff would be returning to England.

The next morning at breakfast Corin announced plans for a picnic, and Blythe felt a childlike anticipation. She had not been on a picnic for ages!

Outside the hotel, two open carriages waited to transport a congenial group of guests to the picnic site. Blythe and Jeff, assisted by Corin, climbed in and found seats along the sides while heavy wicker hampers containing the picnic food were brought out, lifted into the back of the wagon and secured with straps.

Drawn by the largest, sturdiest-looking horses Blythe had ever seen, the carriages rumbled off, leaving the hotel grounds and turning onto forest-lined roads where they climbed into the foothills.

The air was fresh and sweet as they rode by the pungent pines along the steep, narrow roads. The meadows were colorful with golden, blue, and orange wildflowers, the sun slanting through the thick, sweeping pine boughs.

Enjoyment of the outing was a universal language bridging the various backgrounds, and communication flowed easily among the guests. There was an easy camaraderie that left Blythe feeling happier than she had felt since her return from America, and she relaxed in the glow of pleasant companionship and the beauty of the day.

As they rode along, Blythe had a flash of insight about herself. The little ranch girl she had been, naïve and uneducated, had become a woman who spoke at least a smattering of four languages, had traveled two continents, and was comfortable in any setting. How much she had learned! How she had changed!

She looked over at Jeff who had quickly made friends with a small Italian boy and was carrying on some kind of "international" conversation. Corin caught her glance, and they exchanged a mutual message of amusement and understanding.

At length, they arrived at a broad, high meadow where the carriage wagons stopped, and the drivers unhitched the horses and led them away to graze. Two members of the hotel staff spread rugs and cushions and crisp checkered cloths down upon the flower-strewn grass, then unloaded the huge hampers of food.

The mountain air had given everyone an appetite, and the picnic provided by the hotel was bountiful and delicious. Blythe forgot that she had consumed a huge breakfast before leaving and ate as heartily as if she had fasted. There was thin sliced ham, crumbly goat cheese, freshly baked bread, creamy butter, chilled fruit, wine and coffee to drink, and a variety of desserts—flaky pastries filled with apples or berries, and rich chocolate cake. A feast "fit for a king" in any language!

Blythe's heart was suddenly filled with gratitude for the gift of this perfect day. She closed her eyes briefly, lifting up a little prayer, relishing the sound of rushing wind in the tops of the pines, the far-off tinkle of cowbells in the valley below, the warmth of the sun on her back. One of the hotel employees had brought his zither and began to play, and the wistful music spun a spell over the drowsy listeners.

When the shadows lengthened, the staff packed up what was left of the lunch and the picnickers reluctantly climbed back into the wagons for the return trip to the hotel.

The following evening, Corin took Blythe to the weekly band concert held in the main town square. It was an interesting event because, besides the lively music for folk dancing, there were also bellringers dressed in colorful traditional Swiss costumes.

They walked back to the hotel in the silvery glow of the moon rising over the lake below, sending luminous mother-of-pearl streamers out over the glassy surface of the water. Blythe realized guiltily that she had not yet brought up the subject of her decision—the decision that would alter Corin's hopes dramatically.

But the silence and serenity of the night seemed far too magical to shatter by such a declaration. Blaming herself for cowardice, Blythe simply thanked Corin for a lovely evening and bid him good night.

Perhaps, she rationalized, her last night in Switzerland would be the best time to break the news that she could not accept his proposal of marriage. That way, since Corin had planned to remain another few weeks to do some more strenuous climbing, he would have time to get over whatever disappointment Blythe's answer might cause. By the time he returned to England, they would be able to resume the relationship that had been so satisfactory, at least to her.

However, even her last night in Switzerland did not present the right opportunity. Quite unexpectedly, it was announced at breakfast that morning that the hotel owner and his wife were celebrating their fortieth wedding anniversary, and all the hotel guests were invited to a gala party.

It was an unforgettable evening of gaiety, music, dancing, laughter, and entertainment of all kinds, and when the next morning Corin saw Blythe and Jeff off on their train to Zurich and

Calais for the Channel crossing to England, there was time only for last-minute wishes for a safe journey and pleasant trip.

When the train whistle signaled imminent departure, Corin leaned forward and kissed Blythe lightly, thrusting a bouquet of flowers and a box of chocolates into her hands, cheerfully telling them he would see them within a month's time.

As the train clattered down the tracks, Blythe followed Jeff's example, pressing her face against the window for a last look at the towering mountain peaks, the forested hills, and the sight of Corin's tall figure on the train platform waving his Tyrolean hat.

In her heart Blythe wondered if perhaps Corin himself had suspected and dreaded her decision, and so had delayed hearing it for as long as possible.

chapter
14

Larkspur Cottage
Kentburne, England

UPON HER RETURN from Switzerland, Blythe found a letter from Richard Pembruck, the realtor in Mayfield. It began:

My dear Mrs. Dorman,

I believe I have found the ideal property to fulfill the requirements and aesthetic desires you expressed for a domicile for you and your young son. Located about thirty miles from Mayfield on approximately twelve acres of woodland, it abounds in gentle wildlife and boasts a clear stream running through it. There are also many old bridle paths which, although now overgrown with brush, could be quickly and easily cleared.

The building on the property, once a hunting lodge owned by members of a private club for gentlemen and their guests, is, I am afraid, in a state of deterioration after years of vacancy and neglect. The roof has fallen through in places; the clapboard siding has rotted and warped; windows are broken; doors unhinged or missing. Major repairs would be necessary to make it again habitable. However, the native stone foundation is sound; the basement with its stone and granite walls has withstood the years well and is dry, the underflooring solid, and the native heart-of-pine floors could easily be sanded and refinished.

The property itself is the prize. Nowhere could you find such self-contained privacy in such a beautiful setting. But to be honest, I would have to say that a new house could be constructed upon the foundation much more easily, faster and less expensively than restoration of the ruins of the present building.

If you want to acquire this property, I could arrange an architect to send you a design and working drawings to consider. I believe this could be done well within the cost we discussed when you were in Virginia.

Since you said you were interested in Virginia's early history, I am sure you'd be intrigued by this building's strange and fascinating history. It is rumored to have been used as a 'safe house' for the Underground Railroad in transporting runaway slaves to the North, chosen because of its isolation and proximity to the river.

The isolation I refer to would not, I hope, deter you from seriously considering acquisition of this property because, although it offers all the privacy you prefer, it is easily accessible from the town of Arbordale by bridge or by ferry. Lest you imagine from this description that this property is situated on a remote island, I hasten to correct that impression by comparing the house to a medieval lord's manor surrounded by a moat.

I also want to assure you that I can see to all the arrangements of the construction, hiring and oversight of the building crew without your having to travel to Virginia. With good luck and good weather, it could be ready for occupancy by next fall when, you stated, your son would be entering school.

This leads me to the next advantage—easy traveling distance of an excellent Christian school for boys that your son could attend either as a day pupil or boarding student.

In addition to all of the aforementioned points in favor of this property, I have made a thorough title search and have found this property to be free of liens of any kind. It was held corporally in the name of the Hunt Club, then, due to lack of payment of taxes, was forfeited to the county.

These back taxes will be waived if the property is purchased immediately. Thus I urge you to come to a decision as quickly as possible. A desirable property such as this, at the price for which it can be obtained at this particular time, will not remain on the market long. I have taken the liberty to place a HOLD payment on it to give my letter time to reach you in England and also time for your consideration of the matter.

I hope to receive an affirmative answer from you soon. I remind you once more that I am anxious to be of service to you in any way. With best personal regards, I am,

Sincerely yours,
Richard Pembruck

Blythe reread the letter twice before folding it and replacing it in the envelope. Mr. Pembruck had mentioned the urgency of prompt action. She remembered his telling her when they were together, that wealthy Northerners were still buying up Virginia property at the depressed prices brought about by the fact that most of the original owners had been bankrupted by the war and needed ready cash.

The strange history of this house intrigued Blythe. The fact that it had been a "safe house" on the Underground Railroad gave her pause—it seemed a singular link to Rose Meredith Montrose, Malcolm's Yankee bride, who was strongly suspected of working with those who, at great personal danger to themselves, had helped slaves to freedom.

Mr. Pembruck's reference to a "medieval manor surrounded by a moat" also appealed to her, bringing to mind the Arthurian fantasy that the King, thought to have been fatally injured in the last battle with Modred and the rebel knights, had been taken to a distant island where he miraculously recovered. From this had sprung the legend of "the once and future King" who had declared that he would return to rule England again in all the glory of the ideal Round Table.

What had they called the island? "Avalon"? Yes, Avalon would be the ideal name for a home for herself and Jeff.

Blythe was strongly tempted to sit down at once and write to Mr. Pembruck, instructing him to buy the property in her name immediately. Only one concern remained. What would Corin say to her plan to leave England and return with Jeff to Virginia? Would he feel doubly betrayed when he learned of her decision not to marry him?

Perhaps she should wait for his return from Switzerland. After all, he was her good friend and deserved more than a hasty note. On the other hand, if she waited, perhaps the property would be gone, snapped up by some avaricious Northerner. Everything about the place sounded ideal—a good school for Jeff, the privacy and beauty of a woodland estate, a place to keep horses, room for friends Jeff might want to invite home from school—

What should she do? Perhaps she should consult Edward and Lydia? This seemed the logical next step, since they were so close and adored Jeff. She knew Edward thought it was all settled, that the boy would be attending his old school. They would, no doubt, be heartbroken at the thought of her leaving England with Jeff.

But, no, before she consulted anyone, she would pray. As had become her custom, she got out her Bible and thumbed through it, stopping here and there to read a passage or verse, searching for God's Word to use in her prayer for guidance.

She turned first to the Psalms because she loved them and read them often just to delight in their beauty. In the twenty-fifth, she found words of great relevance for her dilemma: "Show me thy ways, O LORD; teach me thy paths. Lead me in Your truth and teach me. For thou art the God of my salvation: on thee do I wait all the day."

But it was in the thirty-third chapter of Exodus that Blythe discovered the prayer that most nearly met her need: "Lord, show me Thy way, that I might find favor with Thee. If Thy Presence does not go with me, do not lead me from here."

In the combination of both Blythe found her direction. She repeated the passage from Exodus over the next few days as she "waited" on Him.

Within a week she was at peace about the course she should take. She sat down at her desk to write to Mr. Pembruck in Virginia, authorizing him to act in her behalf, to acquire the property, and to contact an architect for preliminary designs for a house.

When she had posted the letter to America, she had to write a second letter. This one, to Corin in Switzerland, telling him of her decision and plan, took much more prayer and thought. She wanted to prepare him before his return, feeling it extremely unfair to delay any longer.

Difficult as it was to write this letter, Blythe knew it was the only honest, honorable thing to do. She loved Corin, but only as a friend, not as a potential husband. Under these circumstances it would be kinder in the long run to make the break cleanly and swiftly and not further prolong the uncertainty for him and for herself.

As she addressed the envelope, Blythe prayed her decision would not prove too painful for this kind and gentle man.

The early October morning sun slanting into the garden touched everything with a lovely golden light. The flowers—blue delphiniums, purple gentians, pink phlox—mingled in vivid colors against the rock wall. It was as if nature had conspired to arrest the certain onset of the cold, dreary English winter with a burst of glorious beauty these last weeks of fall.

Blythe took her coffee from the cottage kitchen to sit on the circular wooden bench around the gnarled apple tree in the middle of the yard. Breathing in the mingled fragrance of the dewy-petaled flowers, Blythe closed her eyes and rested her head against the bark, thinking how lovely and peaceful the morning was and wondering idly what she should do with the rest of the day.

Should she dig up some bulbs, store them for spring planting? Or maybe prune back the rambling rose bushes that clambered in disorderly but beautiful profusion over the stone wall? Surely these lovely days would not last, and she did not want to be taken by surprise by the first frost.

Her mental meandering was interrupted by the sight of Mr. Bryley, the village postman, pedaling down the winding lane on his high bicycle. She waved absently, thinking he would go right past. Blythe did not receive much mail. But today he stopped at the gate and drew an envelope out of the leather satchel slung over one shoulder.

"Mornin', Mrs. Montrose. Have a letter here for you," he announced, leaning his bicycle against the stone wall. "Got a foreign stamp on it, it has. Switzerland, from the postmark," he added, examining the envelope a moment before handing it over to her.

She smiled politely, but Mr. Bryley seemed inclined to visit.

"Nice day, isn't it, now?" he said, tipping his beaked hat to her. "But there was a nip in the air for sure earlier when I started on my rounds. Won't be long 'till fall, I 'spose. Well, I'll be on my way then. Enjoy your letter."

"Thank you, Mr. Bryley," said Blythe, her amusement about to get the best of her. The postman had clearly recognized Corin's bold handwriting and was waiting around in the hope of hearing firsthand that he was right.

No doubt the old fellow would have enjoyed a tidbit to pass along at the next stop: "The master of Dower House is corresponding with the American widow at Larkspur Cottage." Well, she hated to disappoint him, but this was one "secret" that she would not confirm to be bandied about the village.

Blythe took the letter back to the bench and opened it. As she did so, a spray of dried flowers fell into her lap. She picked it up and studied it. It looked something like the tiny star-shaped blossoms of the familiar forget-me-not. She began to read:

My dear Blythe,

You and Jeff have only just left, and yet it seems a very long time since you were here. Everywhere I look reminds me of the happy times we spent together here. Jeff is growing up so fast it is almost alarming, for it confirms the feeling I have more and more of time's rapid passing. It seems just yesterday I first met the young fellow when he was an apple-cheeked infant in a pram! Now, I feel he is much a part of my life, at least, of the past five years.

Needless to say, I feel the same about his mother. It is my deepest desire to make you both a part of my life forever. I know we didn't speak of it while you were here, as I felt a reluctance on your part to bring up the subject, and in deference to that, hesitated to say anything myself. But it was never far from my mind.

I want you to know I love you with all my heart, Blythe. Nothing would make me happier than to spend the rest of my life taking care of you and being the best possible father to Jeff. I believe I could. I think Jeff already considers me a friend and would accept such a change in our relationship if you would do me the great honor of marrying me.

I trust, since I first spoke of this months ago, that you have been considering my proposal and that when I return to England, you will make me the happiest man in all of Britain by agreeing to become my wife.

Perhaps this letter will seem out of character. You've teased me about being a reserved, rather staid Englishman. I suppose you are justified in that observation, but you have never seen me as I am now—a man very much in love, persistently hopeful. I enclose a spray of edelweiss, the Alpine flower known for that same quality of stubborn optimism, growing and flourishing in the starkest of circumstances, appearing to surprise and delight where no other flower dares. I found it surging up between two barren rocks on a steep hillside on the climb I made yesterday.

Tomorrow two other gentlemen, our guide, and I will tackle the most ambitious and difficult ascent I have yet attempted. I face it with anticipation, yet some trepidation. As I confront this challenge, I will remember the valiant edelweiss, overcoming the most obstinate conditions to triumph! It will take us nearly three days, with an overnight in a small hostel midway up the mountain.

You are in my thoughts and prayers, dear Blythe. I look forward soon to saying in person much of what is now in my heart.

Yours affectionately always,
Corin Prescott

Blythe refolded the letter and slipped it into the envelope, sitting there to consider Corin's words. The issue she thought closed, settled, had opened once more, newly intensified with this written declaration.

What a dear person he was, and how grateful she should be that a man of Corin's character and quality loved her, wanted her to be his wife.

She reviewed all the advantages such a marriage would bring her, and especially, Jeff. Jeff needed a father, and he admired and liked Corin tremendously. Their relationship had grown even closer and warmer during the days in Switzerland.

Then why did she hesitate giving Corin the answer he wanted so much to hear?

She had heard it said that some people love once and only once in a lifetime. That there are those few who can never love again with the same passion, the same self-surrendering commitment. Was she one of these? Was her whole life ahead to hold only one love, a love that was unfulfilled, yet filled her so completely there was no room for any other?

Was she being unfair to Jeff by refusing Corin? But wouldn't she be cruel to Corin if she said yes, knowing she would only withhold from him the love he deserved from a wife?

And what about herself? If she agreed to marry Corin, wouldn't that be a sort of sacrilege, in view of her feelings for Rod?

Blythe sighed heavily. Why couldn't things have remained the same, with Corin as their friend—a reliable, dependable companion? Would her refusal end their friendship?

The sound of Dotty's voice floating out from the open kitchen window brought Blythe's thoughts back to the present. A moment later Jeff came running out into the garden, a piece of bread and jam in one hand, followed by his puppy, which was jumping and barking at his heels.

Laughing at the two, Blythe was reminded of the day after they had returned from Virginia—

Corin had invited them to Dower House so Jeff could pick out the puppy he wanted from Jet's litter. He had led them out to the kennel where Jet was watching over her rambunctious brood. When Jeff squatted down beside them, all five puppies tumbled over each other, making funny little squeaking noises as they scrambled to reach Jeff's chubby hands reaching out eagerly to pet them.

One by one in turn, he picked up each of the squirming little bodies, laughing as small pink tongues licked his cheeks. Over Jeff's head, Blythe and Corin's eyes met in amusement. Finally, after much deliberation, Jeff made his choice of the only golden one. Picking it up, he cuddled it to his chest, nuzzling the furry head with his chin.

Grinning at the two adults looking on, Jeff's eyes had twinkled mischievously. "I want them all! But I'll take this one, please, sir."

"Good boy," Corin replied approvingly. "That's the pick of the litter. You've a good eye for quality, Jeff." To Blythe he said, "The dog will make a fine companion for him."

Blythe remembered how they had stood there smiling together as the boy and dog rolled over and over on the grass, Jeff laughing hilariously, the puppy trying out his tiny, tentative bark.

And MacDuff *had* become a splendid companion for Jeff, following him everywhere, lying slavishly at his feet under the table at mealtimes, tripping upstairs with him in the evenings, waiting outside the bathroom door while Jeff bathed, sleeping in a basket at the foot of his bed at night. Blythe sometimes found the little animal curled up on the end of the bed when she went in later to check on her son. Then she had to order MacDuff back to his basket, though she suspected that once she was out of the room he probably crept back to this forbidden place. She would never know, she sighed. Neither boy nor dog betrayed the rule-breaking by confirming her suspicion.

MacDuff, wagging his tail, was right behind Jeff as he came up to her now. "Dotty and I saw the postman stop. Did you get a letter, Mummy?"

"Yes, darling, from Corin."

"Is he coming home soon? I hope so. I want to show him some of the tricks I've taught MacDuff and show him how good he minds!"

"Well, I'm not sure how soon, but soon, I think. He says in his letter that he was going on a three-day mountain climb, so he'll have lots to tell you when he does come."

"Oh, good! I do like Corin, Mummy. I liked going climbing with him in Switzerland. Can we go back someday? I'd like to go with him when he climbs one of those really high mountains."

Blythe ruffled his curls. "I'm sure he'd like to take you again, Jeff. He thought you were a very good sport."

After that exchange, Jeff mentioned that Dotty wanted to know if he could go to the village on an errand for her. While baking rock cakes, she had run short of raisins and needed some fetched from the grocery store.

"Yes, darling, run along."

"Come on, MacDuff," Jeff called to his dog, and, with the growing puppy at his side, he went out the gate and started down the lane toward the village.

Blythe watched him go. There was such a manly set to the little shoulders, she thought fondly. As she watched him walking with his hands in his pockets, he was practicing the whistle he had not quite mastered, and the dog trotted alongside. Corin was right. Jeff was growing up fast. Too fast!

Her decision about his future must be made without delay. To stay in England and marry Corin meant canceling her deal with Mr. Pembruck on the property in Virginia, giving up the idea of taking Jeff there to be reared as an American. It was one or the other.

Clasping her hands together, Blythe prayed an urgent prayer for guidance.

"Dear Father God, I need Your help to know the path You would have me take. I have no earthly father to guide me, direct me, advise me. Please heavenly Father, show me what I should do and please make it plain."

For the rest of the morning she worked vigorously in her garden, the energy required leaving none for disquieting thoughts. At noon she went inside, bathed, and ate a light lunch with Jeff and Dotty, then took some flowers over to the church to arrange for altar decorations for the next Sunday's service.

That evening, after Jeff had trundled sleepily upstairs to bed and Dotty had retired, pleading weariness from her day's baking, Blythe settled in an easy chair in the parlor for a quiet evening of reading. She had decided to read all of Dickens's novels, remembering how her father had enjoyed them. Having already completed *David Copperfield* she was now launching into *The Tale of Two Cities*.

With anticipation of enjoyment, she opened the book to the first page, and began reading:

"It was the best of times, it was the worst of times, it was the age of wisdom, it was the age of foolishness, it was the epoch of belief, it was the epoch of incredulity, it was the season of Light, it was the season of Darkness, it was the spring of hope, it was the winter of despair."

Suddenly the sound of the brass knocker on the front door echoed down the hall, startling Blythe so she dropped the book. Who could that be? Puzzled, she took up her lamp and hurried to open it. The knocking came again, this time sounding somehow ominous. Holding the lamp high, Blythe unlatched the door and opened it to find Matthew, Corin's butler-valet, standing on the doorstep.

Something must be very wrong! Matthew's appearance, usually that of an impeccable "gentleman's gentleman," was tonight in complete disarray. His hair was disheveled, his eyes, wild and glazed.

In the wavering light cast by the lamp Blythe saw that his face resembled a plaster cast, gray and stricken. Her heart turned cold.

"Matthew, what is it?" she asked hoarsely. "What's happened?"

Knowing intuitively it must be something terrible as Matthew struggled to speak, Blythe saw the stoic veneer of the well-trained British servant visibly cracking.

"Oh, madam, the most dreadful news—" his voice broke. Matthew fumbled in his coat pocket and brought out a crumpled piece of yellow paper. "A telegram came not more than an hour ago. The master, Captain Prescott . . . madam, an accident while climbing . . . he was . . . they say, trying to help rescue a fellow climber who had fallen to a ledge below. . . Oh, madam, he died in the attempt—"

Blythe felt as though someone had struck her full force in the chest. The pain was blunt and heavy. It took a full minute for the dread news to register. Then she heard herself cry out, "Oh, no! No!"

"Yes, madam, it is true. I went to the telegraph station myself and checked then waited to receive confirmation. The hotel sent word after they brought the bodies back—" Matthew's voice faltered again, and he sagged against the door frame. "I came straight here from the telegraph station, madam. There's no mistake, madam. It is true." The man's voice became a half-sob. "Captain Prescott is dead."

Seeing Corin's faithful servant so undone somehow strengthened Blythe. She reached out and took him by the arm and drew him inside.

"Come, Matthew, come in," she urged. " I'll get you something to bring the strength back. It has been an awful shock, I know."

Even as she functioned, her mind was in denial. Corin dead. It couldn't be true!

She led Matthew into the parlor, seated him there, then, moving as in a trance of denial herself, she went into the kitchen. There she stood irresolutely for a moment, then opened a cabinet where Cook kept the cooking sherry and poured some into a tumbler and took it back to Matthew.

Corin's valet was sitting uneasily on the edge of the chair. Years of the discipline of being "in service" made him uncomfortable in this reversal of his usual position, but his legs felt wobbly indeed, and he realized he would never make it back to Dower House in this condition. Holding the glass with both shaky hands, Matthew drank the liquid slowly.

Blythe reread the telegram that Matthew had turned over to her. The reality of it was all coming together for her now as she read the printed words. *How like Corin to risk his own life trying to save someone else,* she thought.

Even as the truth ground deeply into her heart, no tears came. Probably later, when some of the shock had worn off. Now her job was to try to steady poor Matthew, whose entire life had revolved around Corin. He had served in India with him, had come home to England and nursed him through several bouts of malaria his employer had contracted in the treacherous climate. For more than twenty years Matthew had faithfully cared for Corin and his household. The loss for him must be devastating.

For the next half-hour Blythe tried to comfort him by getting him to talk out some of the raw emotion. Finally, Matthew got to his feet, thanked her solemnly, and walked unsteadily to the door.

"You'll be all right, now, won't you, Matthew?" Blythe asked anxiously.

"Yes, madam, thank you. There's much for me to do. I must get on with it. People to notify, notes to be written, Captain Prescott's solicitor to be contacted—"

"Is there no family, then, Matthew?"

"No, madam, none. Captain Prescott was the last. Both his brothers died earlier." Matthew paused at the door. "If I may say so, madam, you and little Master Jeff was as close to family as the Captain ever had."

Blythe's heart wrenched, her eyes stung with sudden tears.

"Good night, madam," Matthew said, bowing. "And thank you."

"Please . . . if there is anything further I can do—" she hesitated, then added, "and Matthew, I'm sorry . . . so dreadfully sorry."

Her words seemed so inadequate. But Matthew only studied her for a long moment, then bowed again. "I know, madam." Then he turned and walked back down the path, melting into the darkness.

Blythe stood at the open door for a long time, as if she could follow the solitary figure trudging up the road to Dower House. At last, she turned and stepped back into the hall, closing the door.

"Mummy! Mummy!" she heard Jeff's voice calling out.

What had awakened him? She picked up her skirts and ran up the stairway to his bedroom. He was sitting up in bed, rubbing his eyes.

"What is it, darling? Did you have a bad dream?" she asked, leaning over the rail at the end of the bed.

"No, Mummy, I woke up and thought I heard voices. A man's voice. Is Corin here? Did he come back?" he asked sleepily.

A hard lump nearly closed Blythe's throat, but she managed to say, "No, darling, not Corin."

"Oh, I hoped it was. I miss him. I want to hear about his climb." With that Jeff burrowed back into his covers.

Blythe wiped away the tears that rolled down her cheek. There would be time enough in the morning to tell Jeff what had happened. She moved to the side of the bed and stroked the silky curls nestled into the pillow.

Slowly Blythe retraced her steps back down to the parlor. Only an hour ago everything had seemed so cozy and serene—the lamplight, the delicious sensation of beginning a new book she had looked forward to reading. Now everything was changed.

She picked up the volume she had dropped to the floor in her haste to answer the knock at the door. Then, as she held it, the dam of her emotions broke, and she fell to her knees beside the chair and burst into tears. Tears for Corin, who had loved her, and whom she had loved in a special kind of way. Tears for Jeff, who had lost someone important to him. And tears for the faithful Matthew, as well.

It was only much later that Blythe realized gratefully that Corin had never received her letter and had died hoping she would be his wife. Now, she knew that her decision about the future had been made for her.

Blythe stared in disbelief at the impassive face of Corin's solicitor.

"But that's not possible!" she protested.

Returning Blythe's incredulous stare, Horace Brimley replied, "Indeed, it is not only *possible,* madam, it is completely true and legal. Captain Prescott has left Dower House and its contents to you, and the contents of his library to your son, Geoffrey Montrose. I drew up his will myself—and he approved and signed it—only a few weeks before his untimely death." Mr. Brimley removed his nose glasses, fingering the cord with which they were attached to his waistcoat.

"But were there no close relatives? Some family member to whom Captain Prescott could have left his property?"

Sighing heavily, Mr. Brimley shook his head,

"I'm afraid not, madam, none that we could locate. When Captain Prescott first came to us over a year ago, he mentioned that he believed one branch of the Marsh family to whom he was distantly related had emigrated either to the Bermudas or to America. But after we conducted an extensive investigation in order to clear the title to his property, we concluded Captain Prescott was within his rights to dispose of it as he wished." Mr. Brimley cleared his throat and looked somewhat embarrassed.

"If I may be quite personal, Mrs. Montrose, without violating any lawyer-client confidentiality now that Captain Prescott is . . . deceased . . . I believe it was his hope, his fond wish, as it were, that you would become—" Mr. Brimley halted tactfully, then as if rephrasing his thoughts, said, "I believe Captain Prescott was making his will as if you were . . . in the future, to become his spouse."

Blythe felt a jab of painful regret at the lawyer's words, knowing he was truly echoing Corin's hope, but also knowing that it would never have come to that if Corin had lived.

"There was no such promise . . . no engagement," she murmured, feeling her face grow uncomfortably warm under the lawyer's steady gaze.

"Oh, I am aware of that, madam. I meant merely to convey my late client's wishes, the impression I had that, nonetheless, Captain Prescott wanted you and your son to be his beneficiaries. He only indicated that, perhaps, upon his return from Switzerland, he might want to redefine the relationship, not redesignate nor change the will." Mr. Brimley replaced his glasses in the pocket of his waistcoat, and stood.

"Since the land, other than the six acres directly surrounding Dower House, will be sold along with the mansion itself,

Monksmoor Priory, I would suggest that you consider the disposition or sale, whichever you decide, as quickly as possible. The big house is being purchased for a boarding school, and the new owners have some remodeling plans they will be starting very soon. They would be interested in buying Dower House for the headmaster's home, if you were inclined to sell."

After Mr. Brimley's departure, Blythe felt dazed and a little depressed. The news that Corin had bequeathed all his earthly goods to her and Jeff seemed almost a reproach. What he would like to have given her in life, he had bestowed on her in death, and that seemed to her a symbolic kind of bond that she had never sought nor now knew how to handle.

Donning her hooded cape of soft Scottish mohair, Blythe called to Dotty that she was going out for a walk and left the cottage. The air was moist and smelled of autumn. She pushed through her gate and automatically turned in the direction of Dower House.

How often she had walked along this winding lane with Corin, she remembered, feeling anew the loss of this dear friend. His quiet spirit and steady support had always been there, available to her, and now she realized there would always be a vacancy in her heart.

Through the mist she saw the outline of the timbered and stucco structure of Dower House. It had a lost look now, with no smoke pluming from its chimneys, no lights to chase away the early darkness of the fall afternoon. If she knocked on the paneled door, there would be no happy welcome for her as she was led into the cheerful library where a fire would be glowing, warming away the chill, shining on the brass and irons, no one to offer tea and conversation. Corin was gone.

But the house still stood, as it had stood for generations. *Man's passage through life is swift and all too brief,* she mused sadly, *but the things he builds last and linger as memorials of stone and wood to the past, each one's legacy to the next occupants.*

Blythe looked long at the familiar building. Corin's touch was there and before his, Blythe's own ancestor, Jedediah Dorman, the pargeter, had left his own destinctive mark.

She was never sure when the idea struck her. Probably that day or soon after. But once it formed in her mind, no matter how she tried to argue herself out of it, it returned with insistence. Finally, she made an appointment with an architect and a building contractor.

Yes. Yes, it was possible, though it would be costly, to dismantle the structure of Dower House and transport it to America to be rebuilt on Virginia land. She had already received the estimate from Mr. Pembruck for building a house there. The expense of moving Dower House did not exceed that figure by much.

Blythe had lived very simply at Larkspur Cottage for the last six years. The principle of her inheritance from her father had been barely touched, and his many investments yielded yearly dividends that more than covered her living expenses. It seemed right to go ahead with her inspired idea to transplant this ancient house.

With all its treasured memories, as well as its visible link to her own family's heritage, rebuilding the house in Virginia as a home for herself and Jeff seemed a reasonable and inherently valuable thing to do. Blythe hesitated only a few minutes. Then, drawing a long breath, she made her decision, and the unusual project proceeded.

The Maynard Home
Mayfield, Virginia, Fall 1876

FENELLE MAYNARD waited in the small parlor of her family home, moving nervously from window to fireplace. Expecting Rod to arrive momentarily, she was filled with anxiety.

She stared at the newly laid fire, which had not as yet caught, gazing at the struggling flames abstractedly. This would be the first time she had seen her fiancé since she and her mother had returned to Virginia. What she had to tell him she had confided in no one— least of all, her mother.

Their homecoming had been nearly a month later than planned because of a terrible cold contracted by Mrs. Maynard. It was, she declared, brought on by the "horrid" English weather. she had been confined to bed for weeks at their relatives' London town house. So they had taken the last possible sailing date before the onset of winter made an Atlantic crossing treacherous.

Outwardly sympathetic and concerned, Fenelle had been secretly and guiltily delighted to spend more time in England for reasons she now had to explain to Rod.

For all her aunt's and mother's manipulation, Fenelle's "London season" had been an ordeal for her. She had gone dutifully to all the parties, balls and events required of a debutante, hating every moment, wishing she were anywhere else. Then something unexpected and wonderful had happened—

Fenelle drew in her breath. If her mother had not been ill that night it might not have come to pass at all, since little concerning her daughter ever escaped Elyse Maynard's sharp eyes. Although her mother could not have been unaware of the bouquet of red roses and the note that was delivered to her cabin on board ship before they sailed. Of *that* Fenelle was certain.

The piercing ring of the doorbell pealed through the house, and Fenelle gave a little start. She heard footsteps along the hallway as their only servant, Essie, went to answer it.

Looking out the window, Fenelle saw Rod's horse tethered to the hitching post outside the front of the house. She had been so focused on her own thoughts that she missed seeing him arrive.

The parlor door opened and Fenelle whirled around as Rod's tall figure stepped into the room. For a moment they looked at each other, then, in a few long strides, Rod crossed the room, took Fenelle's outstretched hands, and bent down to the cheek she had turned for his kiss.

"Welcome home, Fen," he said.

"Thank you, Rod," she replied, smiling. With a delicate gesture, she motioned him to the wing chair by the fireplace. "It's been a long time."

Taking a seat, he said, "Too long. And how was the crossing?"

"Very pleasant. There was cordial company, beautiful weather, smooth waters." She seated herself gracefully on the loveseat opposite him.

She looks lovely, Rod thought. Her months among English society had given her a polish, a kind of poise she had lacked before. Where Fenelle had been shy and rather hesitant in her movements, she seemed perfectly at ease now, her hands in repose in her lap. Although he was not usually particularly observant of women's fashions, Rod noted that the periwinkle blue dress was well suited to her pale blond beauty and that she was wearing her hair in a new way.

"Rod, I have something to say that will probably come as a surprise," she began quietly.

Immediately Rod was attentive, aware of a firmer tone, a new decisiveness in her voice. Even this was unusual, for Fen hardly ever initiated conversation, responding, instead, to others.

"I wish to be released from our engagement," Fen said, as calmly and directly as if she were commenting on the weather.

Caught off guard, Rod sat up straight in his chair. This was hardly what he had expected. On the way over this afternoon his own emotions were mixed at the prospect of seeing his fiancée again after all these months, especially after his meeting with Blythe. The thought uppermost in his mind had been that Fenelle probably wanted to discuss a mutually agreeable date for their wedding. He had certainly not anticipated her desire to break their engagement.

But his voice was calm as he asked, "You have met someone else? Someone while you were in England?"

She nodded. "That's true. His name is Clive Rensaler. He has asked me to marry him, but I told him that before I could give him an answer, I had to return to Virginia and talk to you. I want you to know that I regarded my promise to you as binding *unless*—but—" Fen paused a second before continuing, "there are things you don't know about me, Rod, things my mother did not *want* you to know."

With a quick, nervous movement, Fenelle rose and walked over to the fireplace, put one hand up to straighten the porcelain figure of a shepherd boy.

"It has bothered me a great deal even from the first, long before I met Clive. I never believed there should be anything concealed from someone you have promised to marry . . . the person with whom you will stand before God and vow to love, honor, and cherish." Her slim fingers twisted the base of the little figure as she went on. "I've been to enough weddings to know that in the marriage ceremony, the minister always asks for anyone who knows any reason why the marriage should not take place, to speak now 'or answer in the dreadful Day of Judgment.' It worried me greatly that I might have to live with that prospect."

Rod frowned. What possible deep, dark secret could this lovely, innocent young woman have that would necessitate such a prenuptial confession?

Fen's eyes were wide and clear, free of guile as she looked at him.

"Rod, I know I was not your first choice for a wife. Not that it mattered to me. I have always admired and respected you. But, truthfully, I have never been in love with you. And if we are both honest, neither are you in love with me. Our marriage—" she halted as if correcting herself—"*this* marriage, if it were to take place, would be a compromise on both our parts. I realize that, as the last of the Camerons, marriage for you was more a necessity to ensure your family line. You want, *need* children to carry on the name, to inherit your estate."

Rod interrupted. "I am very fond of you, Fen, very fond indeed."

She held up her hand, halting any further interruption.

"Yes, I'm sure you are, Rod, and I of you. But it really isn't enough, is it? Especially not if there can be no children." She paused. "You see, Rod, what you don't know and what my mother would not allow me to tell you is that a childhood illness left me with a defective heart. It is most doubtful that I could ever bear children, or at least, healthy ones. If I could even deliver a baby, the doctors are very sure it would not survive—"

Rod opened his mouth to speak, but again Fenelle motioned for him to hear her out.

"No, please, let me finish. I don't want you to blame Mama, Rod. Things have been so difficult for her since the war—Papa's death . . . she was used to so much more . . . Well, you know how it was before—" Fenelle's gesture encompassed the room.

Rod's gaze followed, taking in the small parlor, the worn carpet, the faded draperies, the lighter squares on the wallpaper where paintings had been removed to be sold. The Maynards' fortune had died with the Confederacy.

"Not that Mama would ever have *lied* to you in any way, Rod.

She meant well, wanting only that I be safe and secure. Marriage to you would guarantee that." A small smile lifted the corners of Fenelle's sweet mouth, "As for my . . . condition, in Mama's generation, it would have been indelicate to mention such a thing.

"But, it would be wrong of me to marry you, Rod, knowing this about myself and also being realistic enough to understand you need to have an heir for Cameron Hall. But please don't feel sorry for me. Clive, the man I met in London, knows about . . . me, and it doesn't make any difference to him. As the third son of a very wealthy father, his older brother will inherit everything. Children are not . . . necessary—" Again Fen paused, blushing a little. "It always troubled me that we had concealed from you something so important to your future."

Slowly Fen removed the citrine and diamond ring from the third finger of her left hand, placed it in her open palm, and held it out to Rod.

"Thank you, Rod, for doing me the honor of asking me to marry you. I'm certain that, had I revealed this information and there were no Clive, you would have gone through with the marriage. I know how honorable you are. But it would not have been right. So, now I free you to find someone else you can really love. You see, I know the difference now between affection and real love. I have found that it exists, because I have found it with Clive, and I would not deprive you of that for anything in the world!"

Rod got to his feet and walked over to Fenelle, taking the ring she was offering him. The prongs of the setting pressed into the skin of his palm as his hand closed over it. How ironic this scene suddenly seemed. His thoughts were coming too fast for him to make sense of most of them, but the one thing he knew he must do was assure Fen that he understood. What courage it must have taken for her to confront him without consulting her mother!

"You are a beautiful, courageous lady, Fenelle," he said, meaning every word. "No matter what the circumstances, I would be honored to have you as my wife. But I do give you your freedom, and I wish you every happiness. This Clive Rensaler is a very fortunate man."

Tears sparkled in Fenelle's eyes as she murmured, "Thank you, Rod. I do pray you find the same happiness I have found."

Riding back home to Cameron Hall later, Rod was wrapped in deep thought. What a strange turn of events! How inexplicable the timing of his life! It always seemed too soon or too late. If only Fenelle had broken their engagement sooner . . . before Blythe returned to Mayfield. If he had only known then—

Unconsciously, his jaw clenched, his hands jerked on the reins, causing Sable to toss his head indignantly.

Suddenly an old bitterness of regret rose up like bile. He felt heat flame in his face. Why? Why, he demanded, had not all this happened before he lost Blythe *again*?

chapter

16

Winter Journey

1877

ROD LEANED on the ship's rail and stared moodily out at the restless motion of the slate-gray sea.

It had been a wretched trip. Not that Rod could blame anyone for that. Against all warnings, even his own good judgment, he had chosen to make this mid-winter Atlantic crossing.

Most of his fellow passengers had spent the ten days cabin-bound in utter misery. Only a handful of hardy sailors like himself had ventured out on deck. From experience, Rod knew the best way to prevent seasickness was to get plenty of fresh air, and if one felt the least bit queasy, to walk briskly and breathe deeply.

There was not much conviviality among those few passengers who managed to get themselves to the dining room. Many of the tables remained empty, and the staff stood around without much to do while the diners made quick work of meals. Then they hurried back to bundle themselves in deck chairs and avoid looking at the ocean, which on this passage, had rolled and dipped like some gray, heaving sea monster.

Rod, usually the most congenial of men, had on this occasion welcomed the prevailing lack of company and conversation. The solitude of this strange crossing gave him plenty of time alone to think.

He took out the letter he had received a few months ago, worn from frequent rereadings, and perused it again. The same conflicting reaction assailed him, as it had each time he read it.

Had he debated too long to respond, or was he just off on another "wild goose chase"? Could he, as his mother asked, trust the information this man Burnham had sent? Was it reliable, or was the man some kind of charlatan, taking Rod's money and dangling tantalizing prospects before him with no real proof that he could substantiate them?

"Montrose," as his mother had pointed out, was quite a common name in Scotland and England. How could Rod be sure the "Mrs. Montrose" that the private detective thought he had located was Blythe? What if, when she left Virginia, Blythe had used another name? Perhaps even taken back her maiden name, "Dorman"?

Rod knew it was a risk, knew he was taking a chance, but he could not help himself. If there was the slightest possibility that the man he had hired to find Blythe was on the right track, he had to see for himself.

As the ship neared the English coast, Rod's uncertainty increased. He railed against himself. Why had he waited so long to come? He felt strangely pessimistic, possibly the result of the slow, depressing crossing, he tried to tell himself.

Well, action was the best antidote for this kind of malaise. They would soon dock, and tomorrow he would take the earliest train out of London, bound for a small village a few hours away. Here he would settle, once and for all, if his journey was a 'fool's errand'.

As the train rattled through the countryside the next day, wheels clattering on the track seemed to be repeating the old saying: "Journeys end in lovers' meeting." Where had that come from? And what did it mean? Never superstitious in the slightest degree, Rod tried to shake his gloomy forebodings.

By the time the train pulled into the small Kentburne station, Rod's heartbeat was accelerating. Was this the same little train station with its neat flower beds and gravel paths from which Blythe came and went? Did she stand on this very platform, walk toward the line of passenger wagons hitched to the rail fronting the road?

Rod stopped at the ticket window, then hesitated, not knowing exactly what to ask. He did not want to create a stir by asking for Blythe by name. In such a small village she was sure to be known, and it might be embarrassing to her to have a stranger inquiring about her. Aware of how fast gossip travels, he decided instead to look on his own for the address Burnham had given him—a house called "Larkspur Cottage."

A light mist was falling, and Rod automatically turned up the collar of his coat before taking a deep breath and setting out. *Don't get too excited,* he warned himself sternly. *This* Mrs. Montrose could be a gray-haired old Scotswoman, not Blythe at all. And if it were she? Then, what would he say, what would he do? He swallowed hard noticing how shallow his breathing had become. The constriction in his chest tightened as he turned down the crooked little lane located down a lane just off the main road leading from the town square, marked with a wooden post sign, MARSH ROAD.

His steps slowed, and he moved as if through deep water, hope pumping the adrenalin though his veins, the possibility of disappointment dragging his feet. Then he saw it, the small stone house behind a low rock fence, a picket gate set in the center, a sign on the post: LARKSPUR COTTAGE.

It has a waiting look, he thought, *or was it a deserted one?*

He came closer, leaned over the wall, his gaze focused on the painted door, willing it to open in welcome. His eyes moved to the diamond-paned windows, and he noticed that the curtains were drawn inside. It was then he noticed the sign, COTTAGE TO LET, and his heart turned cold.

The house was empty. There was no one about. If Blythe had ever lived here, she was gone now.

Rod never knew how long he stood there, staring at the cottage. When at last he turned away, the mist had turned into a drizzle. As he began walking back to the village, it became a steady rain.

The village center was forsaken. All sensible people had apparently sought the cozy comfort of their own home and hearth fire. At the train station only the ticket clerk was tucked into his cubbyhole. Silently he issued Rod his return ticket to London, mumbled its departure time, then returned to the newspaper he was reading.

Two-and-a-half hours before I can leave! Rod thought miserably. How to bridge this time here, where he had come to the end of his long hope? He stood on the station platform looking out across the sodden village green. Rain was now coming down in sheets.

Across the green he saw the lights of a tearoom, its wooden sign swinging wildly in the wind. Some warmth and something hot to drink could be found there, he knew. Bending his head, he plunged through the downpour and pushed through the door of the tearoom to find himself its only customer.

After ordering tea and scones, he seated himself by the window, staring out through the rain-blurred window at a distorted view of the street. The very street, perhaps, that Blythe had walked down dozens of times.

Suddenly life seemed as bleak and gray as the scene outside. Loss of hope was almost as devastating as loss of faith, he mused. Without Blythe, Rod's world was bereft of joy, but he had lived in the possibility that someday he *would* find her, would convince her of his love, and spend the rest of his life with her.

Today all that had come to an end. The question now was how to reconcile himself to the rest of his life without even that hope?

chapter
17

Arbordale
Virginia, 1879

THE SMALL COMMUNITY of Arbordale was abuzz. A medieval castle, so rumor had it, was being transported stone by stone from England and rebuilt on Virginia soil! And its eccentric owner was said to be an English lord or perhaps a duchess.

For months, dray wagon after dray wagon had rumbled through the main street from the harbor city of Norfolk to the dock at the narrow point of the river. When the crated contents were loaded onto the ferry and taken across to the wooded island known locally as Hunter's Haven, conjecture ran rampant.

The island itself was so heavily forested that not much could be seen from the town side of the river, so very few had even caught so much as a glimpse of the building. Although many tried ferreting out what was going on over there through workmen on the job, the actual structure remained shrouded in secrecy. As the mystery continued unsolved, curiosity grew, with more and more questions asked and none answered.

Gossip flew faster and more furiously than ever when it was learned that the rebuilding was almost completed and that the owners would soon take possession of the reconstructed dwelling.

When the new residents arrived, however, it was during the

night, with no one in Arbordale the wiser. Prepared for the arrival of possible royalty, the townspeople experienced some disappointment when the true identity of the owner was discovered. Instead of the earl or duke they had imagined, the occupants of the island mansion proved to be an attractive widow and her young son.

For all their effort, Arbordale citizens did not find out much more than that. Through local tradespeople it became known that she had brought a small staff of servants with her, that the boy was attending Brookside School for Boys as a day pupil, and that she kept a small stable and had hired a groom.

Gradually the avid interest in the house on the island diminished as other, more immediate events captured the attention of the townspeople. Still, when they thought of her at all, they wondered where she had come from and why anyone so young and pretty would choose to isolate herself on a remote estate far from the possibility of a social life—the distractions and the cultural advantages offered even by a town the size of theirs.

Blythe was unaware of the speculation that had swirled about her coming. She was busy and reasonably content, for there was much for her to do upon moving in at Avalon. Periodically, furniture from Dower House arrived, and decisions as to its placement had to be made. Then, Corin's library, a valuable collection with many rare first editions, had been sent. When the books arrived, they had to be unpacked and shelved again in the fine oak bookcases that had been rebuilt in the transported room.

In addition, the rest of the house onto which the library and "keeping room," the staircase and balconied gallery from Dower House were added had to be completely furnished. Blythe spent hours thumbing through furniture catalogs and wallpaper books, making selections.

One reward in this year of transition, however, was the reassurance that Blythe's decision to move to Virginia was the right decision. This was the first time a home had been a place of her own choosing. She had never felt she belonged at Montclair, after which came a series of temporary living places—the hotel in Bermuda, the

Ainsleys' London town house, the rented cottage in Kentburne. Through all those years she had experienced a transitory feeling, as if she were "a bird of passage," always on the brink of change. All that time beneath the surface of her daily life, she had felt unsettled, as if she had no real home.

Though Blythe was occupied throughout the hours of the week while Jeff was at school, as soon as he got home, her life revolved around her son.

They changed into riding clothes and rode the many wooded paths on the island. Jeff was becoming an expert rider, and Blythe was learning the finer points of horsemanship not afforded by the early days of riding bareback at her father's California ranch.

Not often, but once in a while, Blythe recalled the times she had ridden with Rod along similar woodland trails. Usually she was able to rein in her wayward thoughts, knowing how dangerous they were to her peace of mind, but most of the time her love for Rod was sealed within her barren heart. Determinedly she did not allow herself the luxury of dwelling on the past, even that part of the past she considered the happiest time of her life.

As the first year at Avalon passed into the second and then the third, Blythe's existence took on a pleasant, if solitary, pattern. Her life, of course, was centered around Jeff. As the little boy grew into a self-reliant youngster, excelling in his lessons at school and evidently popular with his classmates, he would often invite a special friend home for the weekend. Blythe always welcomed Jeff's friends, and soon invitations to Avalon were prized by those fortunate to receive them. The two boys Jeff liked best, the Bancroft brothers from Williamsburg, were favorite and frequent guests, and as Jeff got older, he spent many weekends in their home as well.

At first Blythe was reluctant to let Jeff go where his name might provoke questions, but as the years went by, she felt less and less fear of discovery. Continuing to use her maiden name "Dorman," however, seemed wise, since she did want to avoid detection by anyone known to the Camerons.

When they had lived in Virginia for six years, Jeff celebrated his twelfth birthday by asking Blythe if he could become a boarding student for the coming fall term. His request shocked her because it proved to her that Jeff was growing up, capable of independent thought. In spite of the prospect of lonely weeks without him, she agreed.

Nevertheless, on the September day he left to begin the school year as a boarding student, Blythe was stunned by her feelings. When he gave her his good-bye kiss and hug, she was startled to realize he was almost as tall as she. Holding him at arms' length, she gazed into his face for a long moment, noting that it was losing its boyish chubbiness and becoming the face of a young man.

Jeff's good looks bore the unmistakable mark of his father, but she also saw something of her father, Jed Dorman, in them—his strong jaw and high cheekbones. Before releasing Jeff, she sighed. How quickly the years had passed!

Although Blythe knew she would miss Jeff terribly, she had not anticipated the full impact of his absence. The entire household had operated on Jeff's schedule—the breakfast hour set in time for him to be ferried across the river to catch the Brookside School omnibus, a hearty English tea when he got home at four, a horseback ride together before dinner.

Most of all, Blythe missed their evenings together in the library, with the curtains drawn against the night, the lamps lighted, a fire glowing in the fireplace. It had been such a comfort to see Jeff sitting at the library table, his tousled head bent over his homework when she looked up from her embroidery or book. There were no more such evenings.

Blythe recalled Corin's gentle warning to her, recalling situations of some of his own boyhood friends, only sons of doting mothers. Determined she would never become one of those odious creatures—a widowed mother who loaded guilt on her son for her own misfortune—she resolved to accept cheerfully Jeff's decision to spend an occasional weekend with some friend rather than come home.

Indeed, she attempted to cultivate an interesting life of her own independent of Jeff's companionship. She spent a great deal of time reading not just the popular romantic novels, but books on history and biography, particularly those chronicling the lives of women who had had significant accomplishments. In a time when women's roles were strictly limited, it pleased Blythe to think that some were overcoming the prejudice of both race and gender.

She had always felt her lack of formal education to be one of the subtle barriers separating her from Malcolm, and now that her son would be well-educated as well, she set about to learn as much as possible.

She began to teach herself Spanish, with the idea of one day returning to Spain for a longer period of time. She took up china painting, discovering a talent for it, and spent hours painting delicate flowers on porcelain, then firing and glazing them and displaying them in racks she had built around the wall of the windowed breakfast room. One lovely demitasse set, on which she had created her own design of Virginia's native flower—the pink dogwood blossom—was sent as a gift to Lydia Ainsley.

Nonetheless, try as she might to keep herself busy and occupied during the long winter while Jeff was away at school, as the summer of 1885 approached, Blythe was eagerly awaiting his homecoming and making plans for his vacation.

It had long been Blythe's desire to take Jeff to California, and since the completion of the transcontinental railroad, it was now possible to travel to the Pacific coast in comfortable Pullman cars. The itinerary she planned was extensive—first to Sacramento, where as a little girl she had stayed at a convent school while her father, Jed, was making his fortune in the gold fields of the Sierra mountains. She also wanted to make a sentimental journey to the northern part of the state, to revisit Lucas Valley, the scene of some of her happiest years. There she had grown up, had met, and fallen in love with the stranger who had stumbled onto their ranch, Malcolm Montrose, Jeff's father.

She was anxious that Jeff should know that part of her history and his own background, too, so, when Jeff came home to Avalon the last of May, Blythe had made all the arrangements for them to leave at once for the West—

Part V

All losses are restored and sorrows end.
> *—Shakespeare, from the Sonnets*

chapter

18

London

1885

EVEN IF Garnet had not been expecting her, the slam of the front door, the clatter of sturdy boots on the stairs, then the rush of running feet along the hall outside her bedroom, would have signaled that Faith was home for the holidays.

In the very next moment the door burst open and her rosy-cheeked thirteen-year-old daughter exploded into the room. "Mummy! I'm home!" Then she plunked herself down on the nearest chair and thrust her black-stockinged legs in front of her, sighing, "Oh, heavenly! It's so good to be out of that prison! I can't wait to get out of this wretched uniform!"

She yanked impatiently at the thick tie with her school emblem on the front, then tugged at the wide, square collar under the serge pinafore. "When are we going down to the country? I'm absolutely dying to get on Fazia and ride forever and ever!"

Garnet smiled indulgently at Faith's outburst, while wondering why she and Jeremy were paying such outrageously enormous fees to the boarding school that was supposedly turning this hoyden into a lady! She repressed the urge to lean forward and tuck back the tumbling hair that was falling forward into the wide, dark-lashed eyes. Even at this age, Garnet mused, her daughter gave promise of being incredibly beautiful someday.

Suddenly Faith jerked herself upright, knocking the wide-brimmed blue felt hat askew, and gave her mother a sweeping glance.

"Oh, bother! You're going out, aren't you?" she accused. "My first night home, and you and Papa have a social engagement!" she wailed. "I haven't seen you in nearly three months!"

"I know, darling, and I'm sorry. It couldn't be helped. It is a business event we must attend."

As if taking the explanation as a cue, Garnet got up from where she had been sitting in front of her dressing table and revolved slowly in front of her daughter. Her gown was of the finest royal blue velvet, cut with a portrait neckline that showed to advantage the lovely line of her shoulders. Stylish puffed sleeves narrowed to elbow length, and from a long fitted waistline, the skirt was gathered into a modified bustle and draped into a small train. "How do I look?" she asked.

"You look gorgeous—naturally," Faith admitted reluctantly.

"I suppose I should accept that as a compliment," commented Garnet, lifting her eyebrows.

"Of course, but then you always do!" Faith pretended a scowl. "I shall never be anywhere near as striking looking as *you*. So, where are you and Papa off to tonight? To a ball?"

"Oh, no, not a ball. To a dinner party at the home of your father's publisher. One of the company's American executives is here in London, and Mr. Sewell is entertaining for him."

"Will there be dancing?" Faith's foot tapped unconsciously.

"No dancing, I'm afraid." Garnet shook her head regretfully. "Nothing but a long, eight-course dinner and dainty conversation among the ladies while the gentlemen linger over brandy and cigars discussing the publishing business for an hour afterwards. It will probably be a deadly dull evening with no sparkle, no surprises!"

But as it happened, and not for the first time in her life, Garnet would be proven wrong.

Although the first part of the evening proceeded pretty much according to Garnet's predictions, once the ladies excused themselves from the dining room and gathered in one of the twin parlors of the Sewell's' London town house, the evening became much more interesting.

Expecting the usual exchange of trivia—gossip, comments on the current theater offerings, the doings of the Royals and members of the Court—Garnet settled on one of the sofas, distracting herself by looking around the over-decorated room with her characteristically critical eye.

The interior followed the fashion of all upper-class homes of the time. The furniture, carved and curlicued, was richly upholstered in dark plush fabric and accented with small petit point pillows. Gilt-framed paintings of gloomy landscapes hung about the room, and marble-topped tables held glass domes encasing arrangements of artificial flowers.

As the other ladies took seats, Garnet found herself studying each one, wondering which, if any, would be an amusing conversationalist. Anyone at all would be welcome to ease the tedium of waiting for the gentlemen to join them and to enliven the conversation with more pertinent topics and a little harmless flirtation.

All of the women were exquisitely dressed. *There must be a small fortune in dressmaker fees represented among the less than dozen women gathered in this one room,* Garnet surmised. She had often heard it said among American socialites that a wife was a living advertisement for her husband's wealth. From the look of this assemblage of English wives, the British had drawn the same conclusion.

As the beruffled maid brought around the tray of demitasse and mints, murmurs of individual conversations drifted around the room. As Garnet lifted a tiny cup of after dinner coffee and helped herself to a chocolate wafer, Lucille Edgerton spoke.

"Garnet, my dear, I sat next to your handsome husband at dinner tonight, and he informed me that you are departing soon for America."

"Yes, to visit my mother. We plan to travel with her and my brother to our nephew's wedding in Massachusetts."

"How nice for you. And how long do you expect to be away?"

"Oh, several months, I expect," Garnet replied.

"I suppose when traveling such a great distance, it behooves one to make a real visit of it," Mrs. Edgerton mused. "However, I fear Jeremy will be devastated during your absence."

"Not at all. Jeremy has business to attend to in his New York office, and I will join him after the wedding to sail back . . . to England." Garnet gave a little shrug. "I almost said sail *home*. After all these years, I suppose I am beginning to think of England as home."

"And where did you used to call 'home,' if I may ask?" interjected a pretty woman with a gentle voice and warm smile, whose name had slipped Garnet's memory.

"Virginia."

"Virginia?" the other lady exclaimed, her eyes lighting up. "One of my dearest friends moved to Virginia a few years ago. I do miss her terribly. We were very close. As a matter of fact, my husband and I were godparents to her little boy. We plan to visit her there someday. Where in Virginia are you from, Mrs. Devlin?"

"Oh, a place you've probably never heard of!" Garnet laughed. "Mayfield is very small. The nearest large town is Williamsburg, once the capital of the colonies."

"But that must be very near where my friend moved!" declared the woman, and she got up from where she was sitting to join Garnet on the sofa. "Have you heard of a place called Arbordale . . . or of a school for boys called Brookside?"

"Why, yes . . . I think it's about forty miles from Mayfield," Garnet replied, interested now.

"Wouldn't it be a wonderful coincidence if you knew my friend, then? Her name is Blythe . . . Blythe Montrose."

A queer little prickle tingled along Garnet's scalp, and her stomach gave a small lurch. Her fingers tightened on the handle of the delicate cup she was holding.

"Her son, Jeff, attends Brookside," the lady continued, not noticing Garnet's startled reaction. "She sends us pictures, of course, but I long to see him myself. He is getting to be such a big fellow that I'm afraid he will forget all about us." She paused. "If it would not be too much of an imposition, perhaps if I gave you her address, you might send her a note when you're in Virginia . . . mention that we met? Oh, how rude of me, I don't think I ever introduced myself properly. I'm Lydia Ainsley."

chapter
19

Cameron Hall

Mayfield, Virginia
1885

UPON HER ARRIVAL in Mayfield, Garnet was confronted by two facts
for which she was unprepared. The first, merely disappointing, was
that Rod was in Kentucky on a horse-buying trip, and she would
have a further delay in telling him the astonishing news about
Blythe.

The second reality Garnet had to face was much harder to accept.
She was distressed to see that her mother had aged visibly since their
last meeting. Of course, Kate was nearing seventy. Her mother had
always been there for all of the Cameron family—their strength,
their anchor, their heart—the fact that she would not always be was
a devastating thought.

Still elegant, fastidious in her dress, Kate had become frail. The
arthritis that afflicted her had cruelly twisted her once beautiful
hands, and, as if aware of this, she wore lace mitts to cover their
deformity. She also walked with some difficulty, using a cane.
However, her head was still held regally and the slim shoulders kept
as straight as she could manage. She never spoke of her pain and
would not permit anyone else to. She was, as Garnet newly
acknowledged in a rush of pride and tenderness, a magnificent lady.

The day after her arrival, Garnet sat with her mother in the small parlor adjoining the downstairs bedroom Kate now occupied and wondered if she should share her news about Blythe's whereabouts before telling Rod.

For a while they talked about the forthcoming wedding. Garnet could hear Kate's maid, Annie, singing in a nearby room as she packed Kate's trunk for the journey to Massachusetts.

"It hardly seems possible that Jonathan is old enough to marry!" Kate remarked, shaking her silvered head in disbelief. "The years have gone by so quickly—"

"I know," Garnet agreed as she poured tea into their Spode cups, adding lemon and sugar to her mother's before handing it to her. "Whenever I think of Jonathan—even now—I always remember the day Rose died and I went in to him. He was standing in his crib crying, and I picked him up and held him, realizing for the first time that he was now *my* responsibility. I was never so frightened in my life. Never felt so completely inadequate."

Kate nodded, her eyes misty, remembering.

"Yes, such a tragedy, and yet we must believe it was all for some purpose."

"The fire? Rose's death? The war? Do you really believe that, Mama?"

Kate smiled faintly as she quoted, "'God's ways are not our ways.' I've learned over the years, Garnet, that it doesn't do to question what happens. We just have to accept the events that come into our lives and move on as best we can."

"Oh, Mama, I wish I could have that kind of faith," Garnet sighed. "I try, I really do, and sometimes I think I've reached some kind of understanding—then something happens and I'm . . . angry, or frustrated, or bewildered."

Kate reached over and patted her daughter's hand.

"You've come a long way, darling. I've seen the maturity, the mellowing in you. When I remember how you managed Montclair, the servants, an invalid, the children, all of it, during the war . . .

well, it was rather remarkable. And now you've a wonderful husband, a beautiful daughter—everything you've always wanted."

Garnet set her teacup down.

"But I didn't get the man I thought I wanted," she said in a rare burst of confidence, not sure that her mother had ever suspected her hopeless passion for Malcolm Montrose.

"But you got the man God knew you needed," Kate replied serenely. "Who knows what sorrow would have been yours if you had married Malcolm. Look what happened to poor little Blythe."

It was the opening Garnet had hoped for. "Mama," she said, watching Kate closely, "I know where Blythe is."

Surprise widened Kate's eyes and Garnet rushed on.

"She's been living in England for years! In fact, I'm sure I once saw her on the platform of Victoria Station in London. That was a long time ago, and of course I didn't have the slightest idea where she was living or how to get in touch with her. I was going to tell Rod about it, but then he and Fenelle got engaged and he seemed so happy that I didn't want to risk hurting him again."

"Oh, my dear!" sighed Kate. "Yes, it would only have upset him."

Garnet leaned forward. "What about now, Mama? Is there anyone? Or has Rod resigned himself to permanent bachelorhood?"

Kate waved away the suggestion. "Surely not! Rod is still a handsome man, enormously eligible with all this. He's been master of the hunt for the last two years, and there are always parties, balls, young women who find him fascinating. But—" she shrugged. "In my heart, I don't believe he ever got over Blythe. You said you know where she is now?"

Garnet hesitated a split-second before answering. "Mama, she is in Virginia, not forty miles from here. Outside of Arbordale. And she has a son. Malcolm's son. He attends Brookside School for Boys." Garnet sat back, watching her mother's reaction.

"You're sure? How do you know this?" Kate gasped.

Quickly Garnet filled her in on meeting Lydia Ainsley at the Sewell's dinner party and how she had learned about Blythe.

"What do you think he'll do?"

"I don't know. Maybe he won't want to stir old embers after all these years. That will be up to him to decide."

Garnet looked puzzled. "What I can't understand is why she never got in touch with him when they were both free. Do you think she no longer loves him?"

Kate shook her head. "Who can say? Only Blythe can answer those questions and only Rod can ask them."

"To think she had Malcolm's child after she left here! That means—" Garnet sat up straighter—"that he is . . . Jonathan's half-brother, Mama! Shouldn't Jonathan be told he exists?"

Kate's expression indicated that was something that had not occurred to her before.

"I suppose you're right. But isn't that Blythe's decision to make?"

Garnet's face flushed, her eyes snapping in indignation. "Do you think it was right for her to keep all this secret? Didn't she have any idea what Rod was going through?"

"Garnet, dear, I long ago stopped trying to understand other people's motives for what they do. Blythe must have had her reasons. Maybe it will all be resolved when Rod knows."

"Why did she come back, I wonder? To Virginia and so near Mayfield if she didn't want people to know where she was?" Garnet wondered aloud in spite of her mother's sage comment.

Kate did not venture a guess, and just then Annie came into the room to ask her about some costume she was packing for her mistress, and Kate followed her maid back into the bedroom.

Left alone for a few minutes, Garnet toyed with the possiblity of riding over to Arbordale herself someday before they left for Jonathan's wedding in Massachusetts. She would like to meet Blythe face to face, woman to woman, and find out for herself the truth of why she had left Mayfield the way she did, why she had, in Garnet's opinion, abandoned her brother so heartlessly.

The more Garnet thought about it, the more reasonable it seemed that she should confront Blythe. It was not just to satisfy her curiosity, Garnet rationalized. Blythe *must* have had her reasons, however strange and obscure they might be. Whatever was behind Blythe's mysterious disappearance, wouldn't it be better for Garnet to know before she told Rod what she had found out from Lydia Ainsley? Wasn't it, in fact, her sisterly "duty" to save Rod further humiliation and disappointment?

Garnet had always been impulsive, and, though she assured herself repeatedly that she *had* given the matter much thought, her decision to actually drive over to Arbordale was spur-of-the-moment.

Kate's dressmaker had come to the house for some final fittings of the gowns she was having made to take to Massachusetts and Garnet, on the pretext of having some last-minute errands, went off to town by herself.

At the gate, however, instead of turning toward Mayfield, she determinedly turned her barouche to the left and headed for Arbordale.

However, upon reaching the ferry dock, she was chagrined to be told by the ferry boat driver that the house on Hunter's Island was closed, the residents gone for the summer.

Milford, Massachusetts
June, 1885

Since this was Garnet's and Kate's first visit to New England, they had not known what to expect in the town of Milford. They were pleasantly surprised at its early summer beauty, the impressive houses, beautifully kept lawns, tree-shaded streets, the orderliness of its town center, and its historic buildings.

They were just as impressed by Davida's father, Kendall Carpenter. Mr. Carpenter met them at the train station, saw to their luggage, assisted them into his handsome carriage, and escorted them to the Sheffield Manor Inn where reservations had been made for them to stay during the week before the wedding.

His gracious courtesy reminded Garnet of another former officer, her beloved Jeremy. When she remarked on this to Kate in the privacy of their spacious suite, Kate added, "He was a classmate of Malcolm's at Harvard and came from an educated, well-born family."

"We certainly saw a different kind of Yankee during the war!" Garnet declared, remembering the raids on Montclair that had taken place more than two decades before.

"Well, dear, we must let bygones by bygones." Kate said. Memories of the war years were still too poignantly painful for her to recall.

"Sorry, Mama!" Garnet was at once abject and gave her mother a spontaneous hug. "I shouldn't have mentioned it. To change the subject, I can hardly wait to meet Davida, can you?"

Davida had not been at the train station with her father as she was attending a party in her honor that afternoon, he explained, but she was looking forward to seeing them that evening.

"From Jonathan's descriptions in his letters, she is not only beautiful but also a paragon of virtue and intelligence." Garnet's eyes sparkled mischievously. "So what shall I wear tonight to meet such a model of goodness and charm?"

Kate took off her bonnet, then sat down in one of the cushioned boudoir chairs and smiled affectionately at her daughter, who still had the talent to amuse her.

"Well, I suppose you just *might* find something suitable in the trunkload of fashions you saw fit to bring with you, my dear," she teased.

Garnet turned her attention to the contents of the open steamer trunk the bellboy had just brought up. He had deposited it with such huffing and puffing and exaggerated wiping of his forehead that Garnet had been prompted to give him a more generous tip than she had planned.

Her wardrobe *was* lavish, thanks to Jeremy's unrestricted clothes allowance, enabling Garnet to indulge her penchant for beautiful things. Maybe it was the years of deprivation and poverty brought on by the war that made her now so extravagant, although she always justified it by saying Jeremy insisted on her being fashionably dressed.

Bringing out one outfit after another, Garnet modeled them for Kate, pivoting before the full-length mirror for her mother's opinion. They finally agreed on a jade green moire silk that set off Garnet's gold hair and amber-brown eyes.

Then while Garnet unlocked her leather traveling jewel case to select the right accessories, she asked Kate, "When do you think Rod will get here?"

"It depends on when he left Lexington and what kind of train connections he could make. I'm not sure how often trains come from Boston to Milford."

Garnet picked out earrings of filigreed gold studded with tiny emeralds and a matching brooch. Glancing over at her mother, she noticed Kate looked pale and had leaned her head against the chair back and closed her eyes.

"Mama, you're tired, aren't you? Why don't I have some tea sent up. It will be some time before we're due at the Carpenters for dinner." Garnet walked over to the wall bell to ring for room service.

"I *am* feeling a little weary, dear," Kate admitted.

As if by magic a maid appeared in answer to the bell and took their order for tea and sandwiches. In another few minutes a waiter was at the door bearing a large tray.

As they sipped their tea and nibbled on sandwiches of thinly sliced ham, and cheese, Garnet remarked, "I can't imagine what Rod's reaction is going to be when I tell him about Blythe."

A small frown drew Kate's brows together. "I hope it's the right thing to do, Garnet. I sincerely pray it won't start up all the old heartache again. What if she doesn't want to be found? Have you thought of that?"

Garnet shook her head. "Mama, I *have* to tell him what I know.

The last time I kept silent about her, it haunted me. It's bothered me all these years. There's no way I can keep this from him. What he does about it—" she shrugged. "Well, that's *his* decision."

"Yes, I suppose you're right."

Kendall Carpenter called for the ladies promptly at six as he had promised. Garnet could not help noticing how splendid he looked in evening clothes, remembering with a sharp little tug of memory the last time she had seen him—that day when as a Union cavalry officer, he had ridden up to Montclair and Rose had confronted him on the porch.

Anxious for her husband, Bryce, home on leave and hidden upstairs in the secret room, Garnet had peeked at Kendall from behind the louvered doors while Rose had coolly entertained her former beau in the parlor, successfully distracting him so that the house was never searched. *How brave Rose was,* Garnet thought in retrospect.

When they drove up to the Carpenter's stately pink brick house, a tall, smiling Jonathan stood with his fiancée on the porch steps, and they saw Davida was every bit as pretty and winsome as he had described.

As the carriage drew to a stop, Jonathan came running down to welcome his aunt and her mother. "It's so good to see you, Auntie 'Net!" he exclaimed. "And, Miss Kate, you're as lovely as ever!"

"I can see you haven't lost your southern gentleman's manners!" Kate smiled and reached up to pat his cheek.

Shyly Davida started down the steps toward them.

"And this is Davida," Kate said softly. "Oh, my dear, we are so happy to meet you, so glad about your promise to Jonathan. You have obviously made him a very happy young man."

Jonathan beamed proudly as Davida slipped her hand through his arm.

Davida must look like her mother, Garnet mused, for she bore no resemblance to her strong-featured father. Davida's were delicate, and her eyes were hazel with long, sweeping dark lashes. She had a sweet smile, but there was something stubborn in the set of her firm little chin. This young lady was accustomed to having her own way, Garnet decided. Jonathan was going to have his hands full with this independent little miss—her father's only child, a precious, pampered daughter. *Well, it takes one to know one!* Garnet thought, amused at herself.

But Garnet had no more time to dwell on these fleeting thoughts, for Kendall was ushering them up the steps into the delightful interior of the house, charmingly decorated and exquisitely appointed. Davida's touch, no doubt, Garnet thought, throwing a speculative glance Kendall's way.

There was more here than met the eye, she realized. Evidently, Davida had not only been her father's pride and joy, but also his housekeeper and hostess. Would he be lost without her? Was he giving her up with resentment as well as regret? Or did he not plan to give her up at all?

Garnet had not heard what the young couple's plans were to be when they returned from their honeymoon trip to the Holy Land. As they all sat down in the parlor, Garnet looked around curiously. Were they perhaps planning to move in here with Kendall?

Her curiosity was soon satisfied when she heard Davida say animatedly to Kate, "As soon as we've had some refreshment, I want to take you next door to see Jonathan's and my little house—a wedding gift from darling Daddy!"

So then Kendall was not letting his one lamb stray too far from the pasture, after all! Garnet surmised, unconsciously casting an eye toward Jonathan to see if she could read his thoughts. But he was gazing adoringly at Davida and seemed "pleased as punch" at the entire situation.

After a prolonged inspection of the "doll house" located practically in the back yard of Kendall's home, they went back to have dinner, a delicious meal perfectly served by a crisply uniformed maid.

"I do hope you don't mind having guests drop in," Davida said during dessert. "Everyone in Milford is so anxious to meet

Jonathan's relatives . . . I mean, his *Southern* relatives. They already know the Merediths, of course. I mean, who *doesn't* know the Merediths? They practically run the town, what with the mill and all." Davida's went on gaily. "I understand from Jonathan's Aunt Frances that *she* is giving a reception for you so that others can meet our out-of-town visitors before the wedding."

Garnet did not dare look at her mother. It was a strange sensation indeed to be called "out-of-town visitors" after a lifetime of living in Mayfield and being recognized as one of the most prominent families in that part of Virginia.

A pleasant social hour followed as a dozen or so friends of the Carpenters called to express their pleasure in meeting Garnet and Kate and also to extend congratulations to the engaged couple. After the guests had left, Garnet, seeing that her mother was visibly tiring, made their excuses, and Kendall drove them back to their hotel, offering to come for them the next morning to take them to church services.

Garnet, also feeling the fatigue of travel and the excitement of the day, was eager to retire, but when she went to pick up the room key at the desk, she was informed that her brother had arrived and left a message. Given his room number, Kate and Garnet hurried upstairs, anxious to see him.

A tan, healthy-looking Rod opened to their knock and gave each of them up in an affectionate embrace.

"Come in, come in! I'm just finishing my dinner." He pointed to the table behind him, set for one.

"So late?" Kate asked.

"I just got the last train out of Boston," he explained, drawing up chairs for them at the table. Then he motioned to the wall bell. "May I order something for you . . . chocolate . . . tea?"

His mother held up her hand. "Oh, nothing for me, dear. We have just dined at the Carpenters' . . . unless Garnet—"

"No, thanks!" Garnet shook her head. "I've had a 'gracious plenty,' as we say down home. In fact, I do believe I've had an over-abundance of 'Yankee hospitality'!" she remarked with a touch of her old mischief. "But I am perishing to have a good chat with *you,* brother mine." Cocking her head, she leaned forward. "Was your trip successful?"

"Indeed, yes! But talk about hospitality! I'm convinced those Kentuckians nearly outdo Virginians. They kept trying to load me down with hams and who knows what else! It didn't seem to matter that I still had a long train ride ahead and a wedding to attend." Rod laughed, then asked, "And speaking of *weddings,* how is the happy bridegroom?"

"Delirious and completely dazzled." Garnet rolled her eyes.

"And the bride?"

"Delightful," put in Kate.

"And a little dictator," added Garnet.

"Why, Garnet!" Kate remonstrated.

"Well, she *is,* Mama! Anyone can see she is leading Jonathan around by a velvet cord."

Amused, Rod looked from his gentle mother to his outspoken sister and raised a quizzical eyebrow. "Any other news or report I should hear about?"

Kate looked questioningly at her daughter. Would Garnet now give her brother the startling information about Blythe?

To her surprise, Garnet shrugged indifferently. "You can see for yourself tomorrow. As good a judge of horseflesh as you are, Rod, I'd be interested in your impression of the Carpenters, *père et fille!*" With that, Garnet covered a yawn with one dainty hand and rose from her chair. "I really must go to bed. I'll leave you two to catch up. Good night, Mama. Good night, Rod. We'll breakfast together in the morning, all right?"

Kate watched Garnet move to the door with her usual flair. Evidently she had changed her mind about telling Rod where Blythe was. *That girl has always been unpredictable,* Kate thought. No matter how old, she would never understand her!

Closing the door to Rod's room behind her, Garnet stood indecisively for a moment. It *had* been right to put off telling Rod about Blythe, hadn't it? To spring it on him now might have upset him, diverted his attention from Jonathan's wedding, spoiled this special occasion for them all.

Besides, Garnet was still determined to visit the elusive widow at Avalon herself first and confront her about the silence she had maintained all these years, which had caused Rod such unnecessary pain.

Yes, she had done the right thing, Garnet decided.

chapter
20

Milford Community Church
Milford, Massachusetts

COLONEL (USA Ret.) Kendall Carpenter, hands clasped behind his back, paced the vestibule of the Milford community church. Although a good two hours before the wedding ceremony was to take place, Kendall had fled his normally peaceful household. This morning, because all of Davida's bridesmaids had arrived to help her dress and add the finishing touches to their own bridal costumes, the place was a beehive of activity. Uneasy among so many females, Kendall had decided to come ahead to the church and wait for Davida's arrival.

The tall graying gentleman with the erect military bearing appeared outwardly calm. The truth was, his mental state belied his stoic composure. Not only was he losing his only daughter today but also under strangely coincidental circumstances. The mother of the young man to whom he was giving his daughter—Rose Meredith—had been the real love of Kendall's life.

As a matter of fact, he had not been inside this particular place of worship since *her* wedding to another man twenty-seven years ago. A fact that had left him inconsolable for a very long time.

As he paced, he chastized himself that instead of thinking of his daughter's future happiness he was caught up in the bitterness of his own past unhappiness.

Vividly he recalled that he had sworn to himself he would not see Rose married to his Harvard classmate, Malcolm Montrose. But in the end, he could not stay away. Concealing himself behind a tree in the churchyard, he had watched Rose, a vision in white lace and tulle, descend from the carriage and enter the church on Professor Meredith's arm, followed by her Aunt Vanessa who was carrying the train of her bouffant silk dress.

That long-ago day, Kendall had slipped inside and seated himself in the very last pew of the sanctuary and in a kind of frozen rage had witnessed the ceremony. When the minister asked, "If there be anyone who knows any reason why these two should not be joined together as man and wife, let him now speak or forever hold his peace," Kendall had barely been able to restrain himself from crying out, "I do!"

He had warned Rose that it would be a terrible mistake to marry a slave-owning Southerner in 1858, when a violent storm of controversy over the issue was already separating the northern and southern states. No one knew then that the threat of civil war was so near. Yet only a few years later Rose was, according to Kendall's beliefs, living in "enemy territory."

Impatiently he brought out his heavy, gold watch from the pocket of his waistcoat and consulted it, then glanced through the crack of the swinging doors leading into the church and heard the thrum of the organ chords. Two tall young men, Jonathan and his cousin Norvell Meredith, his best man, emerged from a door at the front and took their place by the altar steps.

Jonathan! Unconsciously, an ironic smile touched Kendall's stern mouth under the trim mustache. *If Fate had been kinder, he might have been my son,* he thought.

He also remembered the unforeseen circumstances under which he saw Rose again after her marriage and of the first time he had seen Jonathan.

Kendall had been one of the first to answer his country's call to arms, rising quickly to the rank of captain, then major. Early in the war, he had been put in charge of troops penetrating Confederate territory to obtain intelligence about the resources of the rebels.

One day, while on an expedition deep into Virginia along the James River and not realizing that his beloved was mistress of Montclair, Kendall, along with his men, wandered onto Montrose land toward the mansion in pursuit of information.

His military mission temporarily forgotten, Kendall spent an hour or more with her trying to persuade her to allow him to escort her to safety in the North. It was then he saw all the loyalty and courage and character of the woman he had loved and lost. It was then, too, he had met her son, Jonathan.

The minute Kendall had seen the child, he knew he wanted him. He had felt a rush of emotion at the sight of this sturdy, handsome little boy with Rose's brown eyes and her lustrous dark hair. And the way the boy demonstrated his own brand of fearless determination in not wanting to shake hands with a "damn Yankee," his father's enemy, had sparked Kendall's admiration, even as it amused him.

His heart had twisted with longing and regret when he had finally taken his leave. It was the last time he had ever seen Rose, for she had been tragically killed in a fire that had nearly razed her husband's home. He had since learned from her son that the accident that had set the place ablaze was caused by Rose's typical defiance of any injustice. Secretly she had been teaching her slaves to read, which was then against the law in Virginia.

Kendall's reverie was broken by the rustle of silk, the whisper of crinoline, the murmur of lowered voices. He turned to see the bridesmaids, in rainbow colors, tip-toeing into the vestibule to line up for the processional. In their midst was Davida in rippling white dotted Swiss ruffles, smiling, radiant.

Swallowing the quick lump that rose in his throat at the sight of her, Kendall, always the soldier, gave her a small salute, then stepped forward to offer her his arm to take her down the aisle to become the bride of Jonathan Montrose.

1886

Spring sunshine poured into the windowed breakfast room of the newlywed's cottage. Looking over at his bride, Jonathan Montrose thought he had never seen a more charming woman.

The light behind her sent dancing sunbeams through her brown hair, giving it a rich, mahogany hue. Roses bloomed in the cheeks of her oval face, and her eyes sparkled as she read off a long list of errands she had to attend to.

Married less than a year, Jonathan found to his astonishment that he loved Davida more now than he could have imagined possible. They had been back from their honeymoon only two weeks, having ended their trip to the Holy Land with an idyllic cruise on the Nile where, released from the duty of required sightseeing, they had reveled in each other and fallen more deeply in love than ever.

"I must consult Mrs. Glendon on how to get the very best cut of beef," his new wife was saying, a slight pucker creasing the creamy brow. "Everything must be simply perfect."

Resignedly, Jonathan sighed. Now that they were back in Milford, Davida was preoccupied with plans for all sorts of entertaining.

"We owe so many people!" she had told him in feigned dismay. "All those who sent wedding presents, our friends as well as Papa's, and of course we must have your Aunt Frances and Uncle John to dinner immediately!"

In a town where Davida was a popular belle, her father, a prominent member of the town council, and his own relatives, the Merediths, employers of large segment of the population at their mill, it was inevitable that they would have "social obligations." Still, while Davida anticipated the discharge of these duties with delight, Jonathan viewed them reluctantly, unwilling to share his beloved with anyone.

With a surreptitious glance in the direction of the kitchen door, Davida leaned forward in case their young maid might overhear herself being discussed and said in a stage whisper, "I shall have to rehearse Molly about the proper way to serve when we have guests. I know Mrs. Glendon has been training her while we've been away, but I must oversee her myself. I don't want any domestic disaster to spoil my first dinner party."

With Davida's enchanting face so close, Jonathan could not resist kissing her rosy mouth and capturing her hand in both of his.

"I absolutely adore you," he said huskily.

"Jonathan!" she exclaimed, pretending to be shocked. "Behave! What if Molly should walk in! Or maybe Papa!"

More likely it would be Papa, Jonathan thought ironically. In the short time they had been back, he had begun to think the blessing of Mr. Carpenter's wedding gift house a definitely mixed one! Ever since their return he was in and out of their home constantly, and not always at the most convenient moments.

Just then, as if on cue, a brief, demanding knock sounded at the front door. They both stiffened, listening, as Molly's footsteps scurried by on the way to answer it. Then they heard Davida's father's unmistakable voice and Molly's reply.

"Yes, sir, they're in the breakfast room."

A minute later, Kendall Carpenter's commanding figure appeared in the archway.

"Good morning!" he greeted them heartily, his eyes lingering lovingly on his daughter. "I haven't come too early, have I? Not interrupting anything, am I?"

"Of course not, Papa, darling!" Davida assured him, hopping up from her chair and running to give him a kiss. "Come and have a cup of coffee with us. I'll have Molly bring some fresh."

"Well, I hadn't planned to stay—" he demurred.

"Oh, you *must*, mustn't he, Jonathan? Do please sit down, Papa."

"Well . . . if you insist." Kendall took a place at the table. "Actually, I just came over to bring your mail." He handed a sheaf of letters to Jonathan.

"Thank you, sir," Jonathan said politely, adding, "I'll have to put up our mailbox soon . . . save you the trouble," he mumbled, knowing this was one of the chores on Davida's list he had not yet done.

"Oh, it's no trouble. I can always bring it over when I pick up mine," Kendall said offhandedly, then turning to Davida. "Well, my dear, what are your plans for the day? I have to drive over to Wilburn on some business, and I thought you might like to ride along, give us a chance to catch up. There's still so much I'd like to hear about your trip."

Jonathan looked up from the mail he was sorting through and glanced over at Davida. He knew Davida had planned to shop for curtain material today, and the one thing he had learned about his bride was that she did not like a change of plans. So it was to his surprise that she agreed.

"Oh, yes, Papa, that would be lovely!"

"Splendid, my dear. We can have lunch at that seafood restaurant that's just opened." Kendall beamed, then neatly ruled out Jonathan's accompanying them. "I suppose you're due at the mill today, my boy?"

"Well, Uncle John didn't specify any hard and fast date for me to start work in the office, but I guess today is as good as any other." Jonathan tried to sound casual, but he inwardly resented having someone else cut his prolonged honeymoon short by reminding him he was now the head of a household and should be busy about the work of provider.

"What time did you want to leave, Papa?"

"As soon as you can be ready, my dear."

Molly, looking flushed, her crisp white cap slightly askew, entered with a steaming pot of coffee and set it down.

"Pour Colonel Carpenter a cup, please, Molly," Davida instructed the little maid, then said to her father, "You sit here and enjoy your coffee, Papa, while I go put on my bonnet and shawl."

Left alone with his father-in-law, Jonathan engaged him in polite conversation in spite of his eagerness to read one letter among the stack received. It was from his favorite cousin, Druscilla Montrose, now Bondurant.

As soon as the sound of Kendall's buggy wheels had faded away, Jonathan opened Druscilla's letter. He smiled as he read the first few paragraphs, his cousin's vivacious personality spilling onto the page. It was the last part of the letter that he had to read twice, however, before the reality of what she was saying actually penetrated.

"Randall and I are deeding to you Bon Chance, along with all surrounding land. It's the original Montrose property, and you, after all, are the rightful heir. Had things been different, you would have inherited it all in due time."

Slowly, out of the past, memories came flooding back. Even with a war going on, Jonathan could remember only a carefree childhood growing up at Montclair with his cousins, Dru and Alair—the orchard where they had played; gentle hands, both black and white, caring for him; the scent of apple blossoms in the spring, the woodsmoke of fall, the spicy odor of apple butter, the aroma of freshly baked cornbread. He thought of the little Shetland pony, Bugle Boy, he had ridden alongside Auntie Garnet and of the time she had taken him by train to Washington to meet his tall Uncle John. From this point, all his memories were of Massachusetts and the family there, because his aunt, with tears in her eyes, had explained that the Merediths wanted to bring Jonathan up along with their own children.

Amazingly, Jonathan was overwhelmed with nostalgia, a heretofore unrecognized homesickness, a longing for Virginia. It seemed imperative to go there at once, as if a part of himself had been lost and now was found. It seemed important to be once more in the land of his birth, to be in the house and on the land of his forebears, to ride through the woods near Montclair, to smell the tobacco drying in the barns, to fish in the sparkling streams alive with trout on the other side of the meadow, to see the burnished brick and gleaming white pillars of Montclair, rising out of the ancient elms . . . to go back "home."

"But, I don't understand," protested Davida. "What does it mean?"

Jonathan's voice betrayed his excitement. "It means that at last

Montclair will be back in the Montrose family! Bondurant had turned it over to Druscilla, and *she* has deeded it to *me!* It would have come to me anyway if my father had not gambled it away—you remember, I told you the story. Both my uncles, Bryce and Lee, were killed in the war, so I, as the only direct descendant, would have inherited it through my father's legacy."

Davida sat immobilized, watching her husband pace back and forth. "Yes, but I still don't understand. What does it mean to *us?*"

"It means, my darling, that we now own Montclair, one of the largest and most beautiful plantations in all of Virginia!" Jonathan exulted.

"Virginia?" she repeated through stiff lips. "Does that mean we must move to . . . Virginia?"

"Of course! Not only *must,* but we are privileged to move there! Oh, wait until you see it, Davida. It was always a magnificent place, but Dru writes that it has been restored to the way it was when it was built by the first Montrose, Duncan, for *his* bride, Noramary Marsh. And now *my* bride will be mistress of Montclair!"

Davida felt something heavy press against her chest. She could neither swallow nor speak. To draw a breath sent a sharp pain through the region of her heart. Move to Virginia? Leave Papa? Milford? All she held dear?

She looked at Jonathan's glowing face, his dark shining eyes. She saw at once that this was not a subject for discussion or debate. He had already assumed she would be as thrilled as he that his ancestral home had reverted to its rightful owner, that it belonged with a Montrose as master.

Her lips trembled into a smile as he came and knelt down in front of her, took both her hands and raised them to his lips.

"Oh, Davida, I thank God I am able to give you this, a home worthy of you, my darling, where we can live on land that was settled by my ancestors, in the home they built for their descendants, where we can raise a family and enjoy all that was meant to be ours—"

Ironically, words from Scripture often misinterpreted as spoken by a wife, took on a personal meaning for Davida—words she had never dreamed she would now have to apply to her own situation—"Whither thou goest I will go, where thou lodgest I will lodge, thy people will be my people—"

Do not be silent at my tears, for I am a stranger—Psalm 39:4
How shall we sing—in a strange land?—Psalm 137:4

chapter
21

Montclair

Fall 1886

DAVIDA'S EYES threatened to overflow. The farther they rode out from the Mayfield train depot, the lower her spirits plunged. They passed deep meadows and vast pasturelands where horses grazed, looking up indifferently as the carriage went rumbling along the country road. In the distance she could see the ridge of blue hills that seemed to enclose her, shutting off any possibility of escape.

Suppressing a shudder, she glanced at Jonathan to see if he had noticed. But her husband was leaning forward in his seat, eagerly looking out the carriage windows.

A feeling of desolation crushed Davida. How could Jonathan be so happy when she was so miserable? And why didn't he sense her misery?

The shock of leaving her beloved home and dear Papa had only begun to penetrate, and she was not prepared for the crush of reality that suddenly hit her. Here she was, far from everything she knew. Beautiful as it was, this landscape was unfamiliar, alien. She ached with the effort of concealing the grief that swept over her, something she could not share with her husband. Worst of all was the possibility that she had made a terrible mistake in agreeing to come to Virginia so that Jonathan could take over his family's plantation.

She winked back the tears. Tears would not console her; they would only make matters worse. Jonathan would be upset, would not understand. Besides, had she not promised to honor and obey him?

The words of the vows they had so recently repeated came to mind, along with the benediction that had been pronounced over them: "May God grant that you two live in such mutual harmony and full sympathy with one another, in accord with Christ Jesus, that together you may with united hearts glorify Him in all you do in your married life."

A wife was supposed to be submissive, sweet-spirited. A wife was not to argue or show anger. But she and Jonathan were *not* in "mutual harmony" nor in "full sympathy" with one another, nor had their hearts been united in this decision!

She recalled Reverend Nevins' also saying: "In marriage there will be sacrifices you will be called upon to make." But she had not imagined such sacrifices would include moving hundreds of miles away from family and friends to an isolated country estate!

She had not wanted to leave the pretty little house Papa had built for them right next door to the house where Davida had grown up, where she could run across the lawn any time to see him or to borrow a recipe from Mrs. Glendon, their longtime housekeeper, or where she could simply cross the common to visit with any one of her girl friends from childhood.

Wasn't there something else the minister had said? Davida tried to remember. "Only love can make it easy, perfect love can make it joy." Well, there was no question about her love for Jonathan. Davida loved him so much that it hurt!

"I think we're almost there!" Jonathan exclaimed. "I believe I'm beginning to recognize the road where we turn off. Yes, I remember! Darling, we're nearly there! Montclair!!"

Davida turned her head to look at him. His face was glowing, and he was smiling. How handsome he was, how much she loved him.

Maybe love would be enough. Maybe love made everything possible. She certainly couldn't change anything now. She had made her choice and married Jonathan Montrose. She had assured him he was all she wanted, all she would ever want, and when she had said it, she had believed it. Desperately she told herself, *I* must *believe it*.

Davida leaned forward and kissed him softly on his mouth. "Oh, Jonathan, I love you."

Davida took her first tour of Montclair, guided by a rapturous Jonathan, who saw everything through the happy haze of a long-delayed homecoming. Later, with all the instincts of a fastidious Yankee housewife, she made a second, more thorough, inspection of the house alone. This time she made the frustrating discovery that the mansion, for all its splendor, had suffered from standing empty for the past eighteen months.

While the Bondurants had been living in South Carolina and she and Jonathan were on their wedding trip, Montclair had stood unoccupied and unattended. In spite of the coverings, the furniture was thick with dust, and in all the vast rooms, unheated for months by the daily warmth of damp-chasing fires, the baseboards and ceiling moldings had collected mildew.

Davida realized a place this size needed a number of servants to keep things in good order, and the fact that it was *she* who would have to hire them and train them, if the work was to be done properly, was daunting.

She thought wistfully of the pretty little cottage her father had so lovingly built for them in the hopes of keeping her close by—of the small, neat rooms, the windows unshadowed by foreboding giant trees that barred the sunlight from pouring in, the tidy lawn bordered by flower beds—which was all that then separated her from her darling Papa.

Always striving to be the "ideal wife," Davida hid her heartbreak. She wished she could share Jonathan's obvious delight in being back in Virginia, but much as she tried to pretend, it was impossible.

So in their first year of marriage, secrets were kept out of love and out of the fear of causing pain to the other—the first link forged in a chain that would build through the years to separate them.

He shall return to the days
of his youth—Job 33:25

Leaving Davida standing in the middle of the front hall to direct the draymen carrying in the crates, boxes and trunks from Milford, Jonathan left quietly by a side door. He walked through the boxwood hedged herb garden, past the stables, out along the meadow, and found the hillside path that led to the Montrose family graveyard.

Pushing aside the scrolled black iron gate, he entered the burial grounds of generations of his ancestors. With a sense of reverence he searched among the headstones, pausing at one or two to read the epitaphs chiseled on them, until at last he found the name he was searching for. In the shadow of the brooding stone angel, he read:

ROSE MEREDITH MONTROSE
1839–1862
Beloved Wife of Malcolm,
Mother of Jonathan
"Love Is As Strong As Death"

As he read that name, Jonathan felt the grip of strong emotion for the mother whom he could not remember. In that moment he experienced the embracing love and tenderness she could no longer bestow. How hard it must have been for her when she realized she was dying to know she was leaving her child.

From the portraits of his mother—the one at his grandfather Meredith's house in Massachusetts of Rose as a radiant bride and the other, hanging in the stairwell at Montclair, of her as a young mother with her child leaning on her knee—himself—Jonathan knew what Rose had looked like. He had often gazed on that face in a kind of awed adoration, studying its contours, its expression, the dark, thoughtful eyes. For him, she would always be not only beautiful, but also forever young.

As fragile as her appearance seemed, however, the things Jonathan knew and admired most about his mother were Rose's strength and courage.

Looking down at her grave, Jonathan realized, perhaps for the first time, that in spite of the two women—Aunt Garnet Devlin and Aunt Frances Meredith—who had tried to substitute the maternal love fate had deprived him of so early, his life had lacked something vital in not knowing his own mother.

Jonathan knelt in the soft grass beside the tomb and wept. It was the first time he remembered weeping for the lovely young woman who had given him life. He had been too young when she died to fully perceive what had happened. Later, the events of his life as he grew up in much different surroundings, had gradually dimmed his memory of the Virginia home where he had been born and lived until he was five years old.

Jonathan did not know how long he stayed there lost in fond thoughts and memories, but the sun was slanting through the maple trees around the fence of the cemetery when he got up from his knees and started down the hillside back to the house.

As he neared Montclair, he could see first the double chimneys at both ends of the house, then the slate roof, and finally the whole house came into view along with its sculptured gardens, boxwood hedges, and the long line of elms facing each other along the winding drive.

"Montclair," he said softly to himself.

A house that descends from generation to generation through a single family begins to have a certain air about it, he thought. Except for the few years it had belonged to Bondurant, Montclair had retained its continuity, its affiliation with the other great James River plantation houses dating back to original King's grants of the last century.

Now it belonged to him and Davida, who had her own strange connection with the Montrose family.

Jonathan came through the orchard to the front and started up the steps of the house, thinking how little aware most people are at the time they make them, how such decisions affect our destinies and those who come after us.

chapter
22

Mayfield
1886

WHEN JEFF returned to Brookside after their California trip, Blythe was once again thrown back on her own resources without the companionship of her son. One favorite pastime was a shopping expedition. Having long ago lost her fear of being recognized, Blythe often shopped in Mayfield.

Not only had *she* changed, but Mayfield itself had changed. No longer the sleepy little town it had been, Mayfield's mild climate and leisurely lifestyle had drawn visitors from the North until it had become a lively metropolis with many new restaurants and stores, guest houses, and other special attractions designed to lure the tourist.

It never crossed her mind, however, that there would be anything unusual about this particular afternoon, nor that on this excursion she would have an unexpected encounter.

Within an hour she had crossed off almost every item on her list as accomplished. As she started back to the spot where she had directed her driver to wait with her barouche, near the town square, she noticed a sign reading ANTIQUES hanging over a little shop she had never seen before.

Corin, who had first given Blythe an appreciation of the value of antiques, had occasionally taken her with him on periodic scavenger hunts for pieces to add to his collection of Jacobean furnishings for Dower House. Since it was still early, she decided it might be fun to go inside and browse around.

She paused in front of the shop, astonished to see something familiar in the window. It was Sara's little desk! She recognized it at once, the lovely inlaid wood, the graceful shape, the turned legs— exactly as it had always stood between the windows in Sara's sitting room at Montclair. How in the world had it turned up here?

The winter Sara had left Montclair to go to Savannah, Blythe knew that Sara had thought it would be only a temporary arrangement until the next spring. None of them guessed that by December of that year, Montclair would have passed out of the hands of the Montrose family and into those of Randall Bondurant, who had won it from Malcolm in the ill-fated card game.

The house with all its furnishings, artifacts, and paintings, as well as Mr. Montrose's extensive library, had been included in the wholesale transfer of the property. With only three days to comply with the eviction notice, Blythe remembered the heartsick haste with which she had packed into a single trunk a few precious things, things of Malcolm's mostly, things that might one day be important to the child she was then carrying.

Probably when the new owner took possession of Montclair, completely restoring and enhancing it, only furnishings assessed as being of great value were kept. Probably the little desk was not one of those. Sara had once told Blythe that this little desk was the only thing she had brought from her girlhood home in Savannah, so its value was sentimental to Sara alone, Blythe judged.

Blythe pressed her face against the glass, shielding her eyes with both gloved hands in order to see better, wanting to assure herself that it really was Sara's desk. Satisfied, she pushed open the shop door and walked into the dim, musty-smelling interior. A bell over the door jingled, announcing her entrance to the woman sitting behind the counter in the back. At Blythe's approach the woman lifted her head and peered over oval-shaped wire spectacles.

"Looking for anything in particular?" she called. "Or do you just want to browse?"

"Oh, I'll just browse for a bit, thank you," replied Blythe, who wanted to examine the desk and also check to see if anything else from Montclair had been placed here for sale.

The woman went back to the newspaper she was reading, and Blythe wandered among the cluttered contents of the small shop, making her way slowly over to the desk.

Apparently she was the only customer. Perhaps this store was seldom frequented due to its out-of-the-way location, for the only other living being was a fluffy yellow-and-black striped cat that uncurled itself from the front display window where it had been sleeping in a square of sunlight. As Blythe drew near, the cat arched its back, stretched thoroughly, then hopped down lightly to search for a new napping place, where it would be undisturbed.

Blythe examined the desk, running her hand over the wood, gritty with dust. The slanted lid was shut, and although there was a tiny keyhole, it was unlocked. The lid pulled down to form a writing surface, she remembered, and behind it was a panel of small pigeonholes. In the center was a small door with a carved fanlight, tiny knob, and miniature keyhole, but again no key. When Blythe tried to open it, it held fast. *What secrets had Sara possibly locked behind that small stronghold?* she wondered fleetingly, before dismissing the idea. Of course Sara would have taken any important papers with her when she went to Savannah.

Sliding open the two shallow drawers under the lid, Blythe noticed an inkpad and stamp. She picked it up, turned it over and saw a trio of scrolled initials, SLM. "Sara Leighton Montrose," Blythe whispered. "This *is* Sara's desk!"

Blythe was not aware that the shop proprietor had come up behind her until she spoke. "Are you interested in this little desk?"

"Yes ... I am," Blythe replied, attempting to control the excitement of her discovery.

"It's quite old, but a fine piece," the woman told her. "Probably made by a plantation craftsman. Many of the slaves in the old days were artisans who made most of their owners' furniture. Unpaid laborers could copy the originals of famous English and French designers for much less money than the owners might spend on a purchase from European markets."

"How much is it?"

Immediately the woman was all business. She named a price. "Actually," she began, and Blythe was afraid she might be reconsidering her offer. "This desk came from Montclair, one of the finest of the James River plantation houses. Used to belong to one of the oldest families around here, the Montrose family. When Mr. Bondurant took over and began redecorating, many of the furnishings were bought by a dealer when they went up for auction. I'm not quite sure how this came to be in here, but I do know this is a good example of the kind of plantation workmanship I was telling you about. Quite rare, nowadays. Nobody seems to know what happened to the slaves who used to do this quality work. All gone up north, most likely."

Blythe followed the woman over to the counter where she wrote up the sale. Opening her purse, Blythe counted out some bills and told her she would send someone to pick it up.

As the shopkeeper went over to the desk to mark it "Sold," Blythe could see through the window a woman standing outside, looking into the shop. She caught her breath. Even though it had been years, Blythe recognized her at once. It was Garnet, Rod's sister!

Blythe's mouth went dry. But there was no way to avoid an encounter, no way of escaping the woman who had always considered her an interloper, who blamed her for stealing the man she loved. Unconsciously Blythe lifted her chin, opened the door of the shop, and walked out to the street.

"Hello, Blythe." Garnet's voice was even, emotionless. "I saw you in town. Actually I followed you. We need to talk."

At her words, Blythe recalled that Garnet's way had always been direct, matter-of-fact. The day after Blythe's arrival at Montclair as Malcolm's new bride, Garnet had abruptly announced that she was leaving and that Blythe would be in charge of caring for the invalid Sara, the house, all the responsibilities she had shouldered during the the years of the war and immediately afterward.

What a shock that had been to the inexperienced sixteen-year-old girl Blythe had been then. From that day Blythe had rarely seen Garnet, for soon after leaving Montclair, Garnet had remarried. This would be the first face-to-face meeting in all these years.

"Yes, I think that would be a good idea," Blythe agreed. "Where shall we go?"

"There's a tearoom nearby. It's out of the way. We'll not see anyone we know there, as we might at the Mayfield Inn. This way." Garnet led the way. Silently they walked down one block and crossed to another.

Sitting across the small, linen-covered table from Garnet, Blythe studied her curiously. Garnet had never been considered a great beauty, but she had a look that Blythe had always secretly envied in other women. Not arrogance exactly, but a sort of assurance possessed only by those of certain breeding and background—an inborn air, a natural elegance.

It had nothing to do with fashionable clothes, although Garnet's were unmistakably that. Her stylish suit was surely from Worth's, Blythe surmised, her furs undoubtedly sable. And her hat, ornamented with velvet leaves in which a small feathered bird nestled, had most probably come from the Rue de la Paix in Paris.

"Tea and blueberry muffins?" Garnet asked Blythe while a crisply uniformed waitress stood, pad and pencil in hand, waiting to take their order.

"Fine. Yes," murmured Blythe, aware of the startling coincidence in running into Garnet and the challenge it presented.

The waitress left, and Garnet proceeded to take off her beige kid gloves, one finger at a time, staring at Blythe. *How maddeningly youthful and beautiful she still is*, Garnet thought. *Not a single line to mar that creamy complexion, nor a gray hair in those glorious copper waves glimpsed under the simple felt bonnet.*

Beneath her confident surface, Garnet had always been intimidated by beauty. In a quick flash of memory, she remembered how stunned she had been by Rose Meredith's appearance when she had first seen her the day Malcolm brought her to Montclair. Strangely enough, Malcolm's second bride had affected her in the same way.

The silence stretched between the two women, accentuating all the uninfished business between them, all the hidden rivalry, the old hurts inflicted by the mere existence of the other.

It was Garnet who broke the tension at last. "I know about Avalon and about your son." At Blythe's startled look, she went on, "I met Lydia Ainsley in London through mutual friends, and when she heard I was coming to America for my nephew's wedding— well, it's no use going into all the details. She told me where you are living."

The waitress was back, setting the teapot on a trivet and placing the muffin basket in the center of the table before placing cups before each of them.

When she had gone again, Garnet continued, "Anyway, I did go over to Arbordale before we left for Massachusetts to call on you, but I was told you'd gone away."

"Yes, Jeff and I went to California—"

"California?" Garnet's eyes widened.

"I was born there," Blythe explained, "and lived there until—" She halted, leaving the rest of the sentence to Garnet's completion. After hesitating a second, she finished, "I wanted Jeff to see the place where I grew up."

"Jeff?"

"My son's name is Geoffrey. He's called Jeff."

"Malcolm's son." Garnet's tone indicated a fact rather than a question.

"Yes."

"Is that why you ran away?" Garnet asked bluntly.

"Yes. I didn't know what else to do . . . after Montclair—"

"You know you hurt my brother cruelly, don't you?" Garnet interrupted.

Her teacup half-raised to her lips, Blythe felt her throat constrict. "I'm sorry, I—"

"He *loved* you, he wanted to help you. Didn't that *matter,* didn't it mean anything to you?"

"I didn't think I had the right—"

"Love gave you the right." Garnet said coldly. "Why didn't you at least contact him after you were settled, let him know where you were, that you had a child? Have you any idea what he's been through all these years?"

It was Garnet's turn to be surprised. "I saw him once, you know, when I came to Mayfield. Mrs. Montrose thought I should bring Jeff. Quite by accident, Rod and I ran into each other at the inn." Blythe's voice trembled as she recalled that wrenching encounter. "I thought the best thing to do was vanish from his life forever—" She paused. "I thought by this time . . . Isn't he married?"

"No, he never married. And it's probably a good thing. He's never gotten over *you.*"

Blythe's hand shook as she placed her cup on the saucer. "I'm sorry," she said again, knowing she was repeating herself, unable to react to this latest news about Rod.

"I haven't told Rod about you," Garnet said finally. She leaned forward, looking unflinchingly into Blythe's eyes, and demanded, "Do you love my brother? I have to be sure of that before I tell him where you are. I don't want him to be hurt any more than he already has been."

Blythe felt heat rush into her face, then the blood drained away from her head, leaving her breathless and dizzy.

Should she tell Garnet the truth? That she had never *stopped* loving Rod? Or was that really the truth? Was the memory of love more powerful than the reality? Had time and distance and loss embellished her feelings for him, given them a romantic glaze that made their love seem more ideal, more perfect that if they had been able to fulfill its promise?

As Garnet's gaze held her ruthlessly, Blythe quickly weighed her love for Rod, realizing it had remained unchanged since she had first acknowledged it. While Malcolm was alive, guilt had shadowed and subdued it, but in spite of all that had happened, she knew her love for Rod was untouched by all the time that had passed.

Still, Rod's feelings for *her* were a mystery. While they had both grown older, become wiser or sadder with experience, the love she had known was still youthful and unsullied. That's what made it so dangerous, what made a second heartbreak more possible. Rod would surely have changed.

Acutely conscious that Garnet was still waiting for an answer, Blythe put her napkin down beside her plate and pushed back her chair.

"That is something only one person should ask. If Rod wants to know or wants to see me again, that is for him to decide, isn't it, Garnet?" Blythe stood up.

"Then shall I tell him where you are?"

"That's up to you, Garnet. Do whatever you think is best."

With that, Blythe turned and walked out of the tearoom. It was not until she was in her own carriage and on her way back to Arbordale, that the full impact of the experience hit her.

All the old emotions out of the past swept over her. Rod, free? Still in love with her? Was it true, or merely Garnet's imagination, or was it a weapon employed to make her suffer for her youthful mistakes, the wounds she had unintentionally caused?

Whatever had been Garnet's motives, the fact remained that she knew Blythe's long-kept secrets. Whether she would pass them on to her brother, Blythe did not know nor dare guess.

Those who sow in tears shall reap in joy—Psalm 126:5

chapter
23

Arbordale, Virginia
November 1886

"THERE'S A GENTLEMAN to see you, ma'am."

Blythe looked up from the china plate she was painting, a small frown of annoyance creasing her smooth forehead. She disliked being interrupted, especially at such a creative moment. She was working on the very intricate shading of the petals of a pansy, brushing the color from a delicate violet to purple.

"Did he leave a calling card?" she asked Bertha, her housekeeper.

"No ma'am, he jest said you'd see him."

Blythe rose from the high stool on which she sat when at her painting board with a sigh of resignation. Carefully she wiped her brush on the paint rag. Her hands slid tentatively to the buttons down the front of her smock, then she decided it was not necessary to remove it. It was probably only Mr. Pruitt, the carpenter she had hired for the addition she was planning to build.

She had decided to add a conservatory for the cultivation of year-round flowers as models for her china painting. The profusion of blossoms during the brief Virginia spring came and went too quickly for her slow, deliberate painting. Sketches were fine, but she needed flowers all year for inspiration, and having a hothouse seemed the ideal solution.

Tom Pruitt had remodeled an unused passageway of the original house into a studio, doing a superb job, if painstakingly slow job. Like so many real craftsmen Blythe had met in the rebuilding and restoring of Avalon, Mr. Pruitt was unpredictable, his hours unscheduled, his work erratic. He came and went at will, where whim or chance took him. She had had to search him out herself twice, ferreting his out-of-the-way carpentry shop to discuss her ideas for the addition. This was probably one of his characteristic unannounced visits. She'd better make the most of it, she decided, as she started down the hall to the parlor where Bertha escorted rare visitors to Blythe's secluded home.

Before opening the parlor door, she paused for a moment to smooth her hair in the hall mirror although why she bothered, she didn't know. Mr. Pruitt wouldn't notice. The times she had been to his hideaway workshop, he had barely acknowledged her presence, but kept right on working. She had had to project her voice over the sound of his sawing and sanding even to be heard.

As Blythe stepped into the doorway, she saw the back of a tall, broad-shouldered man standing in the bow window overlooking the sixteenth century garden, recreated from drawings of the original ones at Monksmoor Priory. Almost at once, she realized this wasn't the stoop-shouldered figure of Tom Pruitt, bent from years of working over a sawhorse. At her footstep, the man turned and Blythe froze.

Rod! Both hands went to her mouth as if to hush the sound of her gasp. It was Rod! She had fled halfway around the world to avoid him, and he had found her here in the woods of Avalon.

For Rod it was a moment he had dreamed and hoped and prayed for. The woman framed in the arched entrance reminded him of Blythe, as he had first seen her, standing in the pantry at Montclair years before—shy, unsure, eager to be accepted. He knew now that something had happened even then, something extraordinary, the beginning and end of love—lost before he could possess it.

She was still beautiful. Tall, slender, her wide eyes were the same velvety brown. Her mouth was parted slightly in surprise, soft and vulnerable, and the color rising into her cheeks was warm as peach glow.

"Blythe!" He spoke her name, and she felt that same heart-throbbing response to his voice, the conviction that her name had never sounded so beautiful.

"I've searched for you . . . everywhere . . . dozens of places . . . and here you were . . . all this time . . . all these years. I didn't know—"

Rod's words fell on numbed ears. Blythe struggled with the reality that he was actually here in the flesh, standing a few feet away from her in her own hidden house.

Her eyes moved over his face, noting the changes the years had wrought—the face that haunted her memory and invaded her dreams, the clear, truth-telling, truth-demanding eyes, the firm yet sensitive mouth under his mustache, the thick russet hair now liberally sprinkled with gray. It *was Rod*, and he was *real,* and he was *here*!

Instinctively she knew he had come to ask questions she might not want to answer. How could she convince him that what she had done at seventeen she regretted a few years later, and had wept tears of sorrow and remorse for it ever since?

But suddenly there was no need for words. In a few short strides Rod had closed the distance between them. He took both her hands in his. He was so close she could smell the clean, woodsy scent of his skin, see the depths of his eyes as they gazed into hers.

"My dearest Blythe, my love," he said huskily, and she was shaken to her very soul.

He drew her to him, bringing her hands down to encircle his waist, then pulled her into his arms. With the relief from more than decade of yearning, Blythe leaned against him, feeling the blessed comfort of his embrace. She put her head on his shoulder, felt his hand on the back of her head, then underneath her hair, caressing the nape of her neck.

"Dearest love," he murmured. "At last—"

Overcome with emotion, Rod's hand stroked the silky softness of her glorious red hair. He let his fingers tangle in it until finally, worked free of its restraining pins the satin weight of it fell loosely from the coiled knot.

Instinctively, Blythe lifted her face for his kiss, a kiss deep with love and longing, tenderly sweet, yet demanding response. That response came without hesitation, with equal yearning and ardor.

In that kiss was all that each had carried in their hearts all the years apart. It was renewal and commitment, an unspoken pledge and passionate promise. With it came the undeniable knowledge that they belonged together, now and forever.

Explanations could be made later, forgiveness sought and unconditionally given, plans made, the future discussed. All that mattered now was the soaring freedom of claiming and receiving the love that had been denied so long.

For hours they sat together in front of the fireplace in the paneled parlor of Avalon, speaking quietly, sometimes sadly of the past and hopefully of the future.

The present was so thrilling, so unbelievable, that it was hard to express—but they tried, tongues stumbling over words.

"I have always wondered if there could come a time when one could truly say, 'This is a perfect moment, I am as happy as I could ever imagine or want to be' . . . Now I know it is possible. This is that moment—" Blythe whispered.

It seemed so foolish to her now, all the uncertainty she had felt, thinking that Rod might have forgotten her, ceased to care about her and love her. How close they had both come to marrying someone else, to making the greatest mistake either of them could have made.

Blythe's heart swelled with gratitude as she remembered the biblical prayer of Mizpah: "The Lord watch between me and thee while we are absent one from the other." Surely the Lord had watched over her and Rod and brought them to this moment of reunion.

I will restore the years the locust has eaten—Joel 2:25

chapter
24

Mayfield
Cameron Hall

FROM A DISTANCE Cameron Hall looked just as Blythe remembered it, as they drew nearer, she saw that the scars left by the war had nearly healed.

The mansion stood serene and stately, peaceful now and proud, the aged bricks turned to rosy-gold by the sun, the fluted white columns rising majestically above the wide green expanse of lawn. It embodied everything about Virginia and Mayfield that Blythe had admired, yet been awed by, loved, and yet still feared. *This time is different*, she comforted herself. *This time, I am returning to become the wife of the master of Cameron Hall.*

Blythe turned to Rod, grasped his hand tightly. Looking into her eyes, he smiled at her, a smile full of love, understanding, and pride. Her heart lifted, and all her earlier doubts fled.

Kate Cameron was waiting for them on the porch and embraced

Blythe fondly. "Oh, my dear, it's been so long . . . too very long. Welcome home, Blythe."

"Yes, I do feel welcome," she said gratefully, her heart full. For the first time in her life, she truly felt she had come home.

"There is someone who is looking forward very much to meeting you," Kate continued as she led the way into the drawing room. "Jonathan is at Montclair now. He and Davida are coming for dinner. I thought you'd like to meet them your first night back, a real family occasion," then added— "except for Jeff, unfortunately. When will he be here?"

"At the end of the term," replied Blythe. "He's at Brookside, you know."

"Yes, of course. A very fine school."

In the drawing room Kate seated herself and pulled the wheeled tea cart toward her. "Does Jeff know about Jonathan?"

"Yes, we've discussed everything—the people, his relatives, Montclair—"

"I'm so eager to see him. Rod says he is a fine boy."

"Hardly a boy any more, I'm afraid." Blythe smiled ruefully. "Nearly sixteen."

"Sixteen?" Kate shook her head, "It seems impossible. The years *do* go by so quickly, don't they? Geoffrey. What a wonderful name! You know what it means, don't you? Geoffrey means 'gift of God'." Kate smiled at Blythe. "Giving him that name was surely an inspiration."

"In a way," Blythe conceded. She had chosen Jeff's name for other reasons, but somehow this unknown one seemed best.

"Is he . . . is he at all like Malcolm?" Kate asked impulsively. Then she glanced almost apologetically at Rod for bringing up Blythe's first husband. But Rod seemed oblivious to anything but Blythe, gazing at her as if he thought she might disappear, holding her with the strength of his love.

By way of answer, Blythe asked, "Would you like to see his picture?" Her hands already on the clasp of her handbag, she opened it. "It's his latest, taken for the school yearbook."

"Oh my! Yes, indeed!" Kate replied. She took the small photograph Blythe handed her and studied it intently for a moment, then lifted her head. "They're very much alike, Jonathan and Jeff. I think you'll notice. The same features, the same dark curly hair. Except for the eyes. Jonathan inherited Rose's eyes, but Jeff has the Montrose look about him, I think."

Kate poured the tea from the silver pot, then set it down suddenly, her eyes bright with tears. "Oh, I cannot tell you how happy I am! After all this time, here we are together! The Lord is so good, so gracious. I feel so blessed."

She reached out a hand to each of them. Rod took the hand extended to him, lifted it, and kissed the fingertips.

"So do I, Mama," he said, his eyes only for Blythe. "So do I."

"And have you set a date for the wedding yet?" Kate asked as she gave them their cups.

The two exchanged a look, but it was Blythe who replied. "June, when school is over for the year. I—I've asked Jeff to give me away." The color deepened in her cheeks, and beneath the long curve of lashes shadowing her eyes, she gazed shyly at Rod.

With a tiny catch of her heart, Kate realized that this marriage for Blythe was as if the first had never existed. Rod was her first love, her forever love, the love of her womanhood, not the girlish infatuation her "love" for Malcolm Montrose had been, a blind attraction that had been disillusioned and shattered by the man himself.

"I will restore the years the locust has stolen—" Kate quoted to herself. *Surely the Lord has done just that for Rod and Blythe,* she thought gratefully.

chapter
25

Mayfield
Cameron Hall

Rod was impatient to get married immediately and had to be persuaded to wait until the announcement could be made and invitations sent out, allowing time for Edward and Lydia Ainsley to make travel arrangements for their trip to Virginia, since Blythe had asked her old friend to be her matron-of-honor. Finally Rod conceded that for Blythe to have the wedding of her dreams, time was needed, and he would grant it, albeit reluctantly.

If the time dragged for the eager bridegroom, for Blythe there seemed not enough hours in the day to accomplish all she had to do—making a dozen lists, planning flowers and menus, shopping, fittings—

At last it was May, nearly six months since they had found each other again, and Blythe spent the two weeks before the wedding packing her personal belongings and arranging for the move of some of the furniture, paintings, and other possessions from Avalon to Cameron Hall into the wing she and Rod were to occupy after their marriage.

In spite of her renewed happiness, Blythe felt some sadness at leaving the house that had come to mean so much to her. Of course, the property had been deeded to Jeff and would become his when he reached twenty-one. In the meantime there were the years of his continued education ahead when he would come home to Cameron Hall instead of Avalon. Blythe did not want the house to stand empty and thus deteriorate, but she had not yet decided whether or not to rent it.

Suddenly there were so many decisions to make. *Just when everything seems to be working out, why does life have to become so complicated?* she wondered.

There were the Montrose jewels. Were they still hers now that she was marrying a Cameron? Blythe unwrapped the silk cloth in which she had kept the betrothal ring all these years. Crafted generations before in Scotland of heavy gold worked with clasped hands under a crown holding a glistening deep purple amethyst, it symbolized all of the heraldic grandeur of the gallant Grahams, the clan to which the Montrose family belonged. Sara had given it to Blythe when she had come to Montclair as Malcolm's bride, but Blythe had never worn it.

Next Blythe took out the jewel case containing the Montrose bridal set composed of a magnificent pendant and matching earrings. Opening it, she regarded the glittering rubies and diamonds for a long time. To whom did these belong? Should they belong to Jonathan, to give to Davida? Or should Blythe keep them for Jeff to present to his future bride?

And what about Montclair itself, her former home with Malcolm?

Possession being nine-tenths of the law, Jonathan was established there and, as Malcolm's eldest son, was the logical one to inherit. If the estate had not passed out of family hands for a matter of years, there would have been no conflict, but when it came back— through Druscilla's marriage to Randall Bondurant—who, in turn, had bequeathed it to Jonathan, it presented a problem.

Should not the two sons of Malcolm share equally in the inheritance—thousands of acres of prime Virginia land, enough to divide, enough to build another fine home upon, with land to spare?

Jeff, of course, was Blythe's priority. Was *he* to be left completely out? If she and Rod had children, they, of course, would inherit the Cameron fortune but what about her firstborn?

Blythe sighed heavily, closed the jewel case, and placed it deep in the trunk she was packing. It would be at least five years before any of this must be decided, she told herself. She would think about it later.

Her immediate relief at this justifiable procrastination was mixed with a troubling reminder of that old adage about "putting off until tomorrow what one should do today," causing her vague uneasiness.

June 1887

The garden at Cameron Hall was beautiful that afternoon when many friends of the Cameron family gathered for Rod's wedding to Blythe.

Only a few knew the story of their long love and the years of waiting that had led up to this glorious spring day. For those who did, there was a special poignancy in the ceremony.

Reverend Macabee, who had known Rod since boyhood through his acquaintance with Kate, was one of these few knowledgeable ones and had chosen an appropriate Scripture to read—words that were particularly meaningful to Rod and Blythe.

"Before we join together this man and woman, let us read from the gospel of Mark, the eleventh chapter, twenty-third and fourth verses," the minister began, "'Verily I say unto you, That whosoever shall say unto this mountain, Be thou removed, . . . and shall not doubt in his heart, but shall believe that those things which he saith shall come to pass he shall have whatsoever he saith. Therefore I say unto you, What things soever ye desire, when ye pray, believe that you receive them, and ye shall have them.'"

When Rod and Blythe repeated their vows and exchanged rings, Reverend Macabee read another significant passage before closing, speaking directly to the couple: "And from Matthew eighteen, verse nineteen, 'Again, I say unto you, that if two of you shall agree on earth as touching anything that they shall ask, it shall be done for them of my Father which is in heaven.'"

Those who caught the meaning of this last reading rejoiced even more than all the others who had come to meet the bride and offer their congratulations to the groom. But none were more pleased and proud than Kate Cameron as she stood greeting the guests who arrived in a steady stream from Mayfield for the reception that followed the wedding. She had longed and prayed for the day when her son would take the love of his life as his bride.

"There never was a more beautiful bride" was the sincere comment of many of the wedding guests.

"I could not agree more!" Kate beamed as she accepted the hugs and pleasant exchanges. Her heart was very full as she glanced at the radiantly happy couple standing with her in the receiving line.

Blythe, indeed, was lovely. At thirty-two, her appealing girlish beauty had been transformed into womanly grace. For her wedding she had chosen a gown of rose-cream silk overlaid with Swiss lace. Its fitted bodice flared in the back into tiers of fluted ruffles ending in a short train. Her coppery hair was arranged in a figure-eight, studded with seed pearls and tiny blushed white rosebuds.

As the people in Rod's life filed by to wish them well, Blythe tried to conquer her old feelings of being an "outsider." She knew people were curious about her, knowing she had briefly been married to Malcolm Montrose.

That dark and terrible time for her had also been a difficult period for many of them. At the time of her marriage to Malcolm, most of Mayfield's residents had been reeling from the crushing defeat of the Confederacy and were trying desperately to keep body and soul together in its desolate aftermath. They had heard rumors about his California bride, but most had been too busy, too tense, too involved in trying to survive, to resume the social life they had known before the war. As a result, the scant year-and-a-half that Blythe had lived in their midst had passed with few of them aware of her presence. By the time the shocking scandal of Malcolm's loss of Montclair in a card game had circulated, she had disappeared.

Today, though, Blythe was much too happy to dwell on the past. She could only thank a gracious God who had at last "given her the secret desires of her heart." She felt Rod take her hand and clasp it in his, and she looked at him, her dark eyes bright with joy.

Rod had to tear his gaze away from his bride in order to receive the hearty handshakes and congratulatory remarks of well-wishers.

Slowly the spring sunshine sent long shadows over the garden, and guests were urged inside by their hostess to partake of a lavish buffet, which was followed by dancing in the reopened ballroom of Cameron Hall.

Inside, the rooms glittered with candlelight glowing from all the wall sconces and crystal chandeliers. Huge bouquets of flowers graced the long lace and linen covered tables and bloomed from side tables under mirrors along the walls, doubling the effect of light and color.

Silver punchbowls were set at either end of the buffet table groaning with the weight of platters of Virginia ham, scalloped oysters, lobster salad, a variety of hot breads and rolls, fresh fruit, and an array of desserts, all served on rare Imari china plates.

Providing a soft, melodious background to table conversation was the music of a string quartet. Later, the musicians moved into the ballroom and began playing music for dancing.

Tradition calls for the first dance of the evening to be the bride and groom's alone. Reunited after so many painful partings, Rod and Blythe circled the floor, lost in each other. Gradually, two by two, the wedding guests paired off and joined them so that soon the newly polished floor was filled with circling couples.

"Do you have any idea how happy I am?" Rod asked Blythe.

She smiled happily. "It's like some kind of dream. I keep thinking I'm going to wake up any minute!"

"It's no dream, my darling. It is real. You are here in my arms, and we are dancing at Cameron Hall on our wedding day."

When the music ended, still holding hands, they joined Kate at the edge of the floor to watch the other dancers.

A lilting waltz began. One couple in particular drew Blythe's attention—a tall young man with tousled bronze-brown hair and a dainty wasp-waisted young girl with flying dark curls, her ruffled skirt and peach satin sash making her appear like some kind of exotic butterfly as he whirled her about the room.

It was Jeff! Blythe saw with surprise. And the pretty girl in his arms was . . . why, it was Faith Devlin . . . Garnet's daughter!

Blythe drew in her breath. Jeff was seventeen and Faith, fifteen? No, more nearly sixteen. Unconsciously, Blythe glanced over at Garnet and Jeremy Devlin who were also enjoying the colorful spectacle, then back at Jeff and Faith, who were totally absorbed in each other. The girl was laughing at something Jeff had said, and it was at that moment Blythe saw something—a luminous, dazzled look in the girl's face—that gave away the game.

At that moment Blythe turned in Garnet's direction only to find that her old rival was staring at her. At once the two mothers were bonded in a unique moment of recognition, understanding, and speculation.

Something indefinable flashed through Blythe's mind. It came and went quickly, but as her glance returned to the handsome young couple, she had a tantalizing glimpse into the future.

And Blythe knew Garnet had seen it too.